I0831827

OUR GRASS WAS GREENER

OUR GRASS WAS GREENER

By

Peter G. Lawrence

First Published in 2006 by Vroe Publishing

Second Edition

Typeset in Garamond by Vroe Publishing

ISBN: 978-0-9556873-0-3

3 5 7 9 8 6 4 2

IN THE BEGINNING...

I suppose it all started on the night of the Colonel's cocktail party. On these occasions David and I, as confirmed bachelors, usually upheld the regimental tradition of 'First in - Last out', and this evening was no exception. Indeed, the lastness was emphasized by the Colonel himself who pointed to a large jug of his potent brew and informed us that unless we did our duty he would be lumbered with drinking it for the next week or so. Too late for dinner in the mess, we headed for the 'Swagman's Stop' and Chicken in a Basket.

Pushing open the door, I spotted a vivacious redhead, deep in conversation with the landlady.

'Hey', I exclaimed to David. 'Look at that. '

David's tactical perception was way ahead of mine.

'Hang on', he said. 'Have you seen the opposition?'

The two escorts, each wearing a Parachute Regiment tie, looked as though London Irish might have rejected them for playing too rough in the scrum.

The Colonel's gin took charge and I headed for the bar. The situation was less threatening than it appeared. Neither of the redhead's Airborne brothers had the slightest objection to someone else buying her drinks. Friendly relations were established. First her sister, then her father were introduced. It appeared that a family gathering was assembling to celebrate the ceremonial opening of a tregnum of whisky, presented by the brothers to their father the previous Christmas. We offered no resistance to their invitation to join in.

It must have been about half past two when I mentioned that we had originally been in search of more solid food. Jo and her sister, Noelle, produced bacon and eggs and we continued with the celebration, much fortified. Later, much later, I groped my way into bed, thankful that it was Saturday and I was not on duty.

I had forgotten that there was a rehearsal of the following week's parade. Sharp at eight the band struck up, just outside my window. The bass drum matched exactly the pulses of pain running through my head. I crawled through the shower and just made it to the ante room. There were half a dozen newly commissioned young officers with shining morning faces, industriously studying the 'Quality' newspapers while the tabloids lay unsullied on the table. I pressed the intercom button to the bar.

'Yes Sir?' queried the loudspeaker.

'Bring me a large horse's neck and three aspirins', I demanded, adding, 'and you'd better take the same to Captain Jones who is probably still asleep.'

A wave of horror swept across the young gentlemen's faces and they hid themselves even more deeply behind their papers.

'Morning, Jeffrey.' The stentorian voice of our Aberdonion Medical Officer did nothing to restore health to a shattered system. 'Where were you last night?'

'I wish I knew. Have you any patent cure for amnesia, Thumper?'

'Not for your sort of self-inflicted amnesia but never mind, you're probably better off not remembering what you were up to.'

His bedside manner was impeccable but his prescription of little help. I explained the problem; how I'd met this gorgeous bird but didn't know where I'd been since leaving the Swagman's. His lack of sympathy was apparent. In fact, had I been the doctor, I would have diagnosed a severe case of hysteria.

Later that day I bumped into Thumper again. He handed me a piece of paper. 'There you are, my boy. Never say a Scot can be beaten. I've been to the Swagman's and I not only know what you were doing but who with. That's her phone number.'

Eight years later I was an unemployed teacher with six children and a socking great mortgage.

The redhead had turned white.

Chapter 1

'I'd much rather drive the mini,' pleaded Jo.

We were on the move. The removal van had left at eight that morning, having loaded the beds, the last bits of furniture in the house. We had breakfasted on our feet, all except Cormac in his carrycot. Now we were ready to go. The children were loaded into the Austin, Cormac securely strapped, in his car chair, to the front passenger seat, while in the back were crammed Phyllis, Anne and Mary, together with our neighbours' teenaged daughter who had bravely volunteered to keep order. Under their feet lay Tiggy, the golden Labrador.

The problem lay in the back of our little minivan: not only were our twelve hens in their crates but also six newly fledged ducklings, a farewell present from the farm up the road. After only thirty minutes the smell was very evident. Although Jo was well past the stage of morning sickness, her figure made it evident that Peters Mark V was on the way and I did not want her to suffer the poultry all the way to Devon. She, however, was adamant and so we set off. It was a three-hour run and I prayed that she would be able to stand it.

I was starting my retirement leave. Before it ended I was to enrol as a mature student at St Lawrence's College of Education. We had fallen in love with an old, rambling vicarage with a stream running past on its way to the Exe. We couldn't possibly afford it but I forgot to mention to the Building Society that I was about to cease being a relatively well-paid officer and start life on a student's grant and they had approved a mortgage. For survival we relied on our wits, something we were to get used to in the years to come.

It was with great relief that I arrived at Jo's brother's house. He was home on leave from Africa with his family, and had offered logistic support for our move. The relief was even greater about half an hour later when Jo's green mini arrived. Jo explained that she was so used to reaching out her left arm whenever she braked, in order to restrain one of the girls from projecting herself into the front of the vehicle, that she had continued to do so automatically and frequently found herself clutching a squawking bundle of feathers. She was trying to give the impression that driving van-loads of revolting chickens around the country was something any six months pregnant mum took in her stride. Her white face disproved that theory and her sister-in-law led her away and tucked her into bed with a glass of brandy. I thought I'd had enough just driving the few miles to Shiel St Peters where I unloaded the birds into their new home, an old wooden barn in the paddock. The removals men were already there and the builder had almost finished installing the Aga, without which, so Jo assured me, life in the twentieth century was impossible.

I explained to the men where the various items of furniture should go. Most of the better pieces had been inherited in one way or another. The living room at our last home had originally contained a three-piece suite, which Jo had obtained for seven and sixpence at the local auction sale. After a couple of years being worked over by three inquisitive infants and a chew-happy puppy this had been reduced almost to bare springs and I had agreed to Jo's making another visit to the Thursday auction. On her return she confessed to having spent as much as twelve and six on another suite. The snag was that, being convinced that the suite would fetch more than she could bid, she had also bought some other job lots earlier in the sale.

As a result we were the proud possessors of, as well as the suite, four arm chairs, five tables, seven mirrors and sundry waste paper baskets, fire irons and other bric-a-brac. She had spent all of two whole pounds and was somewhat shamefaced at her extravagance. I forgave her but was not best pleased next day when it cost as much again to persuade the local haulier to deliver the items. Now, however, all this collection vanished with ease into the rambling rooms and corridors of The Huers.

'Why "The Huers"?' asked the foreman.

'Not sure,' I replied. 'Apparently the couple who bought it from the Church in the first place came from somewhere near Newquay and it's connected with their original home. Anyway, it's shown on the Ordinance Survey map, so I don't think I'll change it.'

Later a much-recovered Jo arrived with the family and we installed them in their rooms. We walked around the house, exploring the odd corners and cupboards. One of these was fascinating, with a little window which looked down into the hall. I staked my claim on the old dairy as a place to store my beer. Outside was just as exciting. 'That level area must have been a tennis court once,' I pointed out. 'A long time ago though. That apple tree must be at least twenty years old.'

'One day we'll restore it,' said Jo. 'Teaching the kids to play tennis would be something to look forward to.'

The walled kitchen garden was overgrown but I thought it would not take too long with the aid of my 'Merrytiller'. We went in and closed the solid old door behind us.

'Let's light the fire,' suggested Jo.

'But it's still August,' I objected.

'Never mind. The place has been empty for a long while. See if you can find some fire wood.'

There were some logs still in the shed, and I soon had a cheerful blaze in the old stone fireplace. We pulled up two armchairs, one on each side and I found the tea chest in which I had packed a bottle of whisky.

'You know something,' said Jo. 'I think we're going to have a lot of fun living here.'

****

'This is a damn good hospital. Anything wrong with your chest, they'll sort it out. Only please don't fall down and break your leg.'

A couple of years earlier I had developed asthma and been sent off to a chest hospital in Sussex, where the services maintained a small unit. The RAF medical sergeant's prophecy had proved to be correct: the problem had been sorted out and I had been invited to have a final check up before retirement. As Jo was now ensconced in The Huers and two of her brothers were holidaying in the area with their numerous families, it seemed a good time to take advantage of the invitation. I set off for Sussex.

The next evening, having spent a day suffering every indignity the medical mind can contrive, I phoned Jo.

'I've had an awful time,' she sobbed. 'All the kids have had squitters. I spent the whole night emptying potties and changing nappies. I haven't had a wink of sleep. You'd think a house eight hundred years old would at least have a ghost. I'd have welcomed one just to lend a hand.'

Blood is thicker than water. Jo's brothers took turns in coming over with their families for the next few days. They looked after the children who played together in the garden. Their wives helped Jo with the cooking and, above all, with the nappies. I had rigged a clothesline, all of one hundred feet long, between two tall trees. It was fully employed while the washing machine worked non-stop. Best of all, Jo was able to catch up on her missed sleep, being packed off to bed each afternoon.

Of course, the Vicar came to call. It was about three in the afternoon. He left his bicycle at the gate and advanced up the drive. Seeing a strange man surrounded by about a dozen children he made the reasonable suggestion that it must be Mr Peters. On receiving a negative reply he inquired whether Mrs Peters was available, only to be told that she was in bed. He retreated down the drive and departed.

Two days later he tried again. This time the scene was the same, the children looked the same but there was a different man. Full of confidence he advanced with outstretched hand.

'Mr Peters I presume?'

'Sorry. No. Mr Peters is away.'

'Could I perhaps have a word with Mrs Peters?'

'Sorry again. She's in bed.'

He didn't try again for a month. This time he knocked at the door. Jo answered, the children clustering around her.

'It really is you, is it? I mean Mrs Peters.'

Jo assured him that it was so and invited him in. She explained that I had gone to college. He hoped that the children would grow up to join the choir. She informed him that they were the wrong brand and would be going to the Catholic church some miles away but that he was welcome to try his hand at me, the only wicked Prod in the family.

He departed, promising to call again.

My church-going never did match up to Jo's. Months later the Vicar paused at the gate to remark on the rate at which the children were growing. I sympathised with him that they were not in his congregation.

'No,' he sighed. 'You're the only one of mine. At least mine's the church you stay away from.'

****

'How on earth,' enquired the P.E. tutor, 'if you were running round the gym when I said "Stop", could you have been in that position?'

'Look,' I explained. 'For the last twenty-five years, whenever I've been ordered to stop, I've stopped in the position of "attention". That's not something I'm going to forget after ten minutes.'

There were, among the 'mature students' at St Lawrence's, about a dozen ex-servicemen who had opted for the Primary Education course. Between us we could muster about two hundred and forty years of adult experience and thirty-eight children. (Any minute now Jo would make it thirty-nine.) I wouldn't go as far as to say we were a thorn in the side of the college authorities but we often got the impression that they would be happier if we were somewhere else. Someone very foolishly invited us to write our first impressions of the college. My opinion that if the organisation were the work of an acting temporary unpaid lance-corporal of three weeks seniority he would be court-martialled for inefficiency was not well received. For a while I thought I would be looking for a different career but it blew over and, when we returned for the following term, we found numbers on the lecture-room doors so that belated students could ascertain whether they were in the right place without interrupting the lecturer inside.

'Has anyone seen Di?' asked Bill.

'Yes,' said Wendy. 'The poor dear's gone home to recover. She's thinking of going back to being a secretary.'

We were sitting in our accustomed corner of the students' bar, discussing our varied experiences while we had been attached to assorted schools for our teaching practice.

'Wherever did she go?' asked Bill.

'Somewhere up country,' replied Wendy. 'When she arrived she found the headmaster was about the same age as her son, wore no tie and a leather jacket and the children called him "Dave". It was all open plan and family grouping and she spent the whole month building a life-sized dinosaur out of *papier-mâché*.'

We were silent for a moment, not in memory of poor Di, but recalling individually some of the shocks we had suffered.

I set off for home only to find Jo white-faced and shaking. She threw herself into my arms.

'Whatever's the matter?' I demanded.

'You remember,' she sobbed. 'You remember the little chest of drawers that used to belong to my father. Do you know what he kept in it?'

'Not a clue,' I replied. 'Come to think of it, he always kept it locked. Probably kept his patients' notes in there. Anyway, what's all the fuss about?'

'Well,' said Jo, 'I was bathing John. The others usually like to be around then but today they were playing upstairs. After I'd finished and put him in his pram I went to see what they were up to. They had been exploring the drawers and it must have been right at the back as I'd never found it, but there was Dad's drugs wallet. It used to go in his bag when he was called out. And there it was with all the phials taken out and the corks broken where Phyllis had tried to open them. I didn't know whether she'd succeeded with any of them and I didn't know how many there ought to be. For a few moments I didn't know what I was doing and by the time I'd pulled myself together Phyllis was too scared to tell me anything. I kept hugging her and telling her "Mummy isn't cross but you must tell her if you opened any of these little bottles", but she was crying too much to answer. In the end I searched the room everywhere but I couldn't find any more phials.'

'You didn't phone the surgery, I suppose?'

'I thought of that, but what could I tell them? That the kids were perfectly fine but they might have eaten strychnine or morphia or any one of a dozen poisons? I've been watching them like a hawk ever since. It's been horrible.' More tears streamed down her cheeks and she seized my proffered handkerchief.

I looked into the living room. Phyllis, Anne and Mary were locked on to 'Jackanory'. Two-year-old Cormac was rocking John's pram with great gusto. Tiggy looked up from his place in front of the fire, thumped the hearthrug twice with his tail and went back to sleep. I got ice from the fridge, gin from the cupboard and mixed Jo a very large, very dry Martini. Then I recovered my senses and mixed one for myself.

Later on I collected a pile of rubbish and lit the garden incinerator. When it was burning well I emptied each phial into the flames. Then I added the wallet for good measure. We spent the rest of the evening going through every bit of furniture we had inherited from Jo's father but found nothing more.

When the children were tucked up and asleep we offered up a prayer of thanks. Then we emptied the gin bottle.

****

'Breakfast!' exclaimed Terry. 'We've never been asked out to breakfast before.'

'Well, there's a first time for everything,' replied Jo.

Easter was early this year. School holidays had started a week ago, on Maundy Thursday, and the weather had been kind to us. Terry, like Jo, was Irish, Catholic and had five children. She did not know that Jo was also a nurse. She was the wife of our doctor, Jack Turnbull and had brought her brood over to play with ours while the two mums exchanged gossip and coffee in the kitchen, surrounded by nappies, ironing and all the other paraphernalia of young families. I, having done my duty with the Sodastream and produced numerous bottles of cola, had made the excuse of potatoes to be earthed up, and escaped into the kitchen garden.

Jo, meanwhile, was confiding in Terry.

'I just daren't face either of them,' she explained. 'What on earth am I to do?'

After the birth of John, Jo had been invited to the surgery for a long interview with Doctor Pushe, Jack's elderly senior partner. He had explained in great detail all the different methods of avoiding pregnancy, extolled the idea of small families and, with his face beaming at a job well done, sent her on her way. Now, only five months later, Jo was sure that all his advice had proved unavailing.

'You'll have to tell Jack,' advised Terry, 'and the sooner the better.'

Jo agreed to make an appointment after the holidays. 'Anyway,' she said, 'never mind that now. You say Jack's not on call on Sunday. Bring the mob over to breakfast and spend the day. We might as well take advantage of this weather while we can.'

At seven thirty on the next Sunday morning Jo set off with the three girls for Mass. I proceeded to demonstrate my skills as chef. John, thank heavens, slept peacefully. Two-year-old Cormac proved to be an ace at setting tablemats. I had to set up a spare table in the dining room to accommodate twelve places plus one each for Cormac in his high-chair and John still in the carrycot. By nine fifteen I was ready. Mountains of bacon, sausages and mushrooms filled the warming oven while a sea of eggs covered the hot plate. Jugs of milk, packets of assorted cereals, slabs of butter and pots of marmalade stood in serried ranks down the centre of each table. I opened the front door and stood on the steps with Cormac as the convoy swept into the drive. In no time at all both families were seated and conversation gave way to the steady champing of jaws.

Afterwards all those old enough helped to transport the remains of the meal to the kitchen. Jack and Jo were left alone in the dining room.

'Are you *enceinte*?' asked Jack.

'She told you!' gasped Jo. 'She's a rotter. I'll never trust her again.'

Jack's eyes twinkled. 'Come over to the surgery tomorrow and we'll have a chat,' he said.

It was a thoroughly enjoyable day. The children rampaged around the garden and Phyllis showed our visitors the shed where one of our hens had hatched eight little yellow chicks. I had killed and plucked a couple of capons and when these went into the oven Jack and I took it as a signal that The White Lion must be open.

Seated around the fireplace in the pub were a dozen or so girls from the students' hostel up the road. Women's lib was all the rage and bra burning the order of the day. Jack and I ordered our pints.

'Ask me where my wife is,' I whispered to Ray, the landlord, and led Jack to the far end of the bar.

'Where's the missis then, Jeffrey?' called Ray.

'Where every good wife should be.' I replied. 'At home cooking her husband's lunch.'

'So's mine,' echoed Jack.

It was as well that Ray hadn't succumbed to the horrible custom of installing a jukebox in the bar. It would never have been audible over the ensuing uproar.

Later on, replete with capon, apple pie and rhubarb wine, we were in the living room. Terry was gazing at the mantelpiece.

'What's that?' she demanded, pointing.

'That's my Mary's Penny,' replied Jo.

'You mean to say you're a nurse?' spluttered Terry.

Jo nodded, with a demure smile.

'Not a midwife as well?'

Jo assented.

'Jack. Did you know Jo was an SRN, SCM?'

'Of course,' replied Jack.

'It just goes to show,' laughed Jo, 'that some members of the Turnbull family can keep a secret.'

****

'The employers will have to accept what the schools produce,' snapped the Maths Tutor.

I had had the temerity to question the wisdom of sending youngsters out into the world, ace at playing with Cuisenaire rods and Venn diagrams but ignorant of their twelve times table. I wondered if the answer fell within the definition of our recently discovered 'St Lawrence's Syllogism' which ran: 'The theory states something. The facts prove something else. Therefore the facts are wrong.' We made our way to the canteen.

'Never mind, Jeffrey,' sympathised Wendy. 'We're free now till Tuesday.'

It had not been a successful Saturday morning. The entire second year body of students had assembled, more or less on time, for our usual Saturday lecture. The tutor had arrived twenty minutes late to discover that there was no blackboard. Later, our maths tutorial had convinced most of us that we were not only witnessing, but about to participate in, the abolition of education. But, as Wendy said, it was Whit weekend and Monday was a bank holiday.

Meanwhile, at home, the Vicar had dropped by to see if I was in.

''Fraid not,' Jo told him. 'Saturday morning is Sex Education at St Lawrence's.'

The Vicar's eye roamed over the lawn where four little Peterses made life hell for Tiggy. From the pram, John announced that it was feeding time or nappy time or both. Jo already showed unmistakable signs that there would be another addition before the year was out. 'You know,' he pronounced, 'that's the last thing I would have thought he was in need of.' He mounted his bike and rode away.

It was a glorious weekend and the Exeter bypass enjoyed its first ten-mile jam of the year. We stayed at home and enjoyed the sunshine. On the Monday afternoon I was cutting back some brambles in a corner of the paddock when I came upon a patch of black feathers on the ground. I could hardly believe it but there could be no mistake. We had only one black hen and only a few minutes earlier she had popped out of the hen house, loudly announcing the production of today's egg. I looked in the nesting box and, sure enough, there was a little brown egg. I felt it. It was still warm. I cursed the foot and mouth epidemic that had led to the cancellation of all hunting last winter, the result being a plague of foxes this spring. We had already lost a drake, a duck, a goose and five hens but this, within feet of where I was working, was the height of impertinence. I called Tiggy and we scrambled through the hedge into the hayfield. The grass was still flattened where the fox had passed and we followed his track until we came to a patch of grass, trodden down in a circle, under which lay the little black hen with a single bite taken out of her.

I was not the only one cursing foxes and the following weekend it seemed as though every farmer in Devon was out with his gun. We didn't see another fox for years and our poultry slept in safety.

****

'Well?' enquired our geography tutor. 'What thoughts cross your mind when you look at this bit of countryside?'

'The first thing you can see,' I remarked, 'is that it's an obvious choice of a beach for an enemy to land on, whether he intended to strike inland or secure a safe anchorage in Torbay.'

'That wasn't quite what I had in mind,' said the tutor. 'Any other ideas?'

'Yes,' replied Alan, the ex Transport Command pilot. 'You could build a jolly good landing strip over there. Level ground, well drained and facing the prevailing winds. Long enough for a Hercules to land and take off.'

'Assuming that war isn't about to break out?' the tutor went on in an encouraging tone.

'Ah!' exclaimed Giles, the one time colonial policeman. 'Now that's interesting. That footbridge over the beach defences. It looks to be level on both sides, but there are twenty-three steps up and only nineteen down on the other side.'

There was a long sigh as the tutor's face looked more and more depressed. 'I was hoping,' he explained, 'for something a little more of a scientific nature. The geology of the site perhaps, or even something botanical. The object of my bringing you all out here is for you to use your imaginations and consider what might be of educational value in the future when you bring a class of twelve-year-olds out for a day's field study. Try to forget your past for a moment.' He stopped abruptly and pointed at the ground. 'What's that?'

'An orchid,' I replied.

'Are you sure?'

'Pretty sure.'

'Is it rare?'

'Well, I wouldn't encourage anyone to stamp on it, but there's a picture of it in the AA "Book of the Road".'

We strolled on, pausing here and there to consider matters of interest as we came upon them until it was time for lunch. In the nearby pub we listened to the news. 'In view of the financial state of the Country,' read the announcer, 'the Government has decided to postpone the raising of the school-leaving age to sixteen.'

We looked at each other in horror. For years there had been an intense campaign to recruit teachers to cope with the increased numbers that would fill the schools in fifteen months' time. The services' resettlement pamphlets had lauded the teaching profession. St Lawrence's was bulging with extra students, all ready to be launched into the world of education next year. Lecturers who for years had been used to classes of half a dozen school leavers with little on their minds but beer and rugger, now found themselves faced by groups of thirty or so, half of them hardened old cynics anxious to get out and earn some money. Now we would not be needed. Geography was not the main subject of our postprandial discussion.

On our return we sought out a friendly mathematician and, with his help, calculated that there would be somewhere in the region of forty thousand fewer jobs for us to apply for. It was not a happy crowd who dispersed that evening.

I reached home to find more disaster. In order to keep the grass in the paddock cut I had invested in a gander and two geese. One of the geese had been eaten by a fox but the two remaining were always hungry and inquisitive. In the kitchen garden the Merrytiller had done its job and rows of assorted vegetables were beginning to look as though we might be self sufficient at least as far as greengrocery was concerned. About tea time one of our little perishers had managed to reach the catch in the door leading into the paddock and left it open. I found two rows of lettuces had been treated to a short back and sides and the geese had just discovered a taste for peas.

Chapter 2

'Try some peapod wine,' invited the constable.

After months of writing letters applying for teaching posts I was to present myself at noon for an interview at a 'crammer' some miles away. At nine o'clock I looked out of the front door and called Tiggy. There was no response but I found his dog-tag lying on the ground. Tiggy had a habit of wandering off but there was always a phone call sooner or later telling us where he could be collected. Now there was no way in which he could be identified. I reported the facts to Jo who had just returned from taking Phyllis and Anne to school.

'Just like his master!' she remarked.

'If his master made a habit of chasing every interesting bitch within ten miles, you'd have something to worry about,' I replied. 'However, as he's lost his tag I'd better report it.'

I set off for the police house in the next village and my knock was greeted by a sturdy looking man in carpet slippers. I explained that I was looking for the policeman.

'It's supposed to be my day off,' he informed me, 'but come in, anyway.' He led the way into the living room.

'Mike Foot,' he announced, thrusting out a massive hand. I introduced myself and explained my errand.

'I'm sorry,' he said. 'I've been meaning to call in at The Huers ever since you moved in but something else has always cropped up. Are you settled in happily now?'

I assured him that we were and he offered me a seat while he went to the office for the appropriate lost dog form. I looked around. The walls were lined with shelves; all filled with bottles except near the fireplace where rows of jars stood with fermentation locks bubbling merrily.

'Nice little do-it-yourself hobby you've got there,' I remarked on his return.

'Do you do any brewing yourself?' he asked.

I admitted to a gallon or two of rhubarb wine at home, and claimed some credit for my beer, which usually proved popular with visitors. But nothing like the quantity or variety displayed on his shelves. He produced two glasses and poured a generous tot into each.

After the peapod we tried oakleaf, then cowslip, then dandelion. While we sipped he telephoned his colleagues for miles around for news of stray Labradors. There was a report of one that had turned up in church in a village near Tiverton the previous evening and listened attentively to the rector's sermon. It was now locked in the rectory tool-shed. I looked at my watch.

'Ye Gods! My interview!'

I drove somewhat erratically home. Tiggy was sitting on the doorstep. I cursed him roundly and rushed in. Jo was furious. I explained as I struggled into my best suit.

'I thought you must have met one of those bitches you were talking about,' she called after me as I dashed out again.

****

'Make no mistake,' said the Head of Department, 'we're not in the silk purse business. Just trying to produce an improved sow's ear.'

Teaching in a 'crammer' had not been a lot of fun. We had about thirty idle little horrors who had had the temerity to fail their Common Entrance Exams. Needless to say, this was not to the liking of their parents who had paid Prep School fees for years in the anticipation that their offspring would, in due course, proceed to Dad's *Alma Mater*. They arrived by Daimler or Mercedes and the conversations in the Principal's study were replete with expressions concerning noses and grindstones, shoulders and wheels, boots and backsides and injunctions not to spare rods. The Principal taught Maths and French with the aid of a stout whangee. An elderly gentleman who sat on the local bench once a week came on three afternoons to teach Latin. Another visitor taught science. The rest fell to me. English, Geography and History lessons followed one another from Prayers to dinner and from dinner to Recreation, which involved my supervising the cross-country run and subsequent shower and tea. Then back to the classroom till seven, when I left for home. Unless, of course, I was on duty when there was Supervised Reading till bed at eight thirty and lights out at nine when I handed my charges over to the tender care of Matron. Still, at least it was employment and I was being paid almost half the Burnham rate for the job.

The children didn't see much of me at this time. I would leave home in the minivan every morning in one direction while Jo set off in the other to deliver the three eldest to school. By the time I returned in the evening they were in bed. Tiggy took a very dim view of my continued absence and would absent himself more and more frequently, often with some possession of mine clasped in his jaws. One evening, about five miles from home, I noticed a black boot standing at the side of the road. I stopped the van, got out and went back to look. Sure enough, it was one of my old marching boots, now used when digging the garden. When I thrust it under his nose he gave a sardonic grin and went to sleep on the hearthrug.

Now I had been offered a post, teaching English in St Jude's College. I had been shown round, before my interview, by John Peterson, the newly promoted Head of Department, who explained that although the main remit of the College was technical training, his department was responsible for ensuring that the students' educational standards, and especially English and Maths, were high enough for them to learn to be lathe operators, electronic repairers or shorthand typists. I liked what I saw, particularly when we came to the College Hall: on the outside of each pair of doors was a substantial handle with a sign instructing one to 'PUSH'. Inside, where one presumably was intended to pull, there was neither instruction nor any handle, only a bronze plate affording no grip whatsoever. This seemed entirely in keeping with the patron saint of hopeless causes. I determined, on the spot, to accept any job I might be offered.

Even this could not go smoothly. I was interviewed on the Monday and, as I subsequently learned, the letter offering me the post was to be in the mail that evening before the final collection. I should, therefore, have received it on Tuesday morning and, in theory, my reply have reached the College by Wednesday. Things don't happen that easily in the Peters household. The letter missed the last post and out in our neck of the woods we never saw the postman before ten thirty. On Wednesday, when it arrived at The Huers, I was on duty and so it came about that I opened it at ten o'clock that night. I promptly wrote my letter of acceptance and posted it first thing next day. It failed to reach the College until the second post on Friday, by which time they were convinced I didn't want the job and John Peterson had phoned to confirm this. Jo, nearly frantic with worry had assured him that I had written, but we had a worrying weekend until, on the following Monday I was able to phone and clear up the problem.

****

'I thought the end of the world had come,' exclaimed Jo.

It was almost the end of term. In September I was due to start at St Jude's. The Principal had gone to London for the weekend, leaving me in charge on the Saturday. We had traded in the old Austin for a Dormobile in which the children were much happier. Instead of the crush, Phyllis, Anne, Mary and Cormac sat on benches on either side of the table, leaving plenty of room for John's car-chair and Jane's carrycot. Tiggy, curled up at the back, was delighted at the prospect of not being trampled underfoot. Jo had packed a picnic and come over to see how I spent my working hours.

We spent a pleasant afternoon. My charges, freed for a while from the classroom, showed a great deal more enthusiasm for cricket than they ever did for their studies and were not too often disposed to query my umpiring. After tea Jo packed the family into the Dormobile and set off for home. Suddenly, as she sped happily along the main road, there was a loud bang, a roaring noise and the children started screaming. The extending roof had extended without warning. Jo said it was like suddenly applying the brake. Luckily she stopped near a garage where the friendly proprietor identified the broken catch and, having no spare, lashed the roof down with twine. Jo set off once more but the wind was freshening and she found that if she did much more than ten miles an hour the leading edge of the roof started to lift once more. She decided that, rather than cause a traffic-jam on a summer's Saturday evening, she would turn off as soon as possible and take the country lanes to Shiel St Peters. She was sure she would meet nothing more than an occasional tractor.

Needless to say, this turned out to be the one day in the year when the local Young Farmers held their barbecue in a large barn near the village. Before she had gone a mile along the lane she had attracted a queue of vehicles, mostly Land Rovers proudly labelled 'Young Farmers do it in Wellies' and all hooting their horns in their hurry to reach the barn before the food ran out. Eventually she turned in at the gate of The Huers, releasing a procession of irate and hungry yeomen to their feast.

****

'I felt like Janus,' sobbed Jo, the tears rolling down her cheeks. 'I had two faces and had to keep changing from one to the other.'

It was Friday and I had arrived home at about half past seven to find several cars, including a police car, outside the Robertses' cottage, opposite our gate. As I got out of the car Jo appeared at the door. I could see she had been crying. I knew the children could be pretty frustrating when the mood took them, but this seemed a very odd result of a happy, laughing, cheerful children's party, which I had understood to be the planned programme for the afternoon.

It appeared that the children, stuffed to the gills with sausages and jelly, were having another round of 'Pass the Parcel' when Jo heard someone pounding on the front door. One gallant mum had volunteered to help in this orgy instead of putting her feet up for the afternoon. Leaving her in charge of the festivities, she set off to investigate and found Mr Roberts, terribly distressed, on the doorstep. Unable to understand what he was saying, she followed him to his home. On the kitchen floor lay Mrs Roberts.

Jo hadn't left nursing so long ago that she couldn't recognise Death when she saw it. She sat the old man in the parlour and, after a while, managed to find the phone number of his Doctor. Having rung him, she was somewhat taken aback when his first question was, 'Has she committed suicide?'

Not for nothing had Jo spent years listening to seasoned Ward Sisters putting down recalcitrant medical officers and it was a chastened doctor who eventually arrived at the door. Meanwhile Jo had sprinted back to the house, beamed encouragement at the now veteran parcel passers, whispered an explanation to Pat, her stand-in, grabbed the whisky bottle and returned to her task of comforting Mr Roberts. She discovered the telephone number of his son, who lived some distance away and succeeded in contacting him. Then she phoned the Vicar who proved a tower of strength. He soon appeared, pushing his bicycle up the path and proceeded to take charge, permitting Jo to return to The Huers just as the first mums arrived to collect their offspring. These departed in a state of mutiny, vowing never to pass another parcel in their lives. Jo poured a couple of very large Martinis and she and Pat collapsed into armchairs in the living room.

By the time I had absorbed all this, the number of vehicles across the road had reduced to one. I walked over and found Mr Roberts in his son's car. The son was in the cottage and explained that his father, who was duc to rctirc ncxt month, had parked his car in Tom Merlin's barn and walked back, over the bridge, to the cottage. Mrs Roberts, hearing the car go past, had stooped down to get her husband's supper out of the oven and collapsed with a heart attack. He was taking the old man home with him.

I was just in time to recover my somewhat depleted whisky bottle before he locked the door and departed.

****

'Cough,' ordered the Surgeon Commander.

Inflation was beginning to have a marked effect on my service pension. Jo and I discussed the problem. Up till now it had been the main part of our income. Now that I had a job, the pay for which, while not munificent, at least afforded a living, perhaps this was the time to commute half the pension and invest the proceeds in something substantial. In the end we decided that this was the right thing to do. I filled in the appropriate forms and, in due course, was invited to travel to London, at my own expense of course, and to present myself at this comfortable office in Queen Anne's Mansions. Here the long retired naval doctor, on his return from an extended luncheon, submitted me to all the indignities to which a lifetime in the service had accustomed me and pronounced his opinion that I ought to live long enough for Her Majesty to show some profit from the transaction.

Some time later an official looking envelope arrived. It contained a substantial cheque. We made an appointment with our bank manager and put our thoughts to him.

'We thought,' said Jo, 'that a house with four or five flatlets or bed-sits would be a good idea.'

'You could do a lot worse,' he opined. 'Only do try to let to students or people who will be moving on reasonably soon. You may have the expense of redecorating more often but, with the present law, long lets are a short walk from the bankruptcy court.'

Jo was in her element. She adored house-hunting and set about it with gusto. She soon had a short list of houses for us to inspect and we settled on an old house which had already been converted into flats, some of which were let. Most important, it was within our price range. We exchanged contracts and looked forward to becoming persons of property. Little did we know what that implied.

Meanwhile, the sun was shining and we were on holiday. The hens were laying and we had new potatoes, peas, beans and salad from the garden. One morning we woke the children early, long before the traffic started to fill the roads. By eight o'clock we were driving gingerly along the potholed road across Braunton Burrows towards one of our favourite picnic spots. The older ones were dispatched to collect fuel while I constructed my field cooker.

'Daddy made an Aga,' pronounced John.

Soon the smell of frying bacon drew them back from splashing happily in the shallows and we settled down to eggs, bacon and sausages, washed down with flasks of coffee.

We spent an idyllic day: sandcastles were built, plastic boats were sailed, rabbits were stalked. Tiggy usually put paid to this pursuit, returning from each foray with a look of baffled indignation. After lunch we set off for home in good time to miss the rush hour traffic on our way. It had all been so peaceful that I had forgotten the proximity of the airfield. As we retraced our route across the burrows there was an enormous roar. Jo screamed. The children wailed. Tiggy barked. An RAF Phantom had passed over us at what seemed like a clearance of three feet.

'Look out!' shrieked Jo.

I jammed on the brake.

'No, no. Go faster. There's another coming. Get out of its way.'

In vain I tried to explain the difficulties of out-manoeuvring a Phantom in a BMC Dormobile. One after another a whole squadron streaked over our heads. By the time we reached the main road the children were regarding the whole thing as a great joke as Jo cowered deeper into her seat at each onslaught.

'Look out, Mummy!' shouted Phyllis as we neared home two hours later.

She pointed skywards to a glider making its soundless way towards Dunkeswell.

****

'I've got an idea,' announced Jo.

I grunted unenthusiastically.

'We ought to go away for a holiday,' she continued.

'That's a good idea,' I replied sarcastically. 'We can easily afford hotel rooms for eight and you can spend a happy fortnight washing nappies in the wash basin while I hang them out to dry on the lines I've strung between lamp posts along the sea front.'

'I didn't mean like that,' she snapped. 'Only Jane is still in nappies. John has one at night but otherwise he's OK. Besides, you can buy disposable nappies at Boots. I was thinking of travelling in the Dormobile.'

'Oh fine! Eight of us in the Dormobile! Living, eating, sleeping, using potties and disposing of nappies! Look. We are here in the heart of Devon. People come here for holidays; they don't go somewhere else in the middle of summer.'

'I do wish you'd listen for once,' pleaded Jo. 'The caravan outside the bungalow up the road is for sale. We could hitch it on the back and that would give enough bed space for us all. We've friends all over the country with enough room for us to park for a night. We could have lots of fun.'

'I think it's ridiculous,' I snorted. 'I don't want to hear any more about it.'

We set off in great fettle. Having practised manoeuvring the caravan on a couple of weekend expeditions, I was confident that I could drive to Essex and back without too many problems. Jane appeared to be comfortable in disposable nappies. There were sufficient tinned rations stowed in the caravan to see us through any emergencies and enough paper, crayons and games to keep the children from becoming bored. Tiggy had a large bone from the butcher. A large anticyclone covered Southern Britain and the fine weather looked set to continue.

'Look, Children!' cried Jo.

A large Rolls Royce swept past on its way up the A38. Its number plate bore the single figure '1'.

'Who's going to be first to see a number "2"?' she went on.

This turned out to be the most popular game we invented and the numbers crept up steadily enough to maintain interest. It was very hot and the engine, situated between the two front seats, acted like a very efficient radiator. Lemonade was distributed at regular intervals and we bowled merrily along until, suddenly, as we climbed steadily up the Mendips, the engine began to splutter. Luckily we were beside a large lay-by and I swung into this as the engine died.

'What's the matter with it?' asked Jo.

'Blowed if I know,' I replied. 'It was just as though we were out of petrol, but the tank is nearly full. We might as well have an early lunch while we're stopped. If you can see to that, I'll have a look at the engine. Anne, you keep a look out down the hill and you, Phyllis do the same up the road. If you see an AA man, let me know.'

Having thus deprived Jo of her two most trusted aides, I removed the engine cover. A wall of heat hit me.

'Oh oh!' I exclaimed. 'I've seen something like this before. Have a look at this, Jo. You see that copper pipe running up to the carburettor? Well that's the petrol lead and it's running right up beside the cylinder-block. And in this heatwave the petrol is vaporising in the pipe, before it reaches the top. We've only towed the caravan on a couple of cloudy weekends, so it hasn't affected us up to now.'

'What can we do?' asked Jo.

'Not a lot. But I bet I'm right and if we let it cool down it'll start perfectly.'

Sure enough, once we had eaten our lunch, the engine started and we went happily on our way until, twenty miles on, the same thing happened again.

'This is nonsense,' stormed Jo. 'We can't go off on a ten-day tour, only progressing in twenty mile hops. You've got to do something.'

She certainly had a point. The problem was: what was I to do? I offered up a little prayer for guidance and it was promptly answered.

'Give me the first aid box.'

I extracted most of a roll of cotton wool and wrapped it round the petrol lead, securing it with insulating tape. The windscreen washer on this type of vehicle had been an afterthought and the reservoir was a plastic bottle in the cab. I disconnected it from the nozzles and fed the lead to the cotton wool so that I could pump water onto it.

It worked a treat and, giving it a few squirts each time we came to a hill, we continued our journey uneventfully. The children had counted car numbers into the sixties and were debating whether we could reach 999 by the end of the holiday when we arrived at our friends' house near Reading. They were somewhat daunted at the sight of us but made us very welcome, nevertheless.

Next day we continued on our way to Essex where we were to spend the weekend with the couple who had been Jo's first employers when she was an agency nurse. They had always been fond of her and she of them and she was as proud as Punch to introduce them to our family. They made us incredibly welcome: I had always preferred champagne in silver pint-pots, and we rewarded them by blocking their drains with disposable nappies.

Next morning Jo awoke with a painful earache. Some of her old friends still worked at the local hospital so she drove over to seek treatment. As far as I could gather it went hard with any other patient that day as an impromptu reunion took place. She returned at lunchtime, well fortified with penicillin, painkillers and other stimulants into the nature of which I did not enquire. We had a marvellously relaxing weekend in spite of the grumbles of the plumber at being called out to unblock drains on a Saturday and were all set to continue our journey on Monday, when we were due to visit Jo's brother.

On our way I noticed that she was sounding rather hoarse and she confessed to having a sore throat. In spite of our stopping at a chemist's shop for Zubes, Jo became more difficult to hear and I was glad to reach our destination and the medical expertise of her sister-in-law. The children amalgamated into an amorphous mass with their five cousins and Jo was tucked up in her bunk.

The next day she was no better, but made a gallant effort in joining a party of friends and relations to see some of their old teachers at a nearby convent. The subsequent description, of Jo surrounded by friends but unable to speak a word, was harrowing in the extreme and I decided to call it a day and return home. Early on Wednesday morning we set off once more. Phyllis was in charge of rations, Anne in charge of games and Mary responsible for car numbers. I drove hard all day, stopping only for short breaks, and reached home in the early evening. Jo was dispatched to bed while Phyllis and I concocted supper and supervised all the pre-bedtime activities. I was very glad to join Jo who, I suspected, was running a temperature.

Next morning I phoned Jack Turnbull who promised to visit after surgery.

'Why didn't you, of all people, realise you were allergic to penicillin?' he demanded.

Jo still couldn't speak but managed to convey that she had never been treated with it before.

'Never mind,' I comforted her as I watched the rain pouring down the path. 'If it hadn't been for that, we'd have been two hundred miles away when the weather broke. Imagine living in the caravan in this. Something to do with clouds and silver linings.'

Jo smiled wanly and went back to sleep.

Chapter 3

'Welcome to the fold,' said Cynthia.

It must have been the biggest meeting the PTA had ever held. The purpose of the gathering was to discuss whether Sex Education should be introduced into the curriculum. The committee chairman had seized the opportunity to persuade some new blood to volunteer and an anonymous voice from the other end of the hall had called out my name. I surrendered as gracefully as I could and was promptly elected. Cynthia, who taught Mary's class, was already a member. We conversed briefly and the meeting was called to order for the main debate.

'We must be quite clear in our minds,' proclaimed the Canon, 'if this instruction is to be practical.'

'My God!' whispered Cynthia. 'I do hope he means "practicable". I don't fancy practical sex lessons with Infants Two!'

It had been a mixed up sort of day. At first it had been quite enjoyable. Praising Rasthi was always enjoyable. When praised she effervesced. Even her caste mark seemed to glow. I did not explain, in front of her classmates, that the part of her essay I had enjoyed the most was the paragraph describing the old night-watchman warming his hands on a hot brassiere!

It being Friday, John Peterson and I followed our usual practice of dissecting the *Times Educational Supplement* at lunchtime. I had first go, in the staff room, before he removed himself and it to his study. Ten minutes before classes began again we compared notes. This week we had a classic. In a letter of no more than ten column inches there were three sentences in which the subject did not agree with the verb and eight instances of a comma used instead of a semi-colon. All this from someone who ran refresher courses for out-of-date teachers. John offered to bet me a quid that we didn't find one to beat it in the next twelve months. I didn't accept.

Jo drove in to St Jude's, swapped her van for the Dormobile and collected the children from school. I caught up on my marking until I was driven out by the cleaners, and then set off for 18, King's Close, to collect the week's rents. This was seldom easy. We were learning the hard way all the stratagems that ingenious minds could devise to avoid the rent collector. My current *bête noire* was Joe Quinn. As an ex-regular with twelve years' service, I had accepted him without further references. Jo wasn't so sure.

'It's because he calls you "Sor" all the time,' she insisted.

'Nonsense!' I retorted. 'He'll be highly disciplined and used to doing everything on time.'

The one thing he always did on time was to vanish on Friday evenings. This evening was no different but, out of a window, I spotted him lurking across the road. I left the house, got into the van and drove away - right round the corner. Five minutes later I walked back and found him in his room. We had a friendly chat during which he assured me how glad he was to see me, and that that he had rushed home especially to catch me and pay his rent on time. We had a slight difference of opinion over my strange custom of preferring cash to a cheque but parted on amicable terms. Then I set off for the P.T.A. meeting.

The meeting lasted a long, long time. Everyone, it seemed, had strongly held views and was going to make them known. In the end the unanimous conclusion was precisely what it would have been at seven o'clock: to leave it in the capable hands of Sister Elfrida. My empty stomach was rumbling by the time I got home. Jo had supper waiting for me and I decided I deserved a couple of pints of home brew.

****

'A cow?' exclaimed Peter French, one of our mathematicians. 'What the hell are you going to do with a cow?'

'Milk it?' I suggested.

None of my friends had thought it a very good idea. Well, none of my colleagues, anyway. At home it was different. Everyone in the village was in favour. They had been very dubious about our scheme to buy a house in town to rent. Dangers lurked in towns. Never knew where you were in town, let alone dealing with strangers wanting houses. But cows; that was different. Everyone knew about cows.

I enumerated the advantages: all the milk, butter and cream we could ever need, a calf a year to be sold at a profit, something to keep the grass down in the paddock. 'And think of the sex education for the kids. Real, practical experience might offset some of the strange ideas they seem to pick up from school lessons.'

Peter was unimpressed. 'Twice a day milking,' he muttered. 'How are you going to cope with that?'

'Oh, I'll do it in the morning and Jo in the evening. Mr Roberts across the way will look out for us if we need to be away. He and his wife used to milk umpteen cows by hand every day, before the war.'

'Well, the best of British to you,' said Peter. 'Don't ever ask me to come and help, though.'

And so Susie joined the family, a five year old, doe-eyed Jersey, in calf and used to being led about by children. Just as well; the kids adored her and followed her everywhere. Jo had spoken to Bob Merlin who had agreed to our grazing her in the meadow opposite once they had cut the hay and, with our little paddock, we reckoned we could feed her. Jo went to an antique shop in Honiton and returned in triumph with a real milking stool while I found a couple of buckets at the hardware store. I think they were intended to be coal buckets, but they could hold about four gallons and were made of a hard, silver plastic with sides that curved gently into the bases, so that they were extremely easy to clean.

Learning to milk was not as difficult as we had expected. Mr Roberts helped us to construct a stall in the old barn, with drinking water, a manger for milk nuts and a chain with which to tether Susie. He assembled cow, stool and bucket in their correct positions and proceeded to demonstrate. Jo and I leaned over him while the children fought over the best vantage points. Then it was Jo's turn. It took her about ten seconds before milk was frothing merrily into the bucket.

I tried. Nothing happened. Once more. Susie stamped her hoof perilously near my toes.

'Tesn't no good just pulling at it,' exclaimed Mr Roberts. 'What ee wants is more like sliding down like.'

'It's easy,' said Jo. 'Look.'

She leaned down and another squirt joined the half filled bucket. After ten minutes I was beginning to get the hang of it and Mr Roberts finished the job, demonstrating how we could be sure that the udders were empty. 'Don't ee ever leave her half done,' he admonished us. 'You'll have mastitis for sure.'

****

'I've had an idea,' announced Jo.

I sank a little lower behind my paper. The bank was making rude noises about the size of our overdraft and I had come to associate Jo's ideas with capital expenditure.

'Well?' she went on. 'Don't you want to hear it?'

I gave the matter deep consideration. The answer was certainly 'No', but my chances of an enjoyable supper would be considerably reduced if I said so. In the end I took the diplomatic option, went to the pantry, drew a pint and a half of home-brew, gave Jo the half and settled back in my chair with the pint.

'Right ho then. Let's have it.'

'Well,' she enthused. 'We own 18, King's Close outright, don't we?'

I nodded.

'But the rents aren't anywhere near what we shall need in a year or two when the kids start at secondary school,' she continued.

I knew precisely what she meant. When we married, the whole country abounded in good grammar and grant-aided schools. Now they were all being abolished. I had sensed the danger while I was at St Lawrence's and my present job confirmed my misgivings; we were getting youngsters of average intelligence who, after ten years of education, were unemployable. In addition, the local 'Tech' had been turned into a sixth form college so that, instead of getting their first taste of responsibility as prefects at sixteen or seventeen, pupils were transformed into undisciplined, scruffy students. Worse, according to John Peterson who had spent many years teaching modern languages, the reward for teaching 3C in the morning was spending the afternoon with the upper sixth. The best qualified teachers had all opted for the college, leaving their less fortunate colleagues in the schools. Jo and I wanted something better.

'If we offered the first house as collateral,' she suggested, 'could we borrow enough to buy a larger house and convert it? It's four years before Phyllis is twelve. By using the rents to repay the loan for that period we might be able to afford school fees when the time comes.'

I could see snags in this. We discussed the subject well into the evening and I broached another five-gallon container of home-brew, but I couldn't come up with any better idea. We agreed to sleep on it.

I should have known better. I slept on it and set off next morning for St Jude's, dropping the children on the way. Jo slept on it and by the time we returned that evening she had the particulars of several potential properties and had made an appointment with the bank manager.

And so it was that we became the owners of yet another property, this time an old hotel, the 'Woodstock'. The builders set about converting it into bed sitting rooms. As soon as they had finished, Jo set to with paint and paper and the whole place began to look bright and cheerful. John and Jane were happily employed with blunt scissors, pencils and the off-cuts of wallpaper.

'All new?' asked the store manager.

'Of course,' I replied.

I had presented him with a list of cookers and mini-fridges and asked 'How much?' It was some time before I realized that he was under the impression that I was trying to flog him the goods and that he, not unreasonably, suspected that they had fallen off the back of a lorry.

In three months the place was ready, advertisements placed in the local newspaper and Jo was whacked.

'Please,' I said, 'take a rest and don't have any more ideas for a long time.'

****

'We thought he'd committed murder,' exclaimed Jo.

We had had a good singsong all the way home, the four eldest and I. We started with 'Old Uncle Tom Cobleigh' when we turned off the main road at Wydshiel and drove up to The Huers on the last verse of 'Little Boy Billee'. Tiggy was on his chain, a sure sign of disgrace. The kitchen was in chaos, feathers everywhere. Jo and her sister, Phyllis's namesake but usually known as Aunty Eff, were draped, exhausted, over the table.

'We were just enjoying a cup of coffee,' explained Jo, 'when John and Jane rushed in shouting that Tiggy had caught a chicken, so we ran out to see. Sure enough, there he was, trotting proudly up the drive with a bantam cock in his mouth.'

At first they concluded that he had chased and caught the bird. Tiggy was seized, reprimanded and chained up. However, it proved to be soaking wet. Tiggy was not in the habit of slaughtering poultry and they began to suspect that his retriever instincts had taken charge and that he had rescued the bird from the river. But who would believe it? The only bantams lived next door and belonged to Sybyl Merlin. As far as we knew, not one of them had ever tried swimming across to The Huers before!

'It's still warm,' said Eff, 'and I can feel its heart beating.'

The two sisters wrapped the bird in a towel and placed it in the warming oven of the Aga, leaving the door open. Jo went off to milk Susie before we were due home. By the time she had finished, her patient looked less bedraggled and more like a normal bantam but was still unconscious.

'I know,' she exclaimed. 'We must give it some brandy.'

'That's a good idea,' agreed Eff.

A raid on my drinks cupboard revealed a brandy bottle, still quarter full. Jo poured a few drops into a teaspoon and then, with Eff holding the unconscious body beak upwards, poured the liquor down its throat. The bird shuddered, then shot straight up into the air, crowing for all it was worth. It flew three times round the kitchen, the sisters in pursuit, and dived behind the washing machine. There it stayed. The machine was too heavy to be easily moved and gentle hands groping behind it were met by savage pecks.

In the end Jo went to find Bob Merlin who moved the washing machine and extracted his rooster, now in the best of health and crowing triumphantly. He set off for home, laughing uncontrollably.

By the time The Ring o' Bells shut its doors that night, everybody in the village knew all about that mad family at The Huers' latest folly. 'Feeding brandy to Sybyl's bantam' was set to become part of the local folklore.

****

'I've never tasted poteen,' remarked Simon.

A fortnight earlier Anne had returned from a holiday. Aunty Eff was visiting cousins in Cork and had offered to take her to Ireland. She had jumped at the opportunity and we had seen them off from Bristol Airport and met them on their return. Anne was white faced and trembling. Her aunt was full of apologies and related in great detail the adventures she had endured, travelling by moonlight across the peat bogs to a *rendezvous* with a purveyor of poteen, returning with two bottles of the nectar. One bottle she had concealed in Anne's suitcase in order to pass through the Customs. Anne, who had listened wide eyed to tales of the gallant brewers outwitting the excise men, was convinced that it would be discovered and she would be cast into durance vile. She soon regained her normal composure and we sped off in the direction of Devon.

Jo had recited the story after dinner. We had been invited by Jack and Terry to meet the new partner, Simon Flint-Jones, and his wife, Corenne who stared at Jo in disbelief.

'You mean to say you had six children under six,' she expostulated. Jo assured her that it was so.

'Planning any more?' asked Simon.

'No,' I told him. 'Not since we found out what was causing it.'

'Oh, do be quiet, Jeffrey,' said Jo. 'Really, I can't take him anywhere,' she explained to the others.

After dinner the conversation turned to drink and Jo mentioned Anne's adventures.

'Jack loves poteen,' Terry assured us. 'Whenever we go over to see my family he vanishes with my brothers and is happy all the week.'

We invited the Flint-Joneses to dinner and to sample Anne's bottle the following Friday evening. It was a great success. Jo prepared one of her choicest meals and the lower the level in the bottle of poteen, the more enjoyably flowed the conversation. Suddenly there was a loud knock on the front door.

'Just passing,' announced Mike Foot, our local bobby. 'Saw the lights on and the Doctor's car outside so I dropped in to see if you were all right.'

'We were introducing the Doctor to poteen,' I explained.

'Good stuff, from what I hear,' said the Constable.

'Come in and try some,' I offered.

'Didn't distil it yourself, I hope?' he enquired.

I assured him that it had passed through Customs, omitting the fact that it had done so concealed in a child's suitcase.

'That's OK then,' he said, placing his helmet on the saddle of his bike. 'I'll come and join you.'

Constabulary tales of the local sinners added enormously to the evening's entertainment. Mike's laugh could easily be heard from one end of the village to the other and any miscreants abroad at that late hour must have thought better of their pursuits and returned to their beds. It was very late indeed by the time we discovered that the bottle was empty. Our guests dispersed, either homewards or back to the beat and we were glad see our bedroom.

Next morning I was not, for some reason, feeling my usual scintillating self and decided to take the children for a walk in Oakshiel Forest. By the time we returned I was feeling human again and a pint of home brew completed the recovery.

'Corenne was on the phone,' announced Jo. 'She couldn't stop apologizing.'

'What on earth for?' I asked.

'Well,' explained Jo, 'apparently, as they arrived home, she asked Simon what that strange light was in the sky. When he told her that it was the dawn she was horrified. She's been castigating him ever since for keeping us up so late.'

I realized straightaway that Corenne and Jo were kindred spirits.

****

'What are you doing there?' demanded Mr Roberts.

'Caponising these cockerels,' I told him.

'Ah! Need to be an expert for that,' he told me. 'Know just where to cut.'

'Things have changed since your day,' I assured him. 'Look, you put one of these pellets into this needle and then you insert it under his scalp. Then you press the plunger and withdraw the needle. The pellet dissolves very slowly and he loses all interest in the hens, just eats and gets fat.'

'Why under the scalp?' he asked. 'Seems a long way from where it matters.'

'I suppose it could be anywhere,' I replied, 'but you don't eat the head so if there was some of the pellet left when you killed it you wouldn't eat that. I hate to think what the effect would be if you did. Anyway, that's the last one so let's go in and have a pint of home brew.'

'What's that on the grass, then?' He pointed to the ground.

Sure enough, there was one of the tablets. But I had been very careful to take only one at a time from the bottle. So it must have fallen from the needle and I had injected one of the birds with nothing but air. There was no way of knowing which bird and I thought it unwise to give each another dose. I left all six in the coop with a liberal ration of corn and we made our way through the kitchen garden to the beer.

The phone started to ring. It was Jo's friend, Pat.

'Why, do you suppose, should Lesley Martin have passed my house lugging a great big suitcase, almost as big as herself and heading for Shiel St Peters?' she wanted to know.

Lesley was a school chum of Phyllis's but she lived at least five miles away. I promised to investigate and made my way out of the front door. There was Phyllis with a large suitcase resting on some old pram wheels that she was securing to her little fairy-cycle with binder twine.

From the ensuing discussion I elicited the information that both girls were fed up with school and had decided to leave home and seek their fortunes in London. We chatted for a while and in the end she agreed that as lunchtime was approaching and Lesley had not arrived she might as well postpone her departure until the afternoon. I went to report all this to Jo in the kitchen but she was chuckling merrily to herself, having listened to our conversation through the window. Then I set off in the van to collect Lesley but found her just arriving back home, exhausted and having abandoned the whole project. A well-fed Phyllis did not seem too disappointed at the news.

Some weeks later I found Phyllis leaning over the capons' coop, admiring one of its inhabitants which, unlike his relaxed and well rounded brothers, was brightly coloured and strutting impatiently to and fro, his scarlet comb and wattles brilliant in the sunshine.

Very gently I lifted the lid of the coop but, in spite of my care, he was too quick for me. In a flash he was out of the coop and, pausing only to chase his father into the branches of an apple tree, was among the hens like a sailor coming ashore in Portsmouth after six months at sea. I knew which cockerel had missed his pellet.

****

'Ten shillings. I mean fifty pence,' shouted Jo.

'Jo, you can't!' exclaimed Corenne.

'Come, come, Mrs Peters,' called the auctioneer. 'We can do better than that. Any advance on fifty p?'

Jo was in her element. Apart from looking at houses, there was no better way of spending a day out than at an auction sale and Mrs Peters of Shiel St Peters was becoming well known for the paucity of her opening bids.

'I never start with more than ten bob,' she explained to Corenne. 'Once or twice I've got away with it. In the old days it used to be half a crown.'

'Come along now,' cried the increasingly frustrated auctioneer. 'Fifty pence I am bid for this fine suite. Will someone make it a pound?'

No one did and Lot 125 was knocked down to Mrs Peters.

'Why do you want a suite of furniture?' asked Corenne.

'I don't really,' replied Jo, 'but some of the furnishings of 18, King's Close were a bit tatty when we bought the place and I'm always on the lookout for anything better. It's Lot number 206 I really want. That's a nice little dressing table and would go very well in Mary's bedroom.'

Lot 206 was bid up to a pound and acquired by Jo.

'Let's go and find some lunch,' suggested Jo. 'I'll just go and pay for those two lots at the office.'

They left the auction rooms, Jo clutching her receipt for one pound fifty. A woman hurried after them.

'Excuse me. Was it you who bought Lot 206?'

'Yes it was,' replied Jo. 'Why?'

'But I wanted it!' exclaimed the woman. 'For my little girl's bedroom.'

'Tough!' said Jo. 'I wanted it too; for my daughter's room. So I bid for it.'

'I was out of the room for a couple of minutes and missed the bidding. Otherwise you'd never have got it,' asserted the stranger. 'I'll give you two pounds for it.'

'You won't,' Jo assured her. 'I'd have bid up to five.'

'Well I'll give you six,' she offered. 'I really want it.'

Jo was about to decline when she realized that five hundred per cent profit wasn't bad for a morning's work.

'O.K.,' she said and walked off with four pounds fifty more in her handbag than when she arrived. On their way home they called in at King's Close where Shelley Bryll was installing a new washbasin.

'Shelley,' she cooed. 'Would you be an absolute darling and pick up some furniture for me on your way here tomorrow in your van?' She gave him the receipt and explained that only Lot 125 was to be collected.

Next morning the phone rang. It was Shelley. 'Oh Mrs Peters,' he cried. 'They've lost your dressing table. They're terribly sorry and they've given me your pound back.'

Having established that Shelley had confused the two lots, Jo phoned the auction rooms and explained.

'You mean he should have collected the three-piece suite?' cried the girl. 'That's a pity 'cos we've got someone here who wants that.'

'He can have it,' said Jo.

'We'll send your fifty pence back,' said the girl.

'Forget it,' replied Jo. 'You've already sent me a quid. Let's call it quits.'

'That was a good day's work,' I remarked later. 'You ought to go into business.'

Chapter 4

'That's what cannabis smells like,' explained Sergeant Pocock.

We had had a number of rather dubious characters applying to become tenants at The Woodstock and there had been a nervous reaction from some of those already in residence. Alan, for example, was a pleasant young man and engaged to a girl in Plymouth. He worked at a wholesale chemist and explained, 'If there was even a suspicion of drug offences at my address, I'd be out on my ear'.

I mentioned this to the charming young WPC who was Schools Liaison Officer, next time I saw her.

'Give me your phone number and I'll have a word with the Drug Squad,' she replied.

The result was a visit from the sergeant himself, equipped with assorted illustrations of drugs in their commonly encountered forms and a number of plastic bags at which we were invited to sniff. Thus instructed, we felt capable of detecting any illicit substances we might come across, and, for a while, whenever I visited either of our houses I wandered about, sniffing suspiciously, until Heather, who occupied one of the ground floor rooms, asked whether I was taking any treatment for such a persistent cold.

Susie, meanwhile, was expecting. She had been dry for some time and we had reached a reciprocal agreement with a family in Wydshiel who also kept a house cow. We had provided them with milk three months ago, when their cow calved. Now we collected a gallon from them each day. It was just about enough for our requirements but there was not enough to make cream and we had reverted to eating New Zealand butter.

On Sunday morning Jo loaded the children into the Dormobile and set off for Mass. I had made my usual joke about how fortunate she was in marrying a wicked Prod so that a delicious breakfast would be awaiting their return, and threatening to convert to Catholicism if she misbehaved. Sunday was the one day when we ate in the dining room, with proper silver instead of stainless steel, and when knuckles were rapped for any breach of table manners. This morning I finished early and took Tiggy for a stroll in the autumn sunshine. In the paddock stood Susie with, at her feet, a newborn calf.

Just then I heard the Dormobile coming down the hill and, rushing back along the path, met the family on the drive and led them to the paddock. I don't suppose there can be many creatures more attractive to a child than a Jersey calf. Or to adults, for that matter. There was a prolonged and joyful gasp and the calf was surrounded. Susie offered no objection to her offspring's admirers and it was soon in danger of being stroked to death. At last I persuaded everyone to come back to the house and a less than delicious, dried up breakfast. Even so, this was wolfed in no time flat, and we received a succession of requests: 'Please may I leave the table?' followed by the scamper of feet on the path to the paddock. For the rest of the day we were in no doubt as to where to find the children. Or I Jo.

The following Friday I was collecting the week's rents. One tenant had proved reluctant to be around on Friday evenings and there was no reply when I knocked at his door. Opening it with my master key,

I looked in. On the windowsill stood a number of pot plants. 'Nice,' I thought and then paused. They were certainly not geraniums. In fact they reminded me of Sergeant Pocock's photo album. My phone call resulted in the arrival of D.C. Foster who confirmed my suspicions but there was no sign of the horticulturalist that evening. I returned next morning in the company of Sergeant Pocock but the room was empty. So was the electricity meter.

****

'You're a right boozy lot,' remarked Moira.

Every Saturday, weather permitting, we would load children, dog and a picnic into the Dormobile and set off on an exploration. Over the months we visited most of the well-known attractions in the West Country. Cricket St Thomas, the Model Village, Slapton Ley, all suffered an invasion of our horde. To assist in retrieving losses, all six were dressed in identical outfits, which aroused much amusement wherever we met other tourists. On the way home in the evening we often stopped at the White Lion where we enjoyed a pint or two while the children regaled themselves on Coke and crisps, guarded by Tiggy.

Now it was Parents' Evening at the school. We had chatted to Sister Elfrida who seemed satisfied with the four entrusted to her up till now and enquired after the health of the two she had yet to endure. We set off on the rounds.

'You see Mr Richards and Moira Butlin. I'll see Miss Jones and Cynthia,' said Jo. We parted and joined the queues of parents admiring the work pinned around the classroom while awaiting our turn to talk to the class teacher.

Moira taught Junior 1 and we had met when she was preparing Phyllis for her first communion. Now Anne was her responsibility.

She was showing me her work, part of which was the 'Monday Diary' in which the secrets of the weekend goings on in thirty families were exposed to Teacher's eyes. For week after week each entry started, 'We went to the pub'.

A couple of weeks later Moira called me into the classroom when I collected the children in the evening. 'Now I really know what you get up to at the weekend,' she smirked, handing me Anne's 'Diary'.

The previous Sunday had been wet and Jo and I had set to and tackled a minor problem that had been irritating us for some time. None of the rooms at The Huers was square; none of the walls was vertical and none of the floors horizontal. As a result of the latter, the bedroom carpet had 'walked' and was now wrinkled against the far wall. We decided to do the job properly: roll up half the carpet, move the furniture, roll up the rest of the carpet, move it to its proper position, tack it down, unroll it, moving the furniture back and tack down the other edges. We had just reached the stage when the rolled up carpet was jammed against the door when the door handle rattled.

'What's the matter?' I roared.

'I want to come in,' called Phyllis.

'Well you'll have to wait.' I continued struggling to straighten the recalcitrant carpet.

Anne's major report for that weekend read: 'Mummy and Daddy locked themselves in the bedroom and wouldn't let us in.'

When I reported this to Jo she merely remarked that if I spent my life acting like a sex maniac I mustn't grumble if the children thought I was one. 'Moira is certainly going to be convinced that you dragged me into the bedroom with only one thought in your mind.'

'Not her,' I replied, perching myself on the arm of the settee. 'She's clever enough to know that if anything happened it would be you who hurled me onto the bed and had your wicked will of me.'

'Fibber!' cried Jo, hurling across the room and knocking me off the arm and onto the settee where she pummelled me unmercifully.

'Stop!' I shouted. 'You'll do me an injury in a minute.'

'I hope I do,' she muttered, punctuating each word with a well-aimed blow. 'You are the biggest liar I ever met.' She paused for breath.

'Mummy,' said Phyllis.

We both turned. From the doorway six pairs of unblinking eyes regarded us accusingly.

We shooed the mob back to bed. 'You know what will happen now,' I said. 'Next week's diary will report, "Mummy and Daddy woke us up by wrestling on the settee".'

****

'Have some champagne,' offered Heather.

By the look of her room it had been quite a party. Crates of empty champagne bottles were stacked high in the corner and every vacant space held an empty glass.

'What are we celebrating?' I asked.

'My Decree Nisi,' she giggled. 'The happiest day of my life.'

'Well, if that's true I'll drink to it.' I raised my glass.

'It's been a lovely day,' she went on. 'A lovely, lovely day. And tomorrow I'll be in Taunton.'

'Taunton?' I queried.

'Somerset are playing Glamorgan,' she explained.

'I didn't know you were a cricket fan.'

'I certainly am,' she exclaimed. 'Haven't missed a test match in twenty years. You just ask anyone. England, The Aussies, The West Indians. Ask any of them. They all know Heather. Look!' She lifted her skirt waist high. Each of her thighs was liberally tattooed.

'Look closer,' she insisted.

I thanked Heaven that Jo was at home at The Huers. If she'd walked in just then she would certainly have got the wrong impression. Heather's tattoos consisted of a great many signatures, one or two of which were familiar.

'That was the Australian tour before the last. The Saturday night during the Lords Test. The English team on the left; Aussies on the right.' She giggled again. 'Pour me another glass and I'll show you Fred Trueman's autograph.'

I made, to coin a phrase, an excuse and left hastily, quite forgetting to collect Heather's rent. Outside the door stood Miriam and Fiona, two sisters who shared another ground floor flatlet.

'Are you all right?' asked Miriam solicitously.

'Only just,' I replied. 'Were you out here all the time?'

'Most of the day,' nodded Fiona. 'We've been trying to keep an eye on her. It started when we had to rescue the milkman this morning.'

Each Friday from then on I knocked with trepidation at Heather's door but she remained a pillar of rectitude. Nevertheless, I heaved a sigh of relief when she announced that she was emigrating to New Zealand. I wondered which part of her anatomy the Kiwis would be invited to autograph.

****

It was a lovely summer's morning. The bird's song was drowned by the jackdaws screeching through the branches of the old Macrocarpus. Halfway up sat our tawny owl, ignoring the jackdaws having their morning hate. I left the bucket by the door and walked across the road to the meadow. 'Susie,' I called, opening the gate. Susie trotted happily up from the stream and stood patiently while I looped the halter over her head.

We strolled peacefully back, over the road and up the drive. Suddenly the halter was tugged upwards and I glanced round to see quarter of a ton of cow rearing up over me. Just in time I leaped to one side and her hooves crashed down where I had been standing.

'Steady on, Susie,' I cried. 'What on earth's the matter?'

Susie threw herself from side to side and I shortened my grip on the halter just as she tried to rear up again. This time I managed to hold her. 'Calm down!' I shouted. 'There's nothing to be frightened of.'

'What's the matter?' Mr Roberts appeared at the gate. He had asked permission to leave his car in our drive overnight.

'I don't know. She must be frightened of something but I haven't a clue what it is. She was perfectly calm when I caught her in the meadow.'

Susie reared again, catching me unawares and snatching the end of the rope from my grasp. She galloped over to Mr Roberts's car, reared up and brought both front hooves down on the bonnet.

The old man let me know in no uncertain terms what he thought of my abilities as a herdsman and we both rushed to grab the halter. When I was holding it securely again he walked round and lifted up her tail. 'Tes like I thought,' he proclaimed. 'She's bulling. You want to phone the A.I. people bright and early or you'll be too late.'

Susie was as placid as could be as I milked her. I left her tied in the stall, with an extra helping of nuts to keep her happy, and explained the situation to Jo. She was to phone the A.I. Centre at Shiel Meadton at eight sharp and arrange for Susie to be 'done', specifying a Jersey bull.

A month later I was in the staff room when Peter French came in. 'Hullo Jeffrey,' he greeted me. 'How is that cow of yours getting on?'

'Fine,' I replied. 'Kids are being awkward though. They've all decided to go off milk. Typical! Can't say I'm too sure about the sex education either.'

'How's that?' he asked.

'Well,' I explained. 'They seem to have developed a curious theory. Apparently what happens is that one morning Mummy jumps on Daddy. Then Daddy ties Mummy up in the shed. Later on a little man in a white coat and a bowler hat comes to the kitchen door, picks up a bucket of water and a bar of soap and goes round to see Mummy. Nine months later she has a little baby.'

'I think you're going to have problems there,' opined Peter.

****

'My name isn't Frank Jordan,' shouted Frank Jordan. 'It's Immanuel Aedifico.'

'Oh no it isn't,' I replied. 'You have no intention of ever building anything at all, let alone God with us here on Earth. In fact you are an idle, loafing bum who has discovered that by looking and acting pathetic you cause other people, who work hard all day to make a living, to have sympathy and share that living with you. Well hard luck, Jordan. I'm one bloke with damned little sympathy, certainly none for scroungers like you.'

He gave me a look of pure hatred. 'I don't want to talk to you,' he muttered and walked out.

In spite of careful vetting, we had some odd characters among our tenants. Frank Jordan was one of the oddest. He had arrived the previous week as the result of a phone call. Jo took the call, looked blank and handed the receiver to me.

'Mr Peters?' asked the voice. 'You don't know me but I'm the Rural Dean. We have an unfortunate young man with us who has fallen upon hard times. I wonder if you have any accommodation available. Of course, we would pay his rent.'

Frank had arrived, bearing a cheque for a fortnight's rent drawn on a charitable organisation's account. By the weekend he was comfortably settled in. We had a number of young, impressionable, female students living in the Woodstock. Frank lacked for nothing in the way of cups of tea, hot meals or washed and ironed shirts.

'He's so hard done by,' exclaimed Fiona.

'Yes,' echoed Penny. 'That rotten university. Just fancy! They wouldn't listen when he tried to explain the problems he was having. They just threw him out because he failed his exams.'

'And what about that horrible employer?' continued Miriam. 'Can you imagine just sacking someone for no reason whatsoever?'

I began to suspect that all was not well and decided not to pay the Dean's cheque into our bank. I hoped that by not accepting any rent we would not be establishing a contract.

'Oh!' cried Shirley. 'He's so funny. Do you know what he did last evening? We were all talking to him when he stood up and said, "All right, Girls. Get your clothes off and let's have an orgy!" '

'And did you?' I asked.

'No. Of course not,' replied Fiona. 'But he made it sound like fun.'

I went to Frank's room and explained to him the rules of the establishment. He tried his imitation of a religious freak to no avail and stalked out in high dudgeon. I wondered how best to give him his marching orders.

I need not have bothered. The next evening's local paper bore headlines: 'Uproar in Cathedral'. It appeared that an interloper had mounted the pulpit in Exeter Cathedral and harangued those present with a sermon on the delights of sex. When led away by the police he had given the name Immanuel Aedifico.

We never saw him again.

****

'There ought to be something we could do with all this buttermilk,' said Jo. 'It does seem a pity to waste it.'

It was late evening, the children were in bed and we had just finished making butter with the Kenwood. Most of Susie's milk was used in one way or another. Bags of cottage cheese flavoured with garlic or chives hung dripping in the larder. Jugs of creamy Jersey milk half filled the fridge. Another pound and a half of yellow butter, lightly salted, was about to join them. There remained the buttermilk, refreshing to drink it was true, but the family was saturated with refreshing drinks.

The doorbell rang.

'Who can that be this late?' I wondered.

'Not a clue.' replied Jo.

I opened the door. There stood Harry Hodgson who ran a small-holding just over the hill. Behind him his pickup reflected the lights from the kitchen window.

'Hullo, Mr Hodgson,' I greeted him, somewhat puzzled. We seldom had casual callers after dark. 'Come in. Can we do anything for you?'

Under the kitchen strip-lighting it was obvious that Harry was not on a social call. He wore heavy boots, overalls and an old jacket and looked as though he could do with a good night's rest. 'Would you like some piglets?' he demanded.

'Piglets!' we echoed.

'If you don't want 'm I'll have to knock 'm on t' head.' he explained.

'Oh no!' shrieked Jo. 'You can't do that. Poor little things.'

We sat Harry down at the table with a pint of my home-brewed beer and he gave us a lecture on the economics of pig breeding. Making a living from a couple of acres, a husband and wife team could find twenty five hours worth of work needing doing every day of the week, even if no catastrophe occurred. If, as had now happened, a sow were to die farrowing there was no spare time to hand rear piglets. If one were lucky one might persuade another sow to accept one or two but any others would have to die. Harry, like all the rest of the village, knew that we were quite mad and might be prepared to take on almost anything.

Jo had been reduced, if not to floods of tears, at least to mournful sniffles into a 'man-sized' tissue by the thought of the doomed orphans. I could see what was going to happen.

'Aren't they sweet!' she cooed, gazing down. Beside the Aga, nice and cosy, stood a tea chest at the bottom of which, on a bed of straw and bulging with warm milk, slept six minute pink bodies. Rinsing in the sink were the babies' bottles I had hoped were a thing of the past.

In the public bar at the 'Ring o' Bells' they had heard of our latest lunacy and were laying bets that none of the piglets would survive.

There was nothing sweet about the atmosphere in the kitchen next morning and the piglets were squealing their heads off. I threw open the windows and both front and back doors and set off to milk Susie, glad to be out in the open. When I returned with two gallons of fresh milk Jo was in the throes of feeding six fighting children and six squealing little pigs. It was difficult to tell who was making the most noise. We agreed that pigs and humans could not share the kitchen so, in my lunch break that day I obtained a heat lamp and, on my return, made a warm home in the shed.

'I don't like the look of this one.' Jo was cradling a pathetic looking mite, much weaker than the others.

'Not a lot we can do bar feed them,' I said. 'I'll pop in and have a word with Bob. He'll have finished milking by now.'

'Bob says they should be fed every four hours,' I announced on my return. 'Worse than flipping kids!'

Later that night my morale was at an all time low. 'If anyone had told me I'd be hand feeding baby pigs at one o'clock in the morning I'd have thought he was mad,' I grumbled.

Jo was on an errand of mercy, saving infant lives, and was in her element though one little life looked very precarious indeed.

Next morning I had to tell her that we now had only five survivors. She was silent for a moment and surreptitiously wiped an eye. 'What will you do with the body?' she asked.

'I might give it to Jim Butlin for dissection,' I suggested. Jim taught A-level biology at a local grammar school. 'I'll pop it in the deepfreeze till I see him.'

Jo exploded. 'You're not going storing dead bodies in my freezer,' she fumed.

'But Darling........' I explained patiently that the freezer was already full of dead animals. 'Trout,' I said. 'Lamb chops, beef steak. All sorts of things.'

I buried the little corpse in the rose bed.

The landlord at the Bells cleaned up on his bets. Five little pigs were soon thriving and housed in a sty. We were still lunatics though. Everyone knew that one must get one's porkers to five score as soon as possible or all profit would be gone. We foolish people were still fattening ours months later. The idea that we regarded them as mobile dustbins rather than business was too outlandish to be worth contemplating.

Chapter 5

'We ought to have a puppy,' suggested Phyllis. 'It would be company for Tiggy.'

'It would have to be a bitch,' asserted her sister.

'Anne!' exclaimed Phyllis. 'That's rude.'

'No it isn't,' insisted Anne.

'It is,' claimed Mary. 'Sister Elfrida was very cross with Wendy when she called Sally a bitch when we were doing R.E.'

' "Bitch" isn't a rude word, is it Daddy?' persisted Anne.

'Only when you use it to be rude to someone,' I assured them. 'Why should it have to be a bitch, anyway?'

'Well,' said Anne. 'Then when it grew up we could have lots of puppies.'

The afternoon had provided some light-hearted entertainment, something which didn't often happen. My class had been discussing one of the stories of Brensham Village in which the local newspaper figured prominently.

'What,' I asked them, 'does the author mean by "The Intelligencer"?'

'I know,' called a voice from the back.

'Come on then, David,' I replied. 'Tell us.'

'The Intelligencer,' he pronounced confidently, 'are all them posh people what think they know everything.'

'That's a brilliant definition,' I assured him. 'And the fact that it's quite wrong doesn't make it less so. It's just a slight error of pronunciation.'

'Ah!' exclaimed David. 'It's because of where I come from.'

'Oh yes,' I replied. 'We all know where you come from, David. You can always tell a Brummie by the shamrock in his turban.'

To my surprise he had never heard this before and fell about laughing. At the end of the lesson he couldn't wait to tell John Peterson what 'That Mr Peters' had said.

I was still in a happy mood when I collected the children from school. The sun was shining and I opted to take the long route home through Oakshiel Forest even though Susie would be getting impatient. On Shrove Tuesday Anne had announced her intention of milking Susie every day in Lent. Now, with only a week to go, we should have hurried home so that she could carry out her resolution, but I stopped and let Tiggy out to chase us for a couple of hundred yards. This led to Phyllis's suggestion.

'Well, we'll think about it,' I promised.

I should have known better. By the time Anne had finished milking and led Susie back to the field across the road the others, playing on Jo's love of all things small, had sold her the idea of a new puppy.

On Saturday we set off for the kennels to inspect a litter of golden Labradors. At first it seemed that we would never be able to make a choice and Jane was in tears on learning that we couldn't take the lot. In the end we settled for a very pale bundle of fur, which looked set to be smothered with affection before we reached home.

'What shall we call her?' asked Mary.

'Whiskers,' said John

'That's daft,' exclaimed Cormac. A fight was about to develop.

'Her mother was called Sherry.' Jo was reading from the pup's pedigree.

'It must have been a very pale sherry,' I punned.

'More like champagne,' suggested Phyllis.

We all agreed. Champagne of St Peters, Shammy for short, took up residence at The Huers. Tiggy was a bit offhand at first but condescended to share the hearthrug. The children learned the joys of house training.

****

'Hullo Jeffrey,' a man at the bar called as I entered.

I hadn't seen 'Wimpy' Wellington for years but at one time, whenever I had been involved in helicopters in any capacity, Wimpy was never far away. Now here he was in the bar of the White Lion.

'What are you doing these days?' I asked as we propped up the end of the bar on which rested our pints.

'Working for Westlands,' he told me.

'Pays better than teaching, I expect,' I guessed. 'Still keeping up your judo I suppose?'

'Of course,' he replied. 'Never give that up.'

Wimpy was a fanatic, black belt and umpteenth dan. During the Korean War there had been strange tales of a fishing boat with a chopper pad on top, which vanished periodically with Wimpy and a gang of desperados, returning days later from the North showing signs of battle. But when off duty he could always be found wearing his judogi at the high altar of the sport. Rumour had it that he had once thrown the supreme master with a trick so simple that the old boy had forgotten it. The bar filled up around us as we reminisced.

'You're in the way, Dad,' came an unpleasant voice from behind us. We ignored it.

A hand grasped Wimpy's arm and the voice repeated, 'I said, "You're in the way, Dad".'

A spotty faced youth leered at Wimpy. 'Get out the way. I want a drink.'

I didn't really see what happened next but Spotty was on his knees, grimacing with pain as Wimpy held one of his fingers.

'Listen Laddy,' he said. 'You are making it quite clear from your behaviour that you are a little bastard but, as you are neither good looking nor intelligent, you can't be one of mine. So let's have less of the "Out the way, Dad," and more of the "Excuse me, Sir," shall we?'

'Yes,' whined the youth.

'Yes, what?' demanded Wimpy.

'Yes, Sir.'

'Right,' said Wimpy, releasing his grip. 'Now run away and play with your little friends. Don't come back here till you're a grown up.'

Spotty paused in the doorway. 'Sod you,' he shouted and fled.

A ripple of applause ran round the bar.

'Have one on the house,' said Ray.

****

'The truck's stuck in your gateway,' announced the driver's mate.

It had to happen some time. The rest of the village were still convinced that anyone who fattened pigs slowly must be mad. We, regarding our pigs as mobile dustbins, were not perturbed by this and our orphan piglets had turned ever so slowly into round, milk fed porkers. Now they were ready for the table. In our continuing ignorance we accepted Harry Hodgson's advice without stopping to consider the differing requirements of the amateur and professional. Over the telephone we arranged that the meat company's cattle truck should include us on its round of the locality on the following Wednesday. We decided to keep the smallest of the pigs so that we still had an outlet for surplus milk from Susie.

On Tuesday evening we managed to lure the little one away from her siblings and to a makeshift sty by Susie's stall. Next morning I set off with the children leaving Jo with explicit instructions of where the men should park their truck. We returned soon after five. I was puzzled to find the gate propped against the hedge and the gateposts lying beside it. Jo appeared at the door. She seemed dishevelled, to say the least.

Sharp at ten thirty the cattle truck had arrived and parked outside while the driver and his mate came in to recce the scene of action. Jo pointed out the sty and the most obvious route for the truck. 'No problem,' announced the driver and, under the directions of his mate, happily reversed through the gateway and back to the sty where the pigs were loaded aboard with the expertise of long experience. 'Here you are, Missus,' said the assistant, handing Jo a receipt for four pigs. And off they drove.

About ten minutes later Jo looked out of the kitchen window and was surprised to see the truck still in the gateway. As she watched the engine revved and the truck moved forward a couple of inches. The reversing light came on and it moved back a similar distance. She walked down the drive and found the truck well and truly jammed between the gateposts. As it had passed between them on its way in, this was obviously impossible but there it was. I had put the posts in myself when we bought The Huers. They were made of cast iron and bedded in concrete. The truck was solidly fixed between them and part of the framework supporting the sides had already been broken. Any movement of the truck resulted in more damage to the framework. The posts were immovable.

The next few hours increased our telephone bill considerably. The driver had a long conversation with his boss in North Devon. This, it seemed, resulted in nothing more helpful than instructions to solve the problem himself. Jo assured me that she learned more new swear words in half an hour of this conversation than in all the years she had been married to me, or even before that, as an avid follower of her hospital rugby team. The driver went on to phone half the farmers in the Culm Valley to explain why he would be late in collecting from them. Each offered advice, none of it very helpful. Jo kept the driver and his mate refuelled with coffee at regular intervals.

By three o'clock Susie was mooing from the gate opposite. It was milking time but there was no way in which Jo could get her to the shed. Never one to be defeated, Jo sallied forth equipped with milking stool, bucket for milk and another of milk nuts to keep Susie happy, forced her way through the hedge and onto the road and opened the gate into the field. Just inside was a telegraph pole and Susie was secured to this with her halter. The bucket of nuts was placed before her and Jo, squatting on her stool, proceeded to milk.

In the nature of things, the peaceful little country road immediately turned into a busy highway and driver after driver braked violently in order to gape at the sight. More onlookers arrived as the news spread through the village that those lunatics at The Huers were doing something for the telly. The noise swelled to a crescendo when the school bus passed by, the children cheering their heads off. At least, Jo thought they were cheering.

Milking completed, the problem of return was complicated by the necessity of keeping leaves, twigs and other debris out of the milk while scrambling through the hedge. At this point Mr Roberts turned up, took one look, snorted 'Move the gateposts,' produced an iron bar and a sledge hammer and in ten minutes had both gateposts out of the ground. The truck roared away up the road, five hours late on its round. It was then that we drove through the gate. Jo did not take kindly to my remark that she looked as though she had been pulled through a hedge backwards. In fact she was downright rude. The children were most indignant that Mummy hadn't waited so that they could join in the fun.

****

'We could just about save enough by October,' Jo assured me.

The salesman had been very persuasive, but we were used to that. We looked at it from every angle but we couldn't see the catch. The price was ridiculously low and the only proviso was that we should allow him to bring potential purchasers to view it, as it would be the first of its type to be installed in the Southwest.

'Just think!' Jo enthused. 'Our own swimming pool. No more driving all the way to the coast for a swim, and I don't much fancy what is floating in the water when we get there. And we could have some super parties.'

'Pimms by the pool parties,' I agreed. 'Sounds a good idea.'

When the salesman returned we signed the contract and paid one hundred pounds deposit. Work was to begin at the end of September and would take about three weeks.

'You'll never regret it,' he insisted. 'We've sold thousands like this all over the States. Now we are starting in the U.K. with the idea of breaking into Europe in a year or two.'

The autumn duly arrived, and with it the excavator. The children were fascinated and, as we arrived home each evening, they evacuated the Dormobile in double quick time and rushed to see what progress had been made. Even Jane woke up. It was her first term at school and she fell asleep as soon as I picked them up in the evening. Not even our spirited rendering of 'The Court of King Caractacus' would wake her on the way home but pool inspection did.

And fascinating it was, too. The excavator operator worked with such precision that the vertical sides of the hole measured exactly sixteen feet by thirty-two, no more and no less. The sand which formed the floor was smoothed by two men with plasterers' floats till it was as smooth as our drawing room wall. At last came the day when it was ready to be filled. Water poured from the hose and very very slowly the level rose, the workmen gently squeezing out any bubbles that formed under the bright blue lining. At last it was full.

'Can we go in now?' begged Phyllis.

'Not for a few days yet,' replied the foreman.

'Oh please!' chorused the children.

I cocked an eye at him.

'Well,' he said. 'There's nothing in there now but tap water. But before it's ready we've got to put in the stabilizer. If you went in in the next two days it would make your eyes sore. Then we have to super-chlorinate it and you probably know what that's like. But a quick dip right now? OK!'

Never were six swimming suits donned so swiftly. The four eldest plunged happily in at the deep end. John ensured that the floats were properly adjusted round his arms and a life belt round his tum, lowered himself cautiously onto a lilo and floated serenely across the pool with only his toes touching the water. Jane sat on the edge with her feet in the water, splashing anyone who approached.

We were glad that they had had that dip, for the weather turned cold and wet next day. The foreman returned to test the chlorination.

'You've got a bargain there,' he said. 'I don't know how they do it at the price.'

It was five years before I found out. I was enjoying a pint in the Ring o' Bells when the salesman came in. He recognized me and came over to my corner of the bar.

'How's the pool?'

I assured him that it was fine and that he could ask for my endorsement any time.

'Won't be doing that,' he said. 'You never knew how lucky you were. A couple of days after we cashed your cheque we had an urgent message to stop all sales of that pattern. All over the States they started collapsing and the company was up to its ears in law-suits. You, three others in England and one more in Wales had paid your deposits and we were committed to supplying pools so you got the next one up in quality, an old model that had never given any trouble. It should have cost you three times as much.'

'Have a pint,' I invited him.

****

'When I first started,' said the bank manager, 'I'd have thought eight per cent was verging on usury but it's the best we can offer you today.'

That had been eighteen months ago. Now they were charging us sixteen per cent. Far from paying off the loan, every penny we collected in rent went to paying the interest and the Peterses' family fortune looked as far as ever from becoming reality.

'Good luck, Darling,' I called from the Dormobile as we set off one Tuesday morning. 'You show them that we're fireproof, bombproof and in the Drug Squad's good books.' The Council's Inspectors were coming to inspect the Woodstock. We thought we could satisfy them on every point, even to the coin operated washing machine in the basement. We should have known better.

Jo was a picture of gloom when we returned that evening.

'All the rooms are too small,' she informed me. 'I argued and argued but all they did was to wave their silly rule book at me. If I'd had one of those rooms when I was a student nurse I'd have thought it was heaven. Honestly, you'd think we were evicting widows and orphans rather than providing young people with a decent home.'

Phyllis turned to and prepared supper for the others while we sat and calculated costs and income. Nothing gave us any joy at all.

'It would cost a bomb to knock down all those walls and turn all the single rooms into doubles,' I muttered for the umpteenth time.

'And even then,' continued Jo, 'we couldn't charge twice the rent. So we'd be even more in debt and with less money coming in.'

There was no doubt about it. Our only option was to sell, pay off all our debts and start again from square one. We agreed that Jo should go and talk to the commercial department of the estate agents next day.

There was a loud knock at the door.

'Got a little runt 'ere,' said Harry Hodgson, standing just inside the door with a writhing sack under his arm. 'No good to I. Others keep on getting at her-biting and suchlike.'

'Poor little thing!' exclaimed Jo. 'Let me see.'

In the sack was the ugliest piglet we had ever seen. Its ears had been partly nibbled away, its tail likewise. Long hairs were growing from its back. When Harry put it down it hobbled across the kitchen floor. 'Must have hurt its leg and never set right,' he explained. 'Growing them hairs 'cos others wouldn't let it near enough to sow to get warm, I s'pose.'

'We'll give her a happy home!' Jo's eyes were watering.

I retired to the larder for beer. I was used, by this time, to succouring orphan piglets and had reduced the chore of weaning them from bottle to trough to a fine art. The greatest problem now lay in persuading Jo that the time had come, when they reached the magic five score - one hundred pounds in weight - that they must be off to the bacon factory. Mind you, by that time they had lost any charm they may have possessed as infants and had changed to raucous, smelly delinquents, always ready to charge out of the sty gate and into the rose bed, given half a chance.

Harry sank his beer and headed up the hill. I rigged the heat lamp over a bed of straw in the shed, collected a now replete piglet from the kitchen and made it comfortable for the night.

'Will Peggy be all right?' asked Jo, on my return.

'Peggy?' I queried.

'Pegleg Peggy Pig.' said Jo.

****

'That wasn't a very bright idea, was it?' asked Jack Turnbull.

The local paper had been lavish in its praise of the cuisine at a newly refurbished pub on the banks of the Exe. Jo, Terry and Corenne, chatting over their morning coffee, had decided that their respective husbands should treat them to dinner there that evening. And so it came about that the six of us met in the bar and surveyed the queue of would be diners whose taste buds had also been whetted by the article.

'It'll be closing time before we get this lot dealt with,' the landlord assured us. 'Sorry.'

'Not a chance of getting in anywhere else handy at this time of night,' remarked Simon.

A general discussion ensued.

'Come on, Corenne,' I said, 'I'll give you a game of bar billiards. We have two doctors and two nurses here, quite enough professional ability to work out how to keep us healthily nourished without our amateur efforts.'

I inserted a coin in the mechanism at the end of the table and we set about demonstrating our skill in knocking over the skittles we were meant to avoid. Meanwhile the others agreed to return to the Turnbulls' and take potluck. It was a happy choice.

'Look,' cried Terry from the depths of the deep freeze. 'I'd forgotten I had this.'

She emerged bearing a salmon of at least ten pounds.

'How could you forget something like that?' demanded Jo. 'Where did it come from?'

Jack chuckled. 'It's surprising, the things that get left on the doorstep of a popular country doctor. It's going to take a while for you to thaw that out, Love. Then you'll have to poach it in the old fish kettle.'

'A twice poached fish?' I suggested.

Jack chuckled again. 'Shouldn't be a bit surprised' he replied. 'Doesn't do to ask questions. You know what they say about gift horses. Any way, as I said, it'll take Terry a while before it's ready for the table. We'd better see what else I've found on the doorstep lately.'

He plunged into the darkness of the spence and emerged with a bottle of twelve-year-old malt whisky. Throwing a couple more logs on the already cheerfully blazing fire, he poured out half a dozen generous measures. The evening looked much more cheerful than from the back end of a pub queue.

It was late when we returned home, full of poached salmon and malt. Jo's sister, Noelle, had been baby sitting for us and greeted us with a tale of woe.

'That was a lovely meal you left me,' she told us. 'The chops and everything were cooked to perfection.'

She had left the food on the broad stone surround of the fireplace where it would keep warm while she fetched herself a drink. She paid the penalty of not being used to dogs. On her return she shrieked with horror as Tiggy munched his way through her supper with evident delight at his good fortune. Her first reaction was to rescue it but the ferocious curl of his lip as he snarled his defiance dissuaded her.

'I made myself an omelette,' she wailed. 'It was OK but not a patch on lamb chops with mint sauce and mashed potatoes.'

Chapter 6

'How about, "Midsummer Madness - The Peterses' Premier Pool Plunge Party"?' suggested Jo.

'Why stop there?' I asked. 'You could go on, "Plenty of pies, pickles and plonk".'

'Polo, piscatorial pursuits and er - um.' Jo tailed off.

'Passion?' I offered hopefully.

'Not in front of the children,' she objected.

The pool had been in use since Easter. The weather had been warm but, even if it had been snowing, nothing would have kept the children out of the water. Safety rules had been established and dire penalties promised for non-observance. The greatest surprise was John who, up till then, had declined to venture into anything more than ankle deep without an armoury of flotation aids. On Friday evening he edged gently into the shallow end with only a pair of inflated armlets. On Saturday he removed the armlets. On Sunday morning he leapt into the deep end and by that evening was happily diving seven feet down to recover small articles thrown in by other members of the family.

We were proposing to invite our friends to an official opening on Midsummer's Night. As the date approached we got down to the smaller details: the wine merchant was consulted on the subject of two-litre bottles and loan of glasses; the greengrocer promised supplies of salads and fruit. I had discovered an unexpected talent as a pie-man. Woe betide any hen which grew fat on layers' mash in the barn without a corresponding return in the form of eggs. It soon found itself simmering all night in the bottom oven of the Aga, in company with a knuckle of ham and assorted herbs, and next day was converted into a succulent pie that went into the freezer.

In the midst of this, Jo went out one morning to hang out the washing on the line that straddled the paddock. Susie was grazing peacefully, the hens clucked contentedly and the apple trees were still covered in blossom. All was peace and tranquillity. Jo stooped over the washing basket when some instinct caused her to look over her shoulder.

'No, Susie!' she shrieked and dived to one side just in time to avoid the pair of hooves which crashed down into the washing. Susie's second calf had been sold to Harry Hodgson some time earlier and now she was bulling again. Once more the phone call to Shiel Meadton and the visit next morning with requests for soap, water and towel.

'She can't find it much fun,' remarked Jo that evening.

'I don't think I envy the bull much, either,' I replied.

The great day arrived. The sun had shone all week and the pool warmed nicely. It was crystal clear and with only a slight whiff of chlorine from my preparations of the day before. After breakfast I set off in the van for Exeter and the wine merchant's. Returning with my trophies, I found a hive of activity. Jo, ably assisted by Terry and Corenne, was preparing vast bowls of salads while the children, under the direction of Phyllis, had placed tables on the lawn and were piling these with all the cutlery and crockery we had been able to beg, borrow or scrounge from our friends. I appropriated one table for use as a bar and began stacking bottles and glasses.

We ate lunch by the pool and rehearsed for such disasters as somebody's breaking a glass among all those bare feet. John displayed his ability to retrieve a glass from the deep end, while Anne and Cormac were appointed wine waiters and briefed on the importance of maintaining full glasses at all times. Phyllis and Mary were to assist Jo and five year old Jane promised to retrieve every errant paper napkin before it could be blown into the pool and clog the filter.

Wise guests arrived early and parked in our drive; late arrivals had to pass right through the village and walk back. As the numbers grew the wine waiters did their job right nobly and conversation began to flow. In a sports shop I had discovered a pair of swimming trunks decorated with the front covers of 'Playboy', which I thought suitable to the occasion; Jo was not impressed. 'Typical,' she sniffed when I produced them.

At eight o'clock I stood on the edge of the pool and called for order. I got as far as, 'I now declare this pool -,' when a tall blonde pushed me unceremoniously in. 'Open!' I declared as I emerged. Phyllis and Anne charged the blonde and all three landed on top of me. Soon there were more people in the pool than out.

Jo's food, as ever, proved a credit to the establishment. There was a short break from swimming for digestive recuperation and then, as dusk turned to dark, floodlit water-polo took over. The World Series lasted well into the night and, when Mike Foot's panda car appeared at the gate we thought the cheers must have led to a complaint. We should have known better. Mike pronounced the wine drinkable and stayed to cheer the finals. The winners were Tiverton Ladies, by five goals to two but rival supporters complained at the inclusion of Jack

Turnbull in the team. His polo tactics owed much to his experience in Barts' scrum.

Susie was milked late next morning and clearing up was completed at a leisurely pace.

Phyllis summed it up: 'A rude lady pushed Daddy in but we got her!'

****

'I've scored twenty,' exclaimed Jo.

'You can't, Mummy. You can't,' came a chorus from the rear seats.

Whenever I could muster all the children sufficiently early in the morning we drove through the woods on our way to school. We played a game to keep them alert, scoring points for various animals we spotted: one for rabbits and pigeons, two for game birds, three for weasels and birds of prey, four for deer and five for real rarities like foxes and badgers. 'And ten for golden eagles and elephants', Mary had added when we formulated the rules.

We were on the outskirts of Exeter. One of Jo's friends had volunteered to include our mob with hers on a visit to the children's programme at the cinema, giving the two of us a rare chance to see the estate agent and our solicitor concerning the sale of the Woodstock. Jo pointed to a field on the other side of the road. Sure enough, there, beside a circus tent, stood two elephants.

The chorus redoubled. 'Oh, please may we go to the circus? Please, please, please!'

'We'll think about it,' I told them. In the mirror I saw Phyllis give a thumbs up signal to Anne.

'There's not a lot of demand for this sort of property,' the agent informed us.

'That's not what you told us two years ago,' retorted Jo.

'Ah!' he replied. 'Things were different then.'

'How different?'

'Well, then you were buying. Now you're selling,' he explained with not the slightest sign of embarrassment. 'But we have had this offer from a chap in Torquay. We might get him to raise it, though I'm doubtful.'

The solicitor was rather more hopeful. 'House prices are rising quite fast,' she assured us. 'The trouble is that you are looking for a purchaser who can afford to make all these alterations that the Council have specified. But the property itself must be worth much more than you paid for it.'

Slightly cheered, we collected the family from their harassed guardian and returned home, stopping on the way to buy tickets for the next afternoon's performance at the circus. This was a great success, especially the clowns and the three girls who stood on giant beach-balls and manoeuvred them between the gyrating elephants.

On Sunday Jo suggested that Anne might write to her godparents in Africa. When I returned from my weekly pool-hoovering chore she was still engrossed in writing.

'What have you said in your letter?' I asked.

'Dear Uncle and Aunty,' Anne read. 'We went to the circus and saw three ladies with big balls.'

'Your godmother is going to be fascinated,' I assured her.

****

'Please can Rosie come to stay,' requested Jane. 'She's my best friend and she wants to see our house.'

Jo phoned Rosie's mother and it was arranged that she should accompany Jane home from school on the following Wednesday and stay the night. Wednesday evening arrived and with it Rosie. She was gorgeous with big, blue eyes and long, golden hair and Jane led her around our domain with pride. John, conscious of his superiority in age, six, and class, Infants Two, treated her with disdain.

Gradually, in order of seniority, the children were tucked up for the night. Jane and Rosie, the first to bed, were too excited to sleep; the thrill of having or being an overnight guest was too much. We left them still chattering.

Only a little later all hell broke loose with screams from the two little ones and the patter of feet along the corridor towards the boys' room.

Rushing upstairs to investigate I found Rosie crying bitterly and Janc comforting her.

'What has been going on and why is Rosie crying,' I demanded.

'John kissed her!' explained Jane in total outrage.

I could hardly blame him but paternal discipline had to be maintained.

'John, you little monster,' I bellowed down the corridor, 'what do you think you're up to, kissing Rosie and making her cry?'

'It - it wasn't that,' whispered Rosie.

'Well, why are you crying then?' I asked.

'He - he - he stopped,' she sobbed.

Jo and I were still chuckling when we settled down to sleep. Something disturbed our mirth.

'Why is Ben barking?' asked Jo.

'I don't know,' I confessed. 'What's the time?'

We continued the conversation for some minutes, neither of us wanting to be the one to voice what we feared. In the end I got up, pulled sweater and slacks over my pyjamas, and set off to investigate.

Old Mr Roberts who lived across the road had set habits. Since the death of his wife we were always pretty sure where we could find him. If his dog, Ben, was running free then his master was working in his garden or in the churchyard next door. If he were farther afield, Ben would be chained to his kennel by the front door. Only when the old man was in the cottage was the dog allowed inside.

Ben was inside. His steady barking did not vary as I walked up the path, nor when I hammered on the door. I walked round to the back and tried that door. It was locked and there was no answer to my knocking. I walked back down the path, over the bridge and up to Bob Merlin's barn. The shed where Bob allowed Mr Roberts to garage his car was locked, presumably with the car inside. I reported back to Jo.

The police car drove up about half past one and a young constable got out as I opened the door. I had coffee ready and explained my fears as he drank.

'Well, we'd better take a look,' he said, putting down his empty cup.

We prowled around the cottage. Ben kept on barking. The policeman tried the doors and windows.

'I really think he must be in there,' I assured him. 'And if we haven't disturbed him by now then he must be ill.'

It was apparent that the bobby was not keen on breaking and entering but duty called and he went down to the garden shed, returning with a crow-bar. With this he levered the back door open, shattering the lock in the process. Then we searched the house, each encouraging the other to be first into each room, especially the kitchen where Ben awaited us. He was not at all put out and wagged his tail enthusiastically. We searched the bedrooms; we searched the bathroom. Mr Roberts was out.

In the end I apologised profusely while the constable found some nails and a hammer with which he secured the back door. He left a note on the kitchen table and we returned to The Huers. He reported the results of our investigation over the radio, drank another mug of coffee and drove off. I retired to bed, recited the tale to Jo and fell asleep at about three.

We slept late. I milked Susie, shaved quickly, grabbed some breakfast and chased the children into the Dormobile. Rosie had recovered from her ravishment and was all smiles again. Smoke was coming from the cottage chimney but I hadn't time to call. It wasn't until we returned that evening that I learned the truth: that Mr Roberts had spent the night playing pontoon with some of his cronies up the village. Mike Foot had arrived to continue the investigation soon after we left, and reported the result to Jo.

Later that evening there was a knock at the door.

'Permission to go to the pictures please, Sir,' said Mr Roberts, saluting smartly.

'Granted,' I replied. 'But don't overstay your leave again.'

****

'She's your daughter all right,' remarked Simon.

Corenne's parents and two sisters were spending the Christmas holiday with the Flint-Jonses and we had invited them for lunchtime drinks on Boxing Day. There was a roaring fire in the drawing room and Jo's brother, McCormac, was doing sterling duty preparing Dry Martinis. He was just emptying the third gin bottle into the jug when Anne rushed into the room, tripped on the carpet, turned a complete summersault and ended sitting upright with not a drop spilled from her glass of cola.

'There's no doubt about it,' Simon continued. 'That all important sense of the necessity to preserve your drink intact must be in her genes.'

'And we know whose genes they are, don't we?' added Jo.

'You must be a sailor,' asserted Corenne's father. 'Never met a sailor who couldn't defend his tot.'

'Do you sail at all?' asked Simon.

'Used to,' I replied. 'When I was a happy, laughing, carefree bachelor. Can't afford it nowadays.'

'I was thinking of going up to the boat show on Sunday week,' he said. 'How about coming with me?'

We agreed that Corenne should spend the day at The Huers with Jo and I would travel up to London with Simon.

'What about Boots?' asked Corenne. 'We can't leave him cooped up at home for all that time. And he can't go with you; he's always car sick on a long journey.' Boots was their large and bouncy Old English sheepdog.

'He could come over here with you,' suggested Jo. 'But Tiggy is very jealous and we'd have to keep them tied up out of each other's way.'

In the end, Simon and I set off for London with Tiggy in the back of the car while Boots ranged free in Shiel St Peters. We made good speed on almost empty roads and Tiggy achieved every right thinking dog's ambition by spending a penny on Rotten Row. We had an excellent pub lunch and parked near Earls Court.

'Don't think much of yours,' remarked Simon as we eyed the two goose-pimpled, bikini clad girls shivering on the deck of an enormous yacht in the pool.

'If we could afford to buy the boat we could afford fur coats for the crew,' I pointed out.

'Even if we could afford it I don't think Corenne and Jo would let us keep them,' he replied.

We spent a happy afternoon touring the show and it was already dark when we set off, footsore and weary, for Devon. We stopped for tea and a snack at the motorway service area near Heathrow, a gloomy place where the staff padded about looking nervously over their shoulders as though expecting to be charged any minute with being an illegal immigrant. It was late when we arrived home and

Simon and I opened the door and turned right to the kitchen where our wives waited to greet us with drinks and supper.

Tiggy, on the other hand, turned left into the living room and discovered a perfect stranger lying on his hearth rug, in front of his fire. This was more than canine flesh and blood could stand and the resulting fight was spectacular. Without hesitation, eight-year-old Mary, in her nightdress, hurled herself into the mêlée and grasped their collars, only to be hurled aside with a nasty bite on her left hand. Simon staunched her wound while I separated the combatants.

'Don't worry, Jo. She's all right,' Simon called, the blood oozing between his fingers giving little confirmation to his words. 'My bag is in the car. I'll just get it if you hold her for a moment. Oh hell! No it isn't. I took it out so that we could put Tiggy in there.'

His car vanished out through the gate in a flurry of gravel. In record time he was back and leaped out with his bag as a blue flashing lamp passed the gate, stopped and reversed into the drive.

'Oh it's you, Doctor,' said Mike Foot. 'I was just putting the Panda away when a car passed my gate doing about ninety so I thought I'd better catch him but I couldn't till now.'

He sank a large scotch as Simon repaired Mary's hand, then departed. Mary was put to bed with hot milk and hot water bottle while Simon and I partook of our belated supper.

Next morning Corenne was on the phone early to ask Jo about the patient. 'Thank Heavens for that,' she exclaimed on being reassured. 'Last night she looked so white, like a milk bottle with legs.'

****

'We're in the black!' exclaimed Jo.

'Pull the other one,' I replied.

I was sitting at the kitchen table marking some essays. Jo, at the other end of the table, was studying a pile of bank statements, chequebooks and files, trying to calculate our financial position following the sale of the Woodstock.

'Come and look,' she invited.

I walked round and leaned over her shoulder at the mass of figures she was calculating. Gradually it crept over me that she was right. We had made a profit out of the enterprise, a rare event *chez* Peters.

'You deserve a drink,' I told her, heading for the sideboard.

'You have one too,' she insisted.

' "You", in this context, means "we",' I assured her.

'I should have known better,' she sighed.

I had good reasons for hoping she was right. Living out in the country meant that we needed transport that worked. The Dormobile was showing signs of age and spending more and more time in the local garage. I had put off replacing it until now, but it no longer deserved the description 'reliable'. The final straw had been the bus-strike when, in the absence of the school bus from Wydshiel, the poor old thing had been loaded, twice a day, with far more bodies than it had ever been designed to carry. Phyllis stood guard at the back door and supervised the passengers, ensuring that each disembarked at the right place. When it was over, the strain seemed to have been too much and parts failed with monotonous regularity. I began to think of a replacement.

'That short enough for you?' asked the barber.

I nodded my assent and, having paid and been brushed down, walked out. By the kerb stood a Peugeot estate car. I inspected it closely and was much taken with the idea of six seats at the back. At that point the owner arrived and proudly extolled the car's virtues. I was particularly impressed comparing the petrol consumption with the Dormobile's. Petrol prices were soaring, a speed limit of fifty miles per hour was in force and we had all been issued with coupons against the day when rationing would start. I was sold.

That evening I described the car to Jo and her brother, McCormac, who was spending a few days with us. A week later McCormac phoned from his home in Reading.

'I've seen a Peugeot 504 for sale at a garage here. It's a demonstration model, almost new. They'd consider taking your Dormobile in part exchange. Yes, it is the family model.'

The next Saturday a salesman appeared in the drive with the Peugeot.

'Take it for a drive,' he invited us, 'while I have a look at your Dormobile.'

Before we could speak the children had piled into the back seats. We made a short tour and returned well satisfied. In no time at all we had signed on the dotted line and agreed to travel to Reading on the following weekend, when the car would be ready for us.

'Pounds?' exclaimed Jo's brother on the phone that evening. 'I wouldn't have given you two hundred and fifty pence for that old wreck.'

We invited ourselves to stay with him on the Friday night.

'That's fine,' he said. 'I'm meeting the other girls in Camberley for lunch on Saturday. We can make a party of it.'

On Friday evening we chugged our way steadily up the A303. The engine was failing fast, and I instructed Jo to pray every time we came to a hill. I was grateful to the self-sacrificing friend whom Jo had persuaded to look after the children. We would never have made it with a full load. With a sigh of relief I parked outside McCormac's flat, only an hour late.

'Let's be quite clear,' said Jo. 'I am not drinking in McCormac's house.'

McCormac was a bachelor with a reputation for lavish hospitality. He had, over the years, reduced each of his four sisters to a hungover wreck and each had vowed never to repeat the experience. I promised to uphold Jo's abstinence and rang the bell. The door opened and there stood McCormac with a silver salver upon which rested two very large Dry Martinis.

'Just go and get the car and leave me here,' moaned Jo next morning. 'All I want to do is die.'

Fortunately the engine started and the Dormobile groaned its way to the garage. I parked it with relief and, having completed the formalities, drove back in the estate car.

Alka-seltzer did little to restore Jo to her usual self and her three sisters took one look, nodded at each other and overflowed with the sympathy of fellow sufferers. The pub in Camberley provided an excellent lunch but she could not face it. As soon as possible I installed her in the Peugeot and set off for Devon. She slept most of the way; almost her only words, as I cruised along a stretch of dual carriage with my foot resting lightly on the pedal, were: 'You do realize you're doing ninety, don't you?'

By the next morning Jo was fully recovered and drove the children happily off to church. On Monday she phoned me at lunchtime.

'We've had another bank statement,' she informed me. 'It shows interest and bank charges of nearly a thousand pounds.'

We were once more in the red; with a vengeance.

****

'I've had an idea,' announced Jo.

I groaned and buried myself deeper in the crossword.

'Lots of people are doing it. It sounds quite profitable.'

'An affirmative in France. Short sinister writer. Seven letters,' I muttered.

'Betty made enough last year to re-carpet her living room. She gets them through an agency,' Jo went on.

'Anouilh!' I exclaimed.

'No,' replied Jo. 'I don't think it was that. "Friends across the Sea" more like.'

I gave in and fetched some beer. 'What exactly are you talking about?' I asked.

'Foreign children,' she explained. 'Apparently lots of parents abroad send their children over here in the summer to improve their English.'

'You mean like when I had that holiday job at St Lawrence's? I taught a class of French fifth formers. There were two nice girls in charge of them if you remember. We had them out to lunch one Sunday.'

'I don't think we're going to forget them,' said Jo. 'For weeks afterwards Anne told every visitor we had all about "Daddy's two French mistresses". But these aren't over here for lessons. They come as individuals; on holiday with a family who don't speak their language.'

'Well,' I conceded, 'I don't suppose one or two extra would make much difference. And we've got enough spare rooms.'

A couple of weeks later I had just finished milking Susie and was about to wake the children. The agency's West Country representative was visiting to inspect the house and ensure that we were suitable people for delicately nurtured children to stay with.

'Tell them their rooms are to be immaculate,' called Jo.

I walked along the corridor chanting:

' "Awake, for morning in the bowl of night
Hath cast the stone that put the stars to flight,
And lo! The hunter of the East has caught
The Sultan's turret in a noose of light."

'And make sure your rooms are spotless,' I added.

'Must you make such a noise, Daddy?' demanded Phyllis.

'Think yourself lucky,' I replied. 'Not many people are woken by Omar Khayyam. You wouldn't like it if I woke you with a bugle.'

'I'd rather hear The Bay City Rollers,' she agreed and vanished into the bathroom.

'How did it go?' I enquired on our return that evening.

'She loved it,' said Jo. 'Especially the pool. She took one look, borrowed a towel, stripped off and dived in. Didn't come out for half an hour.'

'I wish I'd been here.' I enthused.

'I'm glad you weren't,' replied Jo. 'Her figure was a damned sight better than mine.'

'Impossible,' I assured her.

'Flattery will get you anywhere,' she cooed.

Chapter 7

'Her mother,' said the lady at the agency, 'is a Contessa.'

'Is that good?' enquired Jo.

'Might mean she pays her bills,' suggested the lady.

'Wouldn't bet on it,' replied Jo. 'Anyway, when is she arriving?'

The following Friday afternoon saw the two of us speeding towards Exeter. We were speeding because my ever loving spouse had decided that the clothes I had been wearing to muck out the poultry shed were not likely to give the Contessa the impression that ours was a suitable holiday home for her daughter, and it had taken me a little while to change. We reached the station as the London train arrived.

'That's her,' said Jo. An elegantly dressed, raven-haired lady, accompanied by an attractive child, was walking down the platform. I approached her.

'Excuse me. Are you the Contessa Bellini?' I asked.

'Cor no, Ducks,' was the reply. 'But I don't 'alf wish I was.'

We tried again, this time successfully. Mother was even more elegant than our first guess but the ten year old looked like a refugee from St Trinians. 'This is Gerri,' the Contessa informed us. 'Say "Hello" to Mr and Mrs Peters, Gerri.' Gerri scowled and examined a poster which enquired whether she was pregnant and offered advice if it were so.

We returned home in the Peugeot and Gerri sniffed her way disdainfully round the house in her mother's footsteps. After tea - Jo had polished the Georgian teapot and taken the Royal Worcester tea service out of the glass cabinet for the occasion - it was almost time to take the Contessa back to the station. Gerri began to howl. I seized her hand and led her off to the hen house where a family of newly hatched chicks huddled under the hen. I handed Gerri one of them. For an instant she reacted like any normal child and a look of delight crossed her face. Then she remembered her role of 'about to be abandoned orphan', dropped the chick on the nest and ran back round the path to Mum. We agreed that we would take her to see her mother off to London and, with Phyllis dragooned as unwilling company for Gerri, drove back to town without further interruption. Then the train drew in.

Gerri started to scream. It was quite the most overwhelming scream that the city had heard since the last air-raid warning was sounded, but much more piercing. Everyone turned to stare. Porters emerged from their rest room for the first time in years. Two policemen appeared at the entrance. The buffet emptied, its customers with mouths still full of half chewed rolls. It really was a most spectacular performance.

The Contessa turned back from the door I had opened for her and, seizing Gerri by the shoulders, addressed her in voluble Italian, her voice rising rapidly until it matched her daughter's. In the end she won. Gerri subsided into sniffling silence, her mother stepped aboard the train with a swirl of her Chanel skirt and closed the door, the whistle blew, the train drew out, and we hustled Gerri towards the exit before she could change her mind and start again. We were only just in time.

By the time we were half way home both Jo and Phyllis had been defeated in their efforts to silence the continuous howl that had filled the car all the way from town. I could stand it no longer. Stopping beside the road, I walked round to the other side, opened the door, lifted the source of the noise onto the grass verge and pointed along the road.

'Walk!' I shouted in the voice which had drilled a platoon over the heads of the band of the Scots Guards, albeit a long time ago at the Coronation.

Gerri stopped screaming. Her jaw dropped. 'Walk?' she repeated.

'Too much noise.' I told her. 'Walk.'

She hung her head. I pointed to the car. She got in. We drove home in silence.

Next morning the Contessa telephoned from her hotel to ensure that all was well before catching her flight to Rome. Gerri started to scream.

'That's it,' shouted Jo into the mouthpiece. 'I can't stand this for a whole month. You'll have to take her back with you.'

There was no way the Contessa was going to have her month's peace and quiet aboard a yacht in the Adriatic ruined by her charming daughter. 'Let me speak to her,' she demanded.

Gerri took the phone. Once more the cascade of Italian abuse flowed out. The sullen face became more and more morose. What dire fate lay in store if she caused any more trouble we never discovered but at least the screaming stopped. From then on she became, if not obedient, at least manageable; though anything she didn't want to do was met by 'No understand.' In fact her English nanny, now, no doubt, also enjoying a well-earned break, had ensured that she understood everything she was told. Jo's standard ploy was to wait for me to arrive home and then report on the day's misdemeanours: 'It's a pity Gerri doesn't understand because she has been a very naughty and unpleasant little girl and if there is any more of it she won't go riding tomorrow.'

Gerri loved only two things: riding and food. Each morning one of us delivered her to the riding school where she remained happily till evening. Soon after her arrival she discovered blackcurrant jam. From then on she had no other ambition in life than to live on blackcurrant jam sandwiches, the jam being liberally applied so that it oozed out as she ate. After every indulgence she needed a change of clothes and a shower. When she left we calculated that we had disposed of a seven-pound tin of jam every week.

As the end of her stay drew near she became noticeably more affable and we were able to carry on quite lengthy conversations. We learned that one of her parents' greatest fears was of her being kidnapped and that this was the reason they preferred her to be in Britain when they were away. We enquired what she would do if she were to be kidnapped. 'Oh,' she replied, 'I wouldn't mind a bit as long as they gave me plenty to eat.'

On the morning she was to leave, a large hire car arrived to take her to friends in London. We loaded her luggage into the boot and bade her farewell. As the car was about to move off she cried 'Stop!' and, leaping out, ran into the kitchen and emerged with the final jam sandwich. Our last view of her was of a broad, jam-smeared grin.

****

'There is a film with Marilyn Monroe on the television tonight, Herr Peters,' enunciated Marlene. 'I know you like Marilyn Monroe because you have a picture of her on the backside of your swimming trousers.'

Jo's venture into holidays for foreign children was proving very successful. As far as I could see, that is. How she coped was beyond me but the pattern of our daily routine seemed to vary only a little. Gerri had left us in mid-June and soon after that the continental school holidays began. The agency, so Jo told me, was inundated, and our spare beds were filled with imported children. Luckily the weather was fine and they were generally content to lie around the swimming pool in the sun. Just as well, because, until the end of term, Jo had to run the show without help. After that I was at least on the spot though my suggestions of healthy walks through Oakshiel Forest were more likely to produce mutiny than cries of joy. Nor was I able to raise much enthusiasm for activities such as milking Susie or transferring the contents of Peggy's sty to the rose beds.

The swimming pool proved to be one of our better investments. As long as the weather stayed fine expeditions to places of interest proved to be just the opposite; the trip invariably ended with queries of: 'When can we go home to the pool?'

'Don't worry, Mrs Peters,' Juan assured Jo. 'I shall be very careful.'

'You always say that,' she retorted. 'Just look at the drawing room window.'

Juan had discovered golf. At least, he had discovered an old putter and some much hacked balls and was enthusiastically practising on the lawn. He always started with the best of intentions but, sooner or later, he became fired with Spanish enthusiasm and, following through with professional *élan*, drove a ball through one of our windows. On the first occasion I replaced the broken pane at once, only to see it punctured before the putty was dry. After that I left the damaged glass in place, only deducting a pound from his pocket money on each occasion. After his departure it took me hours to replace every damaged window and I became quite adept as a glazier.

Juan, like most of his compatriots, could not understand the British habit of playing according to the rules. One damp evening, when most of the children were gathered in front of the television, Jo and Anne took on Cormac and me at bridge. This was as good as television to some of our visitors and they wandered round the table peering over each shoulder in turn.

'Why don't you want me to tell you what is in Mr Peters's hand?' demanded Juan in an exasperated tone.

'Because it spoils the game, Juan,' explained Jo.

'How can it spoil the game?' he exclaimed in total incomprehension. 'It makes it easier for you to win.'

'But the object is to win by using your brain,' Jo insisted. 'Not by cheating.'

Juan's lip curled and he shook his head. These mad English were beyond him.

The next morning, Sunday, brought its usual crop of voluble complaints. Jo wasn't worried about Lutherans, Calvinists or other strange beliefs but she certainly had no intention of allowing any Catholic soul to suffer damnation by missing Sunday Mass. The Spanish and Italian children, who had only consented to leave their sunny homes in the certainty that a fortnight in pagan Britain would give them a rest from church, were dragged unwillingly from bed, packed like sardines into the Peugeot and driven off to salvation. On their return a massive breakfast awaited them and they were free until lunchtime.

The weather looked as though it might break but I ordained a barbecue and, having hoovered the pool, lit the charcoal and placed a pair of hefty chickens on the spit. Of course, it started to drizzle but I spurned offers of roasting the birds in the oven.

'A barbecue I said. A barbecue it shall be,' I insisted.

The drizzle turned to rain. Every one else concentrated indoors and, except for an occasional scurry of feet and a quick giggle, I was left on my own. All over Europe there are albums with photographs of a stubborn Englishman barbecuing chickens under an umbrella.

A fortnight later saw most of our visitors leaving for home. The shops were full of 'Back to School' advertisements and Phyllis was being kitted out in her new uniform. Jo was calculating her profits.

'Not as much as I hoped,' she reported, 'but it will help towards Phyl's fees at the Convent.'

I kept my fingers crossed.

****

'I'll be there in about an hour,' said the man at the knacker's yard.

It was Sunday morning and I had had a comfortable lie in so that it was after seven when I set off to the paddock to milk Susie. Up till this year she would have been grazing in the meadow across the road but, after hay-making, Bob Merlin had told Jo that he would be ploughing the meadow in the autumn and sowing winter wheat. We had been unable to find alternative grazing and were contemplating selling Susie if something didn't come up soon.

I looked around the paddock, already short of grass and with hay in the manger to supplement her diet. The hens rushed towards me, in hope of grain. The capons poked their heads equally hopefully out of their coop. But of Susie there was no sign at all. I walked right round the paddock but could see no signs of her escape route. Making my way back to the house I found no hoof marks on the lawn, nor cowpats on the path.

'What's the matter?' called Jo from a bedroom window where she was getting the children ready for Mass.

I explained that Susie had disappeared. Cormac and John stopped their standard morning fight and made helpful suggestions. 'I hope she hasn't fallen in the pool,' said Cormac.

'Oh hell!' I ran round the end of the house with visions of what those sharp hooves could do to both the cover and the plastic lining of the swimming pool. Again there was not a sign of a cow. The field beyond held a couple of dozen heifers that galloped up to investigate as I climbed over the gate by the river. Between the field and our property was a drainage ditch. Behind the swimming pool area and the kitchen garden it was quite shallow but as I walked up the field it deepened until, outside our paddock, it was a good eight feet deep. At the bottom lay Susie, quite dead.

Jo was just driving off when I returned and I broke the news to her through the car window. The children were more intrigued than upset but I glimpsed a white tissue in Jo's hand as she turned out of the gate.

Bob had finished milking and was hosing down his yard when I called. He gave me the number of the local knacker and, returning home, I arranged for Susie's removal. There was no time for a proper Sunday breakfast when the family returned, just a quick kitchen table job. Then I set off with the appropriately named Mr Bones, guiding him in his truck to the fatal ditch. He rigged ropes and pulleys, and the corpse was winched up into the field and loaded aboard the truck.

Sunday lunch was not particularly merry. I explained to the family that Susie must have seen the heifers chewing away at fresh grass while she was on dry hay and pushed her way right through a dense tangle of brambles, which had closed up again behind her, not knowing that on the other side lay the deep ditch.

'The grass really was greener on the other side,' sniffed Jo.

Within a week the children had reverted to demanding milk with everything.

****

'You can't possibly mean me,' exclaimed Jo.

I had not recovered from my bad temper of that morning, caused by a sleepless night and increased by a frustrating day. The sleeplessness was all down to Tiggy. We had gone happily off to bed, leaving the two dogs curled up on the hearthrug. At one o'clock I had been awakened by barks, growls and the crashing of furniture being overturned.

Leaping out of bed, I seized the shillelagh that Colour Sergeant O'Hara had given Jo on hearing of our engagement, with the warning, 'You'll need that to keep him in order.' Thus armed I set off downstairs prepared to do battle with the burglars who had disturbed our peace, leaving Jo with her finger poised over the '9' on the telephone dial.

The cause of the uproar was immediately obvious: Shammy had come into season and Tiggy was doing his nut. She was seated firmly on her bottom under a table while he rampaged about her, set upon seduction. As a result of the pursuit chairs and small tables lay overturned all over the room. He took not the slightest notice of my arrival but continued his assault with unabated vigour while she chastely resisted all his attempts to push her out of her retreat.

We had, of course, bought Shammy in the expectation of mating them, but not at the expense of our night's sleep. I dragged Tiggy out into my workshop and put a rug for him by the boiler. Then I made a cup of tea and set about the devastated living room, finally returning to Jo at about half past two. But sleep was not to follow. My workshop was beneath the bedroom and Tiggy spent the rest of the night howling and whining in frustration. At six we could stand it no longer. I pulled slacks and sweater over my pyjamas and took each dog separately for a walk. Then I left them together in the workshop to get on with whatever they felt like doing while I immersed myself in a hot bath.

After breakfast there was no doubt what Tiggy felt like doing, but Shammy had found herself an even more secure fortress under my work bench and was steadfastly resisting all his blandishments. I loaded him into the back of the car and, urging Jo to return to bed and get some sleep, drove off towards our various educational establishments.

I struggled through the morning without too much difficulty but the afternoon brought my regular encounter with Karl, a recidivistic student whose sole interest in life was the legalizing of the use of cannabis. I was too tired to think up new arguments and decided to surrender.

'O.K. Karl,' I conceded. 'Let's make it legal. Then we put a whacking great tax on it so that only the very rich can afford it; nobody is going worry if they blast themselves out of their tiny minds anyway.'

It was no use. This was obviously not what Karl had in mind and the debate continued its dreary course.

As I opened the door on our return Jo raced from the kitchen. I opened my arms for a tender welcome but the hurry was not for me but the telephone, which was ringing in the living room. I stood in the doorway and listened while Phyllis led the others into the kitchen and began to pour the tea.

'Oh, hello Canon.' Jo's voice combined surprise and welcome.

'Really?' she continued. 'Who has been doing the job up till now?'

'Oh, he would have been very good.' She listened again. 'I'm sure my husband would take it on.'

I raised my eyebrows and was about to interrupt when she shot upright and a look of horror swept over her face. Her eyes met mine and she covered the mouthpiece with her left hand. 'They want me to be a School Manager,' she gasped.

'And a very good Manager you'll be too,' I assured her gleefully.

Jo was again expostulating down the phone. 'But I've never done anything like it. I wouldn't have a clue what to do.'

It was obvious, as the conversation continued, that she was losing the battle. 'I couldn't get out of it,' she said, replacing the receiver. 'But it will be awful. You know how I hate speaking in public. He said they wanted a parent on the board and I thought they meant you.'

'I noticed you were pretty quick to volunteer my name,' I replied. 'But you must have realized that they wouldn't want a wicked prod as governor of a Catholic school.'

Tiggy spent the next few nights in the garden tool shed, more or less out of earshot from the bedroom windows. Whenever he approached Shammy she retreated to some suitable fastness and preserved her modesty until her condition became no longer attractive and we could revert to normal sleeping habits.

Jo set off for her first managerial meeting. She returned shattered. 'Do you know what?' she asked. 'Sister Elfrida is retiring at the end of the school year and next term we have to appoint a new Head. I just don't know anything about interviewing people and certainly not Head Teachers.'

I poured her a Dry Martini. 'Take a couple of these to the interview,' I suggested, 'and you'll sail through it.'

****

'We're having a day out,' said Jo. 'Terry, Corenne and I.'

'Good idea,' I replied. 'Where are you going?'

'To a sale in an old house near Honiton,' she told me. 'We thought we'd look at that in the morning and then have a pub lunch. If there's nothing we want to bid for in the afternoon we can look at some of the antique shops in the town.'

'Well wrap yourself up nice and warm,' I said. 'It's bitter cold and there won't be any heating. Try not to have to phone me at lunchtime. We are being honoured by the HMI's visit and will be having lunch with them.'

'That's something for you to worry about,' Jo sympathized.

'Not really. Mr Browne is a very senior HMI and knows what we are trying to achieve. He's always very helpful. The problem is that he's usually accompanied by a younger Inspector who has been infected by all these modernistic ideas. They can be a pain in the neck.'

The day passed much as I had expected. The students did their best to give the wrong answers as long as an Inspector was present. John Peterson warned me to be on my most tactful behaviour in the presence of Miss Jones who looked as though she had only just left school herself, certainly not old enough to have graduated to the rank of HMI. As it happened, it was Mr Browne who spent part of the morning in my classroom and it was not until lunchtime that I met his companion. Peter French, Heather and I were privileged to join our visitors with John at the Principal's table. I found myself sitting opposite Miss Jones.

'I do think some of your methods are completely outmoded,' she remarked and continued in this vein while I chewed my way silently through the roast chicken. It was not until we were finishing the fruit salad and nearing the cheese and biscuits that my feelings overcame John's warning.

'You really shouldn't have your pupils sitting at rows of tables with neat racks of reference books on them,' she prattled on. 'And a whole hour of English or Maths is much too much. And you really ought to spend time introducing them to ceramics and let them develop their inner selves.'

'Ye Gods, Woman,' I burst out. 'Don't you realize that the poor little devils have spent eleven years in your disorganized classrooms, playing with ceramics and sloshing water around in the Wendy House? And what have you got? A whole generation of unemployable school leavers, that's what you've got. And we've got one year to put all that right and turn them into normal people who can be trained to do a job of work and take their rightful place in the community.'

She was both scarlet and silent for the rest of the meal. Peter winked at me. John glared.

'Mr Peters,' said the Principal later that afternoon. 'Don't you think you might have treated an important guest with a little more respect?'

'Yes, I should,' I replied. 'But I still don't understand how any one with such inane ideas gets to a position of influence.'

I gathered from his subsequent remarks that I was not exactly the flavour of the month, an opinion confirmed by John. My colleagues in the staff room were more appreciative.

'I'll buy you a pint if I see you in the White Lion this evening,' said Peter.

I returned home unrepentant to find Jo in high good humour. The three of them had enjoyed themselves immensely, even though Jo had resisted the temptation to bid for anything. Corenne had discovered an early lot, a croquet set, on which she had set her heart and successfully bid. They had spent an entertaining afternoon in Honiton and returned to collect and pay for the croquet set on the way home. The cashier was sitting shivering in an outhouse from which the windows and doors had long been removed.

'Lot 29, please,' said Corenne, producing her chequebook.

The cashier painfully shuffled some papers with his frozen fingers.

'Better check that it's all there,' suggested Terry.

'Good idea,' said Corenne, opening the box. 'Oh no. Look. There's a ball missing. I think it's a blue one.' She turned to the cashier. 'Have you got a blue ball?'

He sucked his teeth, then blew on his fingers.

'I shouldn't be a bit surprised, Missus,' he assured her.

Chapter 8

'By noon on Thursday; no later.' said the man at the factory.

Peggy had taken a long time to reach five score, the magic weight at which she was due to end her life. Jo was tearful but I was adamant.

'Pigs are no different from potatoes,' I informed her. 'When they are ready you harvest them. We've had this with every damned piglet we've reared. If you had had your way we'd have no room for the kids in the house; it would be full of overgrown porkers by now.'

'I know,' sniffed Jo, 'but she was such a pathetic little piglet.'

'Well she isn't now. She's a fat, ill-mannered porker and she has to go. I'll phone the bacon factory and see if they can take her this week.'

Next Thursday I prepared the van early. I had adapted an old bedspring to separate the front from whatever livestock we wished to carry in the back. All that remained was to entice Peggy out of her corner of the barn and into the van.

I looped a short length of rope around her neck and made appropriate noises in the hope that she would follow me to the door.

She did. Much encouraged I urged her to continue along the path. Not on your Nelly! No way was Peggy venturing out into this strange environment. I pulled. No effect. I pushed. No effect. I cursed. No effect.

'Really, Darling!' Jo had arrived in the middle of one of my richer oaths.

Between the two of us we managed to move Peggy a few yards before she broke away, scaled the grassy bank and reached the bit of the paddock that had once been a tennis court. There she stayed.

'What's up then?' asked Mr Roberts, attracted from his cottage by the noise. We explained. He seized the halter and pulled. I got behind Peggy and pushed. Jo made cooing noises from the lawn. Nothing else happened at all.

'Get your bloody shoulder be'ind 'er,' roared Mr Roberts.

I packed down like a second row forward with my shoulder hard against Peggy's rump and pushed. For a moment nothing moved, then she changed her mind and hurled herself forward. I fell flat on my face while Mr Roberts and the pig rolled, locked together, down the bank onto the lawn, narrowly missing incorporating Jo into the imbroglio.

Leaping to my feet I hurtled after them, grabbed the rope and, now that Peggy was moving, kept up the momentum across the lawn to the van, bundled her in and slammed the door. Then I turned round. Jo was bending over Mr Roberts who was groaning and hugging his chest.

We half carried him back to his cottage and deposited him in the rocking chair by the kitchen stove. 'Must go,' I apologised. 'Got to get her to Taunton by twelve.' We left him, leapt into the van and roared out of the gate, heading for the A38. All went well till we reached the Cullompton bypass. Then - bang!

'What the hell was that?' I shouted.

'She doesn't like travelling, especially at this speed,' replied Jo. 'She's trying to get out.'

'Well do something,' I expostulated, with visions of the chaos that would be caused by an enraged pig careering up the bypass. 'We can't stop now.'

'It's alright, Peggy,' crooned Jo. 'It's a lovely place you're going to: no more sore feet; no more cold wet mornings; buckets of lovely warm swill whenever you want.'

Peggy snorted blissfully, her snout protruding through the wire mesh as she tried to nibble my wife's ear.

My foot was as far down on the accelerator as it would go. Try as I might I could go no faster along the bypass in our old minivan with only a redundant bedspring, jammed across behind our seats, separating us from five score of prime pork, on the hoof and determined to burst out of this unaccustomed sty. Only Jo's calming chatter prevented Peggy from achieving her ambition.

Not for the first time I wondered what the hell I had done to get myself into this situation.

'I feel such a hypocrite,' wailed Jo. 'It's horrible.'

'Never mind that,' I snarled. 'Just keep up the good work. This is no time for silly sentiment.'

We reached the factory and handed Peggy over just before noon. By the time we reached home Jo had worked her way through the box of tissues we kept in the glove pocket. Her only remark to me had been, 'I think you're horrible.'

Outside Mr Roberts's cottage stood the Doctor's car. We parked in our drive and sprinted across the road and up the garden path. The Doctor came to the door.

'Ah! Glad to see you,' he greeted us. 'Perhaps you'll keep an eye on this old reprobate. I don't know what he's been up to but he's broken a couple of ribs at least and is going to feel pretty sore for the next few days. Some cock and bull story about a pig.'

Apparently Mr Roberts kept his pipe in the breast pocket of his jacket and in rolling down the bank while embracing Peggy had broken both it and his ribs.

We may have had a side of pork and a side of bacon but it cost me a new pipe and eight ounces of shag, not to mention the chops and rashers on which he feasted daily. I detected a distinct look of regret in his eye when the Doctor pronounced him fit again.

****

'I don't suppose you'll be out of bed for a fortnight,' pronounced Simon in his best bedside manner.

It had happened quite without warning. The previous evening Jo had been upstairs, tucking the two youngest into bed and I prepared to follow our usual routine and sit down with a drink to, discuss the day's events. Stooping down to the drinks cupboard I locked solid. I could neither stand up straight nor walk. My howls of protest brought first Phyllis and Anne who seemed to think it was some form of entertainment laid on for their benefit, and then Jo who propelled me onto the settee where I remained curled up and in agony.

Jo's phone call to the surgery found Jack Turnbull on duty and, twenty minutes later, his car drew up outside.

'Slipped disc I expect,' he explained, rolling me onto the hearthrug. 'Soon fix that.' I realised just why Barts had been so glad to have him in the scrum as he lowered his fifteen stone onto the small of my back and proceeded to tie my legs in knots. Jo hastened to make sure the girls were out of earshot while I gave my opinion of his treatment with all the eloquence derived from twenty-five years of service life.

After ten minutes or so my back was slightly straighter but no less painful. Jack helped Jo to find a board to place under the mattress and supported me up the stairs to the bedroom. He prescribed a large Dry Martini for the pain, another for Jo to counter her shock, and a Scotch for himself for his efforts. Then he departed, promising to call next day.

In fact it was Simon who appeared next morning to prod me about and confirm Jack's diagnosis. He promised to arrange for a domiciliary visit by an orthopaedic surgeon and left to continue on his rounds.

Jo coped with her usual aplomb. I suspected that she rather enjoyed having a patient at her mercy and to be able to issue the orders without fear of contradiction. Nevertheless, her workload must have doubled. Each morning she took the children to school and collected them in the evening, calling on the way at St Jude's where John Peterson gave her my students' work to be corrected and returned next day.

Tiggy, meanwhile, had worked out that I had been stolen and was looking for the culprit. One morning he realised that it must be the postman, who limped back to his van and set off for base and anti-dog-bite jabs. Jo put a rug for Tiggy in the bedroom. He inspected me with a 'You might have let me know' expression and settled down happily. Subsequent visitors were unmolested.

After a fortnight the orthopod made a second call, in the evening and accompanied by Simon. He and Jo were old friends and, once I had been given permission to leave my bed and she instructions to supervise my daily exercises, he accepted her offer of refreshment in the drawing room. As I joined them, in my dressing gown, a few minutes later, the doorbell rang.

'This place has the best non-stop party I ever came across,' said Mike Foot, accepting Jo's invitation.

'Oh,' he remarked an hour or so later as he was about to leave, 'I almost forgot what I came for.' He drew himself up to his full height and put his helmet on. 'The Superintendent does not intend to prosecute you for letting your dog bite old Fred but if it happens again, action will be taken. Evenin' all.' He mounted his bike and rode away down the drive.

****

'You can't throw me out of here,' shouted Kevin. 'I know my rights.'

I had been visiting the tenants at King's Close on my routine end of month call to empty the electricity meters. We provided the lighting in each apartment but the power circuit ran from a coin meter. Knocking at the door of Number Three, I had received no answer and, on letting myself in, discovered that the ceiling light had been fitted with a three way adaptor and now not only provided light but was connected to a two bar electric fire and a kettle. I walked back to the car and took my camera from the glove compartment. Then I returned and photographed the offending apparatus from several angles.

I had just finished when Kevin Whistler, the tenant, appeared. I pointed out the iniquity of his ways and informed him that he was to vacate the premises by Saturday morning. He protested loudly and finished up by waving his rent book, quoting from the rules printed on the cover.

'Personally,' I assured him, 'I'm more interested in my other tenants' right to sleep peacefully in their beds and not have the building burned down about their ears by a pyromaniac like you. Do you know what this is?'

'Of course I do,' he muttered. 'It's a camera.'

'It is indeed,' I replied. 'And if you're not out of here on Saturday morning I shall take the film to the police station and charge you with stealing electricity. There's proof enough in there to convince any magistrate. For the rest of your life you'll have a conviction for theft on your record.'

I left him dismantling the illicit fittings and returned home to find Jo sitting studying a pile of papers, the dogs on the rug at her feet.

'We are interviewing on Thursday.' She had been dreading the day when the School Managers were to select a new Head Teacher. She had received a stack of assorted forms and curricula vitae and these were what she was studying so carefully.

'You'll have a job to find an equal to Sister Elfrida,' I told her.

'Well you're not much help,' she snapped. 'Why can't you suggest a few suitable questions? After all, you are supposed to be a teacher.'

'True,' I admitted, 'but I've never had to interview a prospective Head. With me it's always been the other way round. I'll have a chat with John Peterson tomorrow. He's been through the mill himself.'

The following Saturday morning I drove to King's Close and bade farewell to Kevin Whistler. He was somewhat chastened, having discovered that the other tenants supported my efforts at fire prevention rather than his rights to free electricity. We parted on reasonable terms but I advised him he should not use my name as a referee. Then I called in at the local paper and advertised his room to let.

At home, between preparing meals and planning what to do with the expected influx of foreign children, Jo was still rehearsing the questions that John had suggested. I thought she was sounding very confident but she confessed to butterflies every time she thought about it. Thursday dawned and I set off with the children after bestowing every blessing and felicitation upon her that I could. We returned that evening to an empty house and the older girls set about preparing tea while I carried out the outside chores like feeding the hens. Tea was taken in the living room to the accompaniment of 'Blue Peter' and then quiet was ordained so that homework might proceed uninterrupted.

Half past six brought no sign of Jo. I inspected the kitchen. In the bottom oven stood a savoury casserole. Beside the stove was a pan of potatoes. I put them on to boil and brought the last of the previous summer's runner beans from the deep freeze.

'Not beans again!' complained Phyllis, ladling out the vegetables.

'Don't worry,' I assured her. 'I'll make sure I grow enough this year to last right through.'

A groan ran round the table.

The evening drew on. The children were packed off to bed in order of seniority. Not a sign of my gubernatorial wife. I poured myself a pint of home brew. Still no sign. I took my supper out of the oven and ate it. Still no sign. I watched the News at Ten. Still no sign. Surely one didn't work in shifts when interviewing and keep going all night!

At eleven the phone rang. Jo sounded exhausted. 'I'll be home in half an hour. Tell you about it then.' She put the phone down.

I greeted her with a large drink, which she downed in record time. I reloaded and poured myself one. Then I suggested supper.

'I don't want any, thanks. About nine o'clock the chairman sent out for sandwiches and I've eaten at least three rounds. And I never want to be on a selection board again. The poor candidates! They were all so good. We couldn't make up our minds. In the end we interviewed them all over again and the man we finally selected really stood out this time. I was afraid they were going to get me to break the news to the others, but the chairman did it. I felt so sorry for them.'

'Well at least you don't have to worry about it any more,' I told her. 'You've got your new Headmaster and you can leave things to him from now on.'

'Thank Heavens for that,' said Jo. 'I'm going to bed.'

By the time I had locked up she was sleeping like a baby.

****

'Portelli is an Italian name,' Martina informed us. 'He will be very handsome and very romantic. I shall come to meet him with you.'

Martina was the first of this summer's visitors. She came from Poitiers and, although as capable as any of lying for hours by the pool doing nothing, it was clear from her conversation and the magazines she read that, in her fifteen year old heart, she would have preferred more virile masculinity than was provided by our eight and ten year old sons.

Her arrival had caused me some moments of concern. Armed with a rather blurred photograph supplied by the agency, I had met her train in Exeter. Having fed coins into the platform ticket dispenser, I waited by the exit as the train stopped and disgorged its passengers. After a while I got the feeling that I was being watched. Looking casually around I realized that the policeman a few yards away was eyeing me with some suspicion; suspicion that was heightened every time he saw this middle-aged bloke trying to chat up any attractive dark haired teenager who passed by. I moved down the platform and, fortunately, the next time I approached a girl she turned out to be Martina.

I led her towards the exit, enquiring loudly as we passed the constable as to whether she had had a good trip, how long had she been travelling and similar polite inanities. As we drove away I saw, in the mirror, the policeman noting my registration number. I vowed that in future Phyllis, Anne or Mary would be appointed 'duty brat' and accompany me to the station even if it did cost an extra four-penny ticket.

Now I was setting off to meet Bruno Portelli. Martina was nowhere to be found and, in desperation, I seized an unwilling Mary as chaperone and drove off with her in the back, still protesting that Martina would be terribly disappointed. In this she was correct. When Jo found Martina in the paddock, asleep in the shade of the apple tree, and woke her up she was furious at having been left behind and consumed with jealousy on hearing that Mary had gone in her stead.

We returned an hour later and Bruno dismounted at the door. Martina came running from the pool where she had been sulking, stopped, shrieked and fled back the way she had come, howling with laughter. Bruno, peering myopically through his glasses from his full height of five feet was unable to discover the cause of this hilarity and followed us indoors.

'She should have known that anyone coming for a summer holiday from Nice to Devon would be more interested in improving his English than in birds and sunshine,' I opined.

****

'I didn't mean to do it,' Juan assured me.

'I know you didn't, Juan,' I replied, 'but you never do intend to break a window. You just manage to be around when it happens.'

'That is very true, Mr Peters. I think there must be some metaphysical explanation.' Juan looked impressively pensive.

'Well, let's put it this way, Juan. If I see you so much as look at a golf club again I'll metaphysical your backside with it.'

The summer was proving long and hot. A hosepipe ban had been announced and I was becoming worried about the water in the pool. Once it evaporated below the level of the filter inlet we would no longer be able to swim and Heaven knew how to entertain our foreign guests then. There were more of them than ever and Jo was flat out catering for them, even with the help of Ulrica, the au pair from the Rhineland. We began to suspect that parents were more interested in enjoying a holiday free from their offspring than in the offspring's' improved English.

The previous year's experience had obviously not deterred Juan from a second visit and he had fallen with joy on the putting irons. With admirable restraint he had stuck to clock-golf on the lawn for at least thirty minutes but, in the end, temptation overcame him and another windowpane tinkled to the floor. He shrugged his shoulders and set off disconsolately to the pool where Martina was revelling in the company of two blond and handsome Swedes who were staying with Simon and Corenne Flint-Jones. They had cycled over and were leaping energetically into the pool, ignoring my plea to avoid splashing water out onto the paving. I gave up. Explaining to a Swede the idea of a water shortage was a non-starter. Water flowed freely from the mountains, didn't it? There was a tap. There was a hose. Why not fill the pool to overflowing?

Existence became one long picnic. Breakfast was eaten in two sittings at the kitchen table but, from then on, life only existed in the open air, except for Jo, Phyllis and Ulrica who laboured long over unending mountains of salad. In the spring I had built a permanent barbecue near the pool and the whole village could sniff the air and tell what 'those lunatics at The Huers' were eating that evening. Dieticians would have disapproved but the children loved it and we assumed that the salads and fruit would provide all the right nutriments to encourage growth and improvement in English.

The summer grew hotter and hotter. The grass turned yellow, then brown. The water level sank towards the filter inlet. Phyllis came up with an idea.

'Why not,' she asked, 'take a hose from the tap in the shed?'

Why not indeed? I cursed myself for not having thought of that myself. Our water supply came from the mains but, many years ago, the vicar had built a well, fed by a spring, on the hillside above the house. The tap in the old shed was still fed by a pipe from this well. I would probably be breaking some bureaucratic regulation or other but I couldn't think that by taking water out of one hole in the ground owned by me and putting it into another I was committing a mortal sin.

I sorted out every bit of hose I could find. There was just enough to run from the paddock, through the kitchen garden, through a convenient hole in the wall and across a strip of lawn to the pool. I spent an hour finding assorted hose junctions and finally connected it all to the tap. From the other end, water trickled into the pool. Triumph!

Late that evening, when all the children were tucked up and asleep, Jo set off for bed. I walked down to the pool and checked that the chlorination was sufficient. On my return, as I passed the kitchen window, I noticed that the lights were on. Peering in I saw a figure pass swiftly from the larder to the cloakroom.

Ever so quietly I opened and closed the doors on my way to the kitchen and crept in. There was not a sound. Silently I crossed to the far side and whipped open the cloakroom door. Six pairs of eyes opened in horror. Sitting on the lid of the loo was Ulrica with, on her lap, a gallon container of ice-cream. In her hand was a tablespoon, the other end of which was in Juan's mouth. Clustered around her were four more of our guests, each awaiting his or her turn for a mouthful of Cornish Vanilla. Never before, or since, have I so much regretted not having a camera in my hand.

Adopting my sternest mien, I chased them off to their rooms leaving Juan to the last. He cheerfully admitted having originated the plan and to supervising the whole operation, carefully ensuring that our children were asleep before he led his patrol on its raid. I managed to maintain an attitude of outraged indignation long enough to explain to Ulrica in simple English that she was supposed to be on our side in imposing good order and domestic discipline and expressed my surprise that a good nineteen year old German girl should be so led astray by the wiles of a fourteen year old Spaniard. Then I saw her safely to her caravan home and just reached the security of our bedroom where I startled Jo by exploding with laughter.

It must have been half an hour before I could recite the whole story without lapsing into incoherent giggling and, in the end, Jo was laughing as much as I. Next morning at breakfast we both adopted our most 'we are not amused' expressions and were gratified that our own mob, as well as Martina and Françoise, who had not been among the culprits, managed to look equally scandalized, at least until they escaped into the garden whence shrieks of laughter pervaded the house for most of the morning. Jo doubled the quantity of ice-cream on her list of requirements from the Cash and Carry.

Chapter 9

'You couldn't lay on some English lessons, I suppose?' asked the girl from the agency. 'Parents pay a lot to have lessons.'

'Hang on a minute,' replied Jo. 'I'll ask my husband.'

'Not on your nelly,' was my response. 'I'm not teaching during the holidays.' My mind went back to John Peterson's conversation with the Chairman of the College's governing body who had asked how long a summer holiday we had.

'Two weeks,' was John's reply.

'What do you mean; two weeks?' demanded Lady Caroline. 'You don't come back till September.'

'That's right,' agreed John. 'A month's convalescence and then two weeks' holiday.'

Jo, meanwhile, was still on the phone. 'I'll think about it and ring you back,' she said and rang off. 'If we could find someone to give lessons for three hours a day the agency could provide plenty of children. We could turn that room next to the bathroom into a classroom.'

I grunted. Jo was showing all the signs of an incipient idea, and I knew from experience what that meant.

'There's a sale at an old mansion near Wellington next week. There might be some suitable furniture in it. Desks and such like. Eff might come with me while you stay and run things here. I'll give her a ring.'

By the next Thursday Jo had enrolled a second year student at St Lawrence's for a month and was in the process of converting a classroom. She set off in the Peugeot with her sister for the sale, returning triumphantly late that afternoon.

'We had a splendid day,' she informed us. 'I found one room with some small tables, plain chairs and a blackboard. They're in the back of the car. But Eff had the best time. Go on, tell them Eff.'

'Oh no,' replied Eff, turning bright red. 'Just don't mention it; never again.'

'Oh do tell us, Aunty,' chorused the children, scenting an embarrassment.

'Well,' said Eff, 'I tried to get into the upstairs room where the sale was going on, but it was too crowded so I wandered outside and there was a man standing on a ladder and bidding through the window so I climbed up beside him. After a while he started bidding for an old clock and soon there was just him and one other bidding for it. He got to two hundred and seventy five pounds and the other man called "Two ninety".' She paused. 'Oh,' she continued, 'it's too much. I can't go on. You tell them, Jo.'

'I could just see what was going to happen,' Jo chuckled. 'The man on the ladder had obviously reached his limit but Eff was intent on encouraging him. I could hear the auctioneer even though I couldn't see him and he was just about to bring down the hammer at two ninety when Eff nudged the man and said, "Say three". So he bid three hundred and it was knocked down to him. Then he looked down at Eff and said, "There you are. It's yours."

'Well,' she went on, 'you can imagine the situation. Eff saying she didn't want it and the man saying she had told him to bid for her. He was bidding for someone else anyway and they'd given him an absolute limit of two seventy-five. In the end he accepted it and went off cursing while I kept out of the way and pretended Eff was nothing to do with me.'

I fetched gin, ice and vermouth and poured three Dry Martinis. 'I reckon that one's well worth a drink,' I told them. 'Cheers.'

****

'So,' said Brian Redhead, 'the government has appointed a minister in charge of drought.'

I stretched luxuriously and considered whether or not to leap out of bed. The sun was streaming through the window, as it had done every morning since May. I abandoned all thoughts of leaping but slid gently from the sheets and gazed out at the view. The fields were brown with only a ribbon of green showing where a few gallons of water still trickled down the course of the Shiel.

'What's the time?' muttered Jo.

'Nearly half past seven.'

'Ugh,' she groaned. 'I suppose it had to be some time. I was on an ocean liner and it took me to Harrods so I could buy an umbrella.'

'Well you won't need it this morning,' I assured her. 'It's scorching hot already.'

'Right ho then,' she said, rolling out of bed. 'Let's go for a swim before the rest of the mob wake up.'

I went downstairs, let the dogs out and put the kettle on before joining her in the pool. We splashed around in unaccustomed peace for a while, then lay on our towels and let the sun dry us.

'I don't want this to end,' I remarked.

'Personally,' replied Jo, 'I shall be jolly glad when the term starts and it will be my turn to have a holiday.'

There was a week to go before that. In a couple of days we would be seeing the last of our visitors. We were going to miss Vanessa, the student teacher who had proved a tower of strength for the last month. Her work was not made any easier by the fact that her German and French pupils bitterly resented having the lessons specified by their parents while the Spanish contingent, led by Juan, relaxed in idleness by the pool.

Soon after midday I brought a basket of newly dug potatoes into the kitchen and stayed to admire the efforts of Jo's team of workers. Suddenly it grew dark. The bathers appeared in the doorway.

'The sun has gone,' cried Elena.

'Just as we had finished our lessons,' exclaimed Emille, arriving from the classroom.

I went to the door and looked out. The sky in the east was blue but heavy clouds covered the rest. A puff of dust leaped from the drive, then another. I walked outside and a fat raindrop fell on my nose.

'This is what we've been waiting for,' I shouted. 'Come on. Everybody outside.'

A score of faces gaped blankly.

'Come on,' I repeated. 'Juan, show us how to do a Spanish rain dance.'

'OK,' beamed Juan. 'Follow me everyone.'

He cavorted across the lawn, followed by our family and his fellow Spaniards and Giovanni from Italy. After a moment's hesitation the French joined in and finally, with muttering and evident disapproval, the Germans. Round and round the lawn Juan led us all. The heavens opened, the rain poured and we hugged each other in delight.

That weekend we waved goodbye as our visitors set off to spread among yet another generation of Europeans their confirmation of the total madness of the English. If only they had stayed long enough to see, on the television news, pictures of citizens patiently queuing in floodwater over the tops of their wellies to fill their buckets from standpipes in the street, their convictions would have been reinforced.

****

'When would you want them to start?' asked Jo.

'Yesterday,' replied the man on the phone.

We had been relaxing, if one could call it that, after the crowded summer. Mary had joined her older sisters at the local convent school. Even Jane no longer qualified as an 'Infant'. I was trying to convince another intake of students that, contrary to everything their previous teachers had told them, spelling and grammar did matter if they ever hoped to be employed. Jo, when not being an efficient

School Manager, was busy with her usual autumn chores, painting and papering. This was a 'Forth Bridge' type of operation; the middle-landing loo was overdue for its second redecoration.

One afternoon the girl at the agency had phoned.

'Your summer school seems to have been a success,' she told Jo. 'You wouldn't consider doing it permanently, I suppose?'

'You mean every holiday?' asked Jo.

'No, I mean every term,' said the girl. 'There are an awful lot of people, all over the world, who want to send their children to English public schools. The schools are, of course, delighted but there aren't many who want to have a special class teaching children who don't know any English, so there is a great demand for small establishments where they can concentrate on the language for a year before starting. They live as part of the family and soak up ordinary conversation. You sound ideal with your own children covering the age range you might expect. How about it?'

We discussed this at great length; I sank three pints of home brew before we agreed to give it a whirl. As usual, the burden would fall on Jo's shoulders. We were a little concerned about our children's reactions. When we first started having foreign visitors we had visions of their growing up into broad-minded citizens of the world, but after three months of never being able to call their home their own, I was afraid they might be developing into outright xenophobes. Above all, where did one find the teachers? Still, the school fees had to be paid and this sounded like a possible way of raising the money.

Next day Jo phoned the agency and discussed what we might charge in fees, how long our terms should be, their commission and many other matters. The day after that she met us on our return home in the evening.

'I'll need you home as early as possible tomorrow. A Mr Fahadi is coming down from London with his two sons to see if we are suitable. I suspect that he wants somewhere to take them right away, though I told him our term didn't start for another week. I didn't tell him we hadn't any teachers, let alone books and so on. They'll need much more than the stuff Vanessa collected for her morning sessions.'

Next day I arrived home, decanted the children and entered the drawing room where Jo was pouring tea for Mr Fahadi and his two sons, Omar and Abdul. By the time we had finished our tea we had agreed that the boys should remain with us while Mr Fahadi returned to London and, eventually, Teheran. We were surprised when he phoned next day and said that he would be back with his sixteen year old daughter who was also to be entrusted to our care. Sure enough, the following evening he arrived with Azari, shy and charming, whose English was already good enough to engage in simple conversation.

I drove Mr Fahadi back to Exeter to catch his train to London. On the way I tried to draw him out on his reasons for educating his family in Britain. He was not very forthcoming but maintained that he wanted his children to live exactly like the English.

'Speak English language. Play English games. Eat English food,' he assured me.

I suggested that he wouldn't like them to eat pork.

'No matter,' he said. 'In Iran eat Iranian food; in England eat English food. Pork, sheep, cow. No matter.'

This solved a problem. We had already had protests from his sons because we had not allowed them to join the others in bacon and sausages at breakfast time. I was able, on my return, to assure them that their father had given his permission for them to partake of these hitherto forbidden delights.

Meanwhile Jo was frantically searching for teachers. Vanessa was due back at St Lawrence's but she introduced Jo to Olive who introduced Belinda who introduced Jenny. It seemed that Devon contained a vast, untapped well of married teachers who were only too willing to put in one or two days a week as long as they could be home in time to meet their children from school and, even more important, they didn't earn enough to pay income tax or put their husbands into a higher tax bracket. Between Olive, Belinda and Jenny the weekly programme was worked out with separate curricula for the boys and Azari, books were bought, and all was set fair for St Peter's Tutorials to enter upon the academic world.

****

'What about you, Mr Peters?'

I stifled a groan. Sister Edwina had press-ganged me onto the Convent School's PTA Committee with precisely those words a year ago. Now the chairman was resigning, his deputy was moving with his family to London and she wanted a reliable replacement. A look of relief spread over the other faces round the table. They knew a call to duty from the Headmistress was not to be resisted.

I had almost given this meeting a miss. Jo and I discovered, by comparing our diaries, that we each had a meeting on the same Thursday evening, I at the Convent, she of the primary school managers. We had arranged for a baby sitter in the form of another mum who agreed to bring her own daughter over and supervise our heterogeneous collection. At the last moment she had phoned to explain that a family crisis had arisen and she was unable to come.

Phyllis was still a couple of months short of her fourteenth birthday and although we knew she was responsible enough to be left in charge of our family on occasions, it seemed a bit much to expect her to take charge of our pupils as well. Azari was sixteen but we could hardly saddle her with the task. Jo's meeting seemed the more important and I was about to cry off mine when Sybyl, our next-door neighbour knocked at the door to ask if we had any jumble for the parish Autumn Fête. Hearing of our plight she promised to keep a phone watch and to pop in from time to time. Jo and I set off on our separate ways after extracting promises of good behaviour all round and after I had shown my old cane to the Fahadi brothers and invited the Peters brothers to explain its purpose. John demonstrated his histrionic abilities so well that one might have thought he spent his life having his bottom whacked. I hoped the Persians were impressed.

Sister having been assured that I would allow my name to be proposed at the AGM in two weeks' time, we settled down to discuss future events, the first of which was the Christmas Draw. I discovered that I would be legally responsible for any malpractice and wondered whether Mrs Jones' receiving a cuddly toy instead of a bottle of port would bring Mike Foot to my door. At last the meeting ended and I was able to return home and phone Sybyl to relieve her of her supervisory duties. All was peaceful, the younger ones were in bed and Phyllis assured me that she had had no trouble. I saw the others safely on the way to their rooms and settled down to wait for Jo.

As ever, Jo's meeting had dragged on late. I heard her car in the drive and went to meet her.

'Just wait till you hear what they have done to me,' she wailed. 'They all ganged together and elected me chairman. I told them "No" but it was no use. I never wanted to be a chairman.'

'Snap!' I said.

I went to the cupboard and poured two very large whiskies.

****

'But I have no relations in England that they could stay with. I thought they would stay with you in the holidays.' Mr Fahadi sounded far away, as indeed he was, and there was a ghostly echo on the line from Teheran.

Jo pointed out that the children lived with us all term and they needed a break.

'So do we,' I called across the room.

'Shut up,' snarled Jo. 'No, not you Mr Fahadi. There is someone here trying to speak to me. I have told him to go away.' She grimaced threateningly in my direction.

In the end Mr Fahadi had his way. He was a very persuasive businessman. Jo went on to discuss fees. Paying up was not one of his favourite pastimes. The concept of fees in advance, we came to know all too well, was quite novel to Iranians. He had persuaded us to accept a month's fees in the first place, rather than a term's, and had been most apologetically in arrears ever since. Postal services invariably lost mail addressed to anyone by the name of Fahadi. Banks were served by the most inefficient and corrupt officials. Telegrams arrived just after he had set out upon a business trip and would be incommunicado for a fortnight.

'He promised to send a cheque at once,' said Jo, replacing the receiver.

'If he does it'll be dated next Easter,' I told her.

The annual excitement was in the air. An advent calendar hung over each bed. The Persians had demanded theirs, though they had no idea what it meant. Cormac, John and Jane were heavily involved in the Carol Service and Nativity Play. Uncle McCormac had phoned to ask what size turkey he should bring. The music mistress at the Convent had been foolish enough to include Phyllis, Anne and Mary in the choir for their Carol Service. Now we would have to explain what it was all about to our three pupils who would convert to guests for the holidays.

****

'I'm not at all happy about Mary,' announced Jo.

Mary could give the most convincing impression of severe illness as the car was about to leave for school in the morning, giving way to miraculous recovery as it vanished through the gateway. Now, however, it was late evening when she reported that she was feeling sick. Her white face and pathetic appearance supported her claim and we decided that she should sleep in our bedroom so that we would be at hand to minister to her in emergency. I obtained a spare mattress and Jo made up a bed on the floor at the foot of ours.

Next morning we awoke from an undisturbed slumber to be assured by Mary that she felt 'a little better', her downcast eyes and mournful expression carefully contrived to prove the opposite. In the end we agreed that she should remain in her makeshift bed for the morning. Of course, as was normal in the Peters' household, this raised problems.

That afternoon Jo was due to attend the first performance of the Nativity play in which Cormac and John appeared as shepherds and Jane as an angel. She had proposed to take our three pupils with her and to give Jenny, who should be teaching them, a lift home on the way. Six would not fit in her little car but I would still need the Peugeot to convey the others to school. We agreed that if I rushed home at lunchtime she would have her team fed and ready to move.

At five to one I was eating a sandwich with one hand, brandishing a mug of soup with the other and urging, through a mouth full of bread and cheese, the motley throng to embark in the two cars while Jo was bewailing the fact that her daily help had the flu and none of the chores such as bed making and general tidying had been completed. All of a sudden a London taxi drew in at the gate. From it emerged a Chinese couple and two children who beamed and shook our hands. The driver explained that they appeared to speak no English but had given him a sheet of the agency's notepaper with our address on it. He had set out with no further instructions and arrived in Shiel St Peters three and a half hours later.

In spite of my, protests Jo proceeded to show them round our establishment. Their smiles faded as they viewed the chaotic scene, from untidy bedrooms to abandoned lunch table. I shouted up the stairs that I could wait no longer. The mother managed to indicate to Jo that a visit to the lavatory would be welcome. I directed father and son to the cloakroom while Jo led mother and daughter through our bedroom to our private bathroom. The mother could no longer conceal the look of horror on her face as she eyed Mary's unmade makeshift bed on the floor. They climbed back into the taxi and drove away, we presumed back to London. I led Jo at breakneck speed in the opposite direction.

We never heard of them again.

****

'I am very sorry, Mrs Peters, I have broken my leg.'

'Oh dear, Mr Fahadi,' said Jo into the phone. 'I am sorry to hear that. How did it happen?' She listened for a few moments, then turned to me and whispered to me, 'He fell off a bus.'

'Not him,' I muttered. 'It would be the bus that was damaged.'

Jo was still listening. After a while she turned to me again and explained, 'He's unable to travel so he won't be in England to take the children away for Easter. He doesn't want us to tell them he has had an accident so as not to worry them.'

I should have been in a good mood. April Fools day had brought a notable triumph. At our weekly staff conference John Peterson had reminded us of the hazards we would face.

'Why don't we turn the tables?' I suggested. 'Look, the first one of us to be told that he or she has left the car lights on.' I went on to outline my plan.

Sure enough, by nine-fifteen Peter French had been informed that the back of his jacket was covered in chalk.

'You are a dozy lot!' he exclaimed. 'Don't you ever read the papers? Surely you remember that the last thing Harold Wilson did before he resigned was to abolish April Fools day? It was causing too much waste of time in the factories. Now settle down, get up to date and get on with your work.

By the first change of classes the news had spread throughout the college.

'Is it true?' I was asked.

'Of course, Colin,' I replied. 'If only you would read something more enlightening than "The Beano" you might know what's going on around you.'

I had returned home that evening in a satisfied state of mind to find Jo on the telephone to Mr Fahadi.

'Let me speak to him,' I demanded.

I took the phone and we exchanged pleasantries.

'Now Mr Fahadi.' I was determined to get down to business. 'Your account with us is now almost a thousand pounds in debit. You promised to settle this when you arrived this weekend. What do you propose to do now?'

There was a pause, followed by a detailed description of the difficulties of getting to banks on one leg.

'I'm very sorry about your leg, Mr Fahadi, but you do not hold a pen with your leg and there is nothing to stop you signing a cheque and telling your secretary to post it to us.'

More protests followed, coupled with promises to do everything in his power to see that the money reached us at the first opportunity.

I returned to the attack. 'Very well, Mr Fahadi. We shall look forward to receiving your cheque in a few days. But I must point out that when our pupils' fees are not paid on time we have to borrow money from the bank in order to pay our teachers. And banks charge interest. In future I too shall charge interest on overdue accounts. From the first of next month, if your account is not in credit, I shall debit it with interest at the same rate that I am being charged by the bank for my Access Card. At present that is two per cent per month.'

'You should do that, Mr Peters,' he smarmed. 'Of course I understand your problem. You will receive payment by next week at the latest. Please give my love to my children.'

'Do you think he really has hurt himself?' asked Jo as I hung up.

'Not him,' I replied. 'He's fireproof. I should have offered to cancel his booking at the Hilton. I bet he never was booked in and never intended to visit us anyway.'

The days passed and became weeks. A cheque for about half what owed arrived in the post. The three Persians recovered from their disappointment and remained with us for Easter.

'They could pass for Christians anywhere,' said Cormac. 'Christmas, Easter, ham sandwiches. They'll be making their first Communion any minute now.'

'I don't want any more of those,' remarked Jo. 'Not after Gerda.'

Gerda, a fourteen year old, blonde, Lutheran Swede, had spent a month with us early in the previous summer term. John had made his first Communion in June and Gerda had asked to accompany the family to church. As we could not leave her at home alone, the alternative would have meant John managing without paternal support. If only, we thought, all 'foreigns' would be so obliging.

Our mistake lay in not making sure that Gerda sat next to me. After the First Communicants, Jo led the rest of her brood down the aisle, leaving Jane and me sitting at one end of the pew. It was not until she returned that I spotted, kneeling at the rail, an unmistakable blonde head. I pointed this out to Jo whose expression changed rapidly from reverence to horror to resignation as she realized that there was nothing to be done. Monsignor had made history as the first Roman Catholic priest to administer the Host to a true blue Lutheran.

Chapter 10

'And this is the chapel,' said Brother Corcoran proudly, 'and here I'll show you our pride and joy.'

We had brought the boys to St Dominic's to see the establishment for ourselves and to let the Headmaster look them over in his turn. The whole school, even empty of pupils in the Easter holiday, was most impressive. I especially liked the science laboratories and the playing fields and Jo approved heartily of the religious background. We were now in the boarding accommodation where we had been joined by Brother Davis, the ebullient housemaster, and I could see little difference between these dormitories and mine of thirty-five years ago; the beds separated by small lockers, and high enough to leave room for a trunk and a tuck-box.

The building had once been a hospice belonging to an order of nuns and the chapel was magnificent. It could have been a fair sized theatre. The Headmaster's pride and joy was the organ, an old cinema organ, and he and Brother Davis recited the story of how they had rescued it from demolition in a northern seaside resort. We were treated to a few bars of what Brother Corcoran called 'Hymn number t'irty t'ree' and then, to John's immense delight, he broke into the latest 'pop' favourite. The boys would have been happy to stay there and then. We agreed to deliver Cormac in September and

John in two years' time, subject to their passing the appropriate exams.

'And,' added Jo in the car on the way home, 'subject to our finding the fees.'

'We'd better find some more pupils for St Peter's Tutorials,' I agreed. 'Some whose parents pay on time for preference.'

On our return home we found letters from various other schools. These concerned the Fahadi brothers whose father had asked us to find a suitable school for them. We had agreed to do so but pointed out that few school bursars would adopt such a tolerant attitude to unpaid bills as we did. He thought Eton sounded very nice but we decided that, if we were to be responsible for transporting them to interviews and the like, we should seek closer to home. There was a cluster of well-known establishments just a few miles up the new motorway, around Taunton and Wellington, and these we had submitted to a campaign of applications. Replies were coming in, most expressing cautious optimism.

Cormac and John described their impressions of St Dominic's with enthusiasm and our two Persians could hardly wait to be off to visit a new school themselves. We used this enthusiasm to good advantage and subsequently their teachers reported a fresh commitment to the mysteries of English grammar.

To Jo fell the task of escorting them to their various interviews, hair brushed, nails clean and shoes polished. She sensed a certain reserve from Headmasters, in spite of assurances that the boys' academic prowess seemed to be of a sufficient standard to make them acceptable. In the end we realized that the schools were much more experienced than we in the problems of extracting fees in advance. Eventually we agreed to enrol them at a suitable school and I sent the necessary forms to Teheran. They were returned, duly completed, but with considerable differences between the dates of birth shown in their passports and those on the forms. Less surprisingly, there was no accompanying cheque to cover their enrolment fees and the purchase of clothes.

'Perhaps you would attend to this for me,' suggested Mr Fahadi when I managed to get him to a phone.

I left him in no doubt that I had no intention of involving us in payments to other establishments on his behalf, nor of clothing his children at our expense. We would have been hard put to find the regulation uniform for our own girls had it not been for the Convent's second hand shop. I invited him to deal directly with the school in all matters from now on and we rang off with polite expressions scarcely veiling our mutual antipathy.

We began to get urgent messages from the school concerning the non-arrival of enrolment fees. I had long telephone conversations with the bursar who agreed that this was not a new problem. He told me that the difference in the boys' birth dates was probably due to the oriental custom of calculating age from conception rather than birth, but the maths were too complicated for me. We settled down patiently to await some form of communication from their father.

****

'Mum,' came the voice of one of the village children standing on the bridge. 'The Peterses have painted their door red, white and blue.'

I chuckled. Our contribution to the Jubilee celebrations was on the way to becoming yet another part of the legend of 'those lunatics at The Huers'. I had spent the previous evening with sheets of crepe paper and drawing pins, turning the front door into a passable Union Jack and now it did look, from a distance, as though I had been painting it. Mr Roberts had appeared with a nineteen twenties edition of the Scouts' handbook to check that I had managed to get it right.

Omar, Abdul and Azari entered into the spirit of things with enthusiasm though they were somewhat baffled by the absence of police enforcing the rejoicings. Jo had taken them to see Cormac, John and Jane in their school pageant and they had spent part of their pocket money on flags to wave whenever suitable. This afternoon would see them put to good use at the Parish sports meeting which was taking place 'by kind permission of Colonel Witherspoon' at Shiel Lowdon.

In the morning I authorised a dispensation of the otherwise immutable rule: no television before five o'clock, and the visitors were afforded a chance to see some of the London ceremonies. After an early lunch we set off in two cars, which were proudly decorated and beribboned in patriotic colours. Arriving in Shiel Lowdon we were directed to the car park and made our way to the sports field where we were greeted by the Vicar who, with the aid of a map on a large blackboard, explained the layout of the field. Our girls led the way with unerring instinct to the pony riding, much to the disgust of John who turned bright scarlet and gasped for breath in the vicinity of anything remotely connected with horses. We left our pupils to be introduced to ponies and let John loose on the coconut shy from which he returned in triumph with two large coconuts.

In due course we were summoned by the ringing of a hand-bell to the sports track and explained the objects of various types of competition. Omar cottoned on in no time and was delighted at coming second in the egg and spoon race. Azari was running neck and neck with Phyllis in the Young Ladies' Sack Race but fell at the last moment and finished fifth.

At last came the crowning event: the bun fight. With whoops of joy the children of three villages descended like an Assyrian cohort upon the groaning tables laid out in the marquee and proceeded to demolish the piles of food. Their parents and grandparents sipped tea and reminisced about previous events, including old 'Gaffer' Wedgecock who appeared to be a little confused as to whether we were celebrating Edward VII or George V. After tea there was a presentation of Jubilee mugs and we made our way slowly through the crowd to the cars.

'Did you enjoy yourselves?' we enquired.

'Our Shah does it better,' asserted Abdul stoutly.

****

'How many?' shouted Jo down the phone. 'You must be joking!'

In her capacity as Chairman of the School Managers, Jo had felt that she ought to organize something out of the ordinary for the pupils. I raised no objections but suggested that it shouldn't cost much. Cormac's fees would be due in September in addition to the three girls already at the Convent. Azari, Omar and Abdul would have left us and so far we had only one tentative booking for next year.

We considered the available facilities. As we lived in the country and had a large garden with a pool it seemed obvious that we should make use of that. Jo telephoned Mrs Stalker, the ever-helpful School Secretary and asked if there was any record of the numbers we might expect to an event run by the PTA.

'Hang on a minute,' she replied. 'I've got a file on PTA goings on. Here it is. Looks like an average number would be about seventy. Can't see anything has ever attracted more than ninety. Don't mention it. Glad to be of help.'

'We ought to be able to cope with seventy,' I said. 'See what Joe has to say.'

Joe Philips, the Chairman of that PTA, was an old friend and an outdoor activities enthusiast.

'Hullo Joe. This is Jo. What do you think of this for an idea?' Jo outlined her plan.

'Great!' exclaimed Joe. 'We could hire a coach, spend a couple of hours in Oakshiel Forest - I've got a good orienteering course there - and then come on to you for a swim and a picnic.'

They discussed details for a while and rang off.

That was some weeks ago. Now the event was getting closer and we were about to order the rations. Jo turned to me in horror.

'They've had three hundred and eighty takers so far and some parents haven't yet replied,' she announced. 'What are we going to do with all those people?'

'Well, we've committed ourselves now,' I replied. 'We'll just have to pack them in somehow. Five hundred rolls; five hundred sausages precooked in the oven and whacked onto the barbecue to warm up; gallons of orange squash and a thousand plastic mugs. Isn't one of the parents an ice-cream seller? We could get him to park his van on the drive. Joe will have to lay on some pretty efficient life-savers around the pool to keep an eye on all those kids.'

The great night arrived. Five coaches pulled up at our gate, discharged their cargoes of families, hot and sticky from Joe's exercises in the forest, and set off to park where the swede lorries loaded in the winter. Three hundred and more Junior Mixed and Infants whooped with joy, donned bathing costumes in a flash and tried to fit themselves into the pool all together.

'Haven't seen anything like it since I was in India before the war,' remarked one grandfather. 'Just like the banks of the Ganges!'

Joe's lifeguards restored a modicum of order and life became less perilous for the infants who had been in danger of total submersion by their bigger siblings. I produced the first tray of smoking sausages from over the glowing charcoal; Cormac carried them to the table where Jo and the girls popped them into bread rolls, added onions from a vast pot and tomato sauce from a gallon jar and wrapped the resulting delicacy in a paper serviette. An orderly queue formed, occasional ears received a parental clip and an admonition to 'Say "thank you" ', and the grateful recipients proceeded to the next table where Azari presided over her two brothers in dispensing mugs of orange squash.

Joe had obviously a better grip on his committee than ever I achieved with mine. A multi-sided football match started on the lawn, a dozen Frisbees sailed in graceful curves over the paddock and teams of similar ages played water polo under the supervision of Joe himself. The ice-cream seller made his fortune.

Dusk fell but nobody made a move. Not one sleepy child wailed in protest at the lateness of the hour. Queues formed in the house outside the loos. Thank Heavens we had four of them, enough for the ladies. I pointed out to the men that the riverbank was screened by bushes. The boys had discovered this for themselves. At last, when we feared that it would be too dark for parents to locate their offspring, the coaches were summoned and the concourse drew away leaving us exhausted but satisfied: it had been a success.

Next morning Jo and I rose early to plan the cleaning up operation. We needn't have bothered. The garden was immaculate. Not one plastic cup, not one paper serviette lay outside the dustbins we had provided. True, the pool was a trifle murky, but that was to be expected and I set to with chlorine and hoover.

About noon Mr Roberts's son appeared in the drive.

'That's odd,' said Jo. 'Where was the old boy last night? Not like him to miss a do like that.

Young Mr Roberts was ashen faced. 'It's Dad,' he told us. 'He's dead. Heart attack some time last night.'

'Just like his wife,' whispered Jo with a catch in her voice. 'Just when we were having such fun.'

I handed her my handkerchief.

****

'He is so sweet that you will want to do nothing but cuddle him.' Jo was reading a letter from Mrs Schulz whose son, Ernst, was to arrive at the weekend.

'Sounds a right little nause,' I said. 'For Heaven's sake don't let any of the kids see that. They'll make his life a misery, especially Juan. When do he and his sisters arrive?'

'On Saturday. Same time as Ernst.'

Before meeting the train from Heathrow I checked that glasscutter, putty and putty-knife were ready for use. Four young Spaniards bubbled onto the platform and took charge.

'Stop, stop, Mr Peters,' cried Juan on the way home. He pointed at the Wydshiel village store. 'Please stop here. My sisters have never had gobstoppers. I must buy some.'

Juan, now fifteen, was handsome enough to cause a flutter among the young females that Mr Bevis employed in his store. When he was joined by three raven-haired beauties, all chattering in Spanish, Mrs Bevis appeared from behind the scenes, presumably to keep an eye on Mr Bevis. When they had bought enough in the way of sweets and fizzy drinks to make them thoroughly sick, and a monstrous ice-cream confection each, to sustain them on the way home, we continued our journey, Juan pointing out the scenes of various misadventures in past years to his sisters.

When we arrived at The Huers a taxi stood in the drive. Beside it a blond youth of about eighteen was talking to Jo. Between them was a boy of twelve. Jo introduced us.

'Richard has brought his brother Ernst to stay with us,' she explained. 'He is going on to North Devon and will be back at the end of the month to take him home again.'

Juan, meanwhile, was showing his sisters the swimming pool and sizing up Omar and Abdul. I cornered him by the barbecue.

'You will see,' I informed him, 'that the clock golf numbers are in the lawn and the clubs in the porch. If you cannot restrain yourself from seeing how far you can drive a ball, please take one up to the paddock and practise there.'

'Do not worry, Mr Peters,' he assured me. 'I am now grown up and no longer do such childish things as breaking windows.'

'Please let me help, Mrs Peters,' said Ernst as Jo supervised the postprandial loading of the dishwasher.

'Go on. Cuddle him,' I whispered.

Jo dug a vicious elbow into my ribs.

There was a tinkle of glass from the other end of the house.

'Juan!' I bellowed as I rushed out of the kitchen.

****

'Mrs Peters. Someone has taken my watch.'

This was what we always feared. A thief among so many children. We would need all our brains, all our tact and a lot of luck. Jo accompanied Michelle to her room and together they searched it, but to no avail. The watch had vanished.

'It is those *pieds noirs*,' muttered Michelle.

'What did she mean, "*pieds noirs*"?' asked Jo when Michelle had left the kitchen.

'I expect she means the Persians,' I replied. 'That's all we need. As it is, every one of those kids is going to be suspicious of each of the others. Now we're going to get racial bias creeping in as well. You'd better warn "Cornish Cream" to keep an eye open'

'Hush!' Jo admonished me. 'One of the kids might hear you call her that.'

'Cornish Cream' had come from a village in the middle of Bodmin Moor. She was nineteen and worked hard, helping Jo in the kitchen. She slept in the caravan, peacefully away from the children.

'Why "Cornish Cream" ' asked Jo when I christened her.

'Thick and delicious,' I replied.

This summer holiday was not going well. At the beginning we had heard from their prospective school that Mr Fahadi had not paid the enrolment fee for his sons and that the offer of places had been withdrawn. He had written that he would soon come to England and sort matters out and had actually enclosed a cheque that covered most of what he owed us. Nevertheless, the boys were reduced to tears as they saw Cormac being prepared for his new school while they were not. Anyone who could wield a needle was enlisted into the team sewing nametapes onto his clothes. We did our best to cheer them up, helped by Azari whose South Coast College had not, apparently, met the same problems yet, but we could hardly tell them that it was all because their father never kept his word.

The next item to vanish was a large packet of toffees from Dolores, Juan's elder sister. This was a great loss, as she had no money to buy more. The family had arrived with sufficient money for a month's stay. With typical Spanish nonchalance they had spent it all on their first weekend and remained at The Huers thereafter.

'So we have no money; so we lie by the pool in the sun,' was Juan's laid back comment.

'Please may I trim the lawn, Mrs Peters?' asked Ernst. 'At home I like very much to help in the garden.'

'No wonder he gets cuddled,' I remarked when Jo explained why I had arrived home to find Ernst wielding the shears. 'I wish some of our kids would offer to help occasionally. You're all right with the girls but I think the boys will grow up to be flat-dwellers with nothing more horticultural than a window box.'

Small items continued to vanish but there was no clue as to the identity of the thief. The day before most of the visitors were due to depart, Isabella, from Rome, reported that a ten-pound note had been taken from her purse. There was still no clue that would help us. Everyone was indignant at the loss and sympathetic to Isabella but never a sign of guilt.

Saturday arrived and I set off with the Spaniards in good time to catch their train to Reading and their flight from Heathrow. At the station I checked the timetable and led them to Platform Three. The train drew in, I saw them aboard, bade them farewell and left them settling into their seats.

'The train at Platform Three is about to leave. Please close the doors and stand clear,' crackled the Station Announcer and continued: 'This train stops at Taunton and Paddington only.'

'Oh no!' I sprinted back down the platform - too late! I watched the train bear its unsuspecting travellers towards London, knowing that they had tickets from Reading to the airport and almost no spare money.

A visit to the enquiry desk produced the information that all trains were running late and, even if they had waited for the train that did stop at Reading they would have been too late at Heathrow. I didn't wait to find out precisely where the cow had been on the line, or possibly the points were frozen this August day. I phoned Jo and told her what had happened.

'Do we know anyone in London who might help?' I begged her.

She promised to try and I returned home. On my arrival she was beaming.

'I managed to contact an old nursing friend who married a surgeon and still lives in Paddington,' she told me. 'She's going to meet the train, lend them enough money and see them in a taxi to the airport. How's that for sorting out your cock-ups?'

We were still raining blessings on Jo's friend when 'Cornish Cream' walked in. She carried a pillowcase. The bottom was full of toffee papers.

'I was stripping the beds like you told me,' she explained. 'This was Ernst's.'

Ernst denied any possibility. It could not be his pillowcase. It was all a mistake. He didn't like toffees.

'Nevertheless,' I told him, 'I want to see your suitcase.'

This produced voluble protest and suggestions of violated rights. The inspection of his suitcase produced all the missing items except the ten-pound note.

'Show me your wallet,' I demanded.

Inside was a ten-pound note. More protestations, but in the end he had to admit that he possessed no notes except those locked in Jo's drawer for safety.

'Oh, this is an awful job,' complained Jo at her writing desk. 'It's going to kill his poor mother who thinks him an angel. But we must tell her so that she will know in the future.'

Jo's friend phoned to say that the Spanish family were safely on their way to the airport. Jo was still thanking her when a taxi arrived with Ernst's brother.

'I'm afraid there has been some trouble,' she told him. 'He had some things belonging to other people.'

'Oh, not again!' exclaimed Richard.

'Again!' Jo exploded. 'Do you mean to say this has happened before?'

'Yes,' admitted Richard. 'Last year, when we stayed in Cornwall.'

'Well I do think we might have been warned,' said Jo. 'Here is a letter. Please give it to your mother.'

'Life is full of surprises,' she exclaimed as we watched them drive away. 'Do try to catch the right trains in future.'

I poured her a large drink to make my peace. 'You've earned it,' I assured her.

'Well, that disposes of the slave labour accusations,' said the girl from the agency.

They had received a letter of complaint from Mrs Schulz in which she asserted that her poor son had been forced to work in the kitchen at every meal and then in the garden for the rest of the day. To cap it all he had been falsely accused of theft. Jo explained with a history of Ernst's visit.

'She's asked us to find somewhere else for her little dear next summer,' said the girl. 'We'd better make sure that whoever he stays with is warned.'

Chapter 11

'Do the dead rise out of their graves and walk about in the night?' demanded Juanita.

I knew, the first moment I saw her, that we were going to have problems with this one. Her mother was a ravishing Spanish beauty and she showed, at fourteen, every promise of excelling the parental example. She was destined, we were told, for an English education including university so that she would be bilingual by the time she joined her father in the world of high finance.

Her parents departed in their hired Daimler and Jo set about making her feel at home but was taken aback at her reaction to the view of the churchyard opposite.

'Certainly not,' she said in answer to Juanita's question. 'Do they do that in Spain? We wouldn't allow such things to happen here.'

Our little school was growing. Omar and Abdul were still with us and their father was still promising to come to England and 'Put everything right'. Azari had joined her south coast college; in her place we had Alessandra from Turin and Suzuki from Yokahama. Our daughters once again moved bedrooms and, in the absence of

Cormac, now safely ensconced at St Dominic's, Omar had a room to himself.

Juanita's arrival soon threw poor Suzuki into a state of mild shock. The Spanish concept of *mañana* was totally alien to her ideas of school work while Juanita's theory that the first ten minutes of any lesson should be devoted to a discussion of the costume she had selected for that day was beyond belief. Suzuki could be found in the classroom any time between breakfast and supper and the standard of her English improved daily. As far as Alessandra was concerned, we could not understand why her parents had sent her to us; her written work was better than most fourth formers and we wrote to her parents suggesting that we enrol her at the convent with our girls. They could not believe our opinion, but after her mother flew over and discussed the matter with her teachers and with Sister Edwina, it was agreed that she should start there after Christmas.

'Please Mrs Peters, may we come to Church with you?' asked Omar one gloomy Sunday morning.

The two boys often made this strange request. We imagined that it gave them a change from Shiel St Peters and they usually behaved themselves.

I waved goodbye as Jo drove the laden car out of the gate, and began the preparation of Sunday breakfast. On her return the children exploded out of the car.

'Daddy, Daddy,' they chorused. 'Mummy nearly did something terrible.'

Jo looked too upset for me to start pulling legs.

'It was awful,' she whispered.

I sat her in the old armchair. 'Let's hear all about it,' I encouraged her.

'Well,' she started, 'it was a nasty dull morning. I'd stopped to talk to several people and when we got into the car there was nobody left in the car-park. I started up and reversed back in front of the little convent next to the church. Suddenly I felt a slight bump and thought I had touched one of the stones at the edge of the tarmac. I'd just made up my mind to reverse over it when Omar and Abdul started shouting.

' "Oh my God!" they went, both together. "Oh my God! Stop, Mrs Peters. Stop. Oh my God!"

'On they went, non-stop, so I got out to see what they were shouting about and found I'd knocked over a little old nun. She was so old and frail and just lying dazed on the tarmac. She had been making her way back from the church to the convent with her head buried in her prayer book and her back to me and I'd hit her. I was so frightened! I thought I must have killed her.

'Anyway, I picked her up and helped her to the convent door and some of the others came out and I told them what had happened. One of them gave her a real dressing down.

' "There you are," she told her. "I'm always telling you to look where you're going or you'll get knocked down, aren't I?" and all the other nuns nodded in agreement and started on at her.

' "No, no," I cried. "It wasn't her fault; it was mine." But they took no notice and kept on telling her how silly she was while all I wanted to do was to get a doctor to her. She had limped all the way to the convent and I was sure she was hurt. After a minute or two someone produced a cup of tea and gave it to her and she began to sit up and take notice.

‘ “Please,” I asked her, “let me get hold of a doctor to look at your leg.”

‘ “Leg!” she exclaimed, “Nothing wrong with my leg.” And with no further ado she leaped off the chair, lifted her skirt and proceeded to dance a jig all round the room!

‘In the end I left her there. I gave them my address and phone number and made them promise to ring if anything went wrong. She was the oldest nun there and I’m sure the shock was enough to kill her.’

For the rest of the week Jo phoned the convent daily for progress reports, but she had no need to worry. Her victim made splendid progress and never missed a Mass.

The following Sunday the family were once again seated on their pew when the voice of one of our oldest friends rang out from behind them: ‘Standing behind Mrs Peters we are closer to God than anywhere else on earth!’

****

‘That’s Mummy’s car,’ said Mary, pointing to the car some distance ahead of us on the road back to Shiel St Peters. ‘Where has she been at this time of day?’

We turned into the drive as Jo and Juanita were getting out of the little hatchback. Heather, looking worried stood at the door. Juanita turned towards us as we pulled up. She had a large plaster on her forehead and a black eye.

‘My word, Heather,’ I exclaimed. ‘She must have jolly well provoked you.’

Heather was as gentle as she was minute and couldn't have been provoked into swatting a mosquito, let alone inflicting grievous bodily harm on one of her pupils.

'Shut up, you idiot,' chuckled Jo. 'It was all Juanita's own doing.'

'Oh, yes indeed,' twittered Heather. 'Though I do blame myself. I should never have left her alone to finish her work. Whatever must you think of me?'

'For Heaven's sake don't go on like that,' pleaded Jo. 'You'll only encourage Jeffrey to make more stupid remarks. Phyllis, you see Juanita off to bed and I'll bring her a cup of tea in a minute. Don't try to get her to talk. She's had some pills to sedate her. Heather, you get away home; you're quite late enough as it is. And thanks for staying while I took her to the doctor's.'

An unceasing flow of conversation from a loquacious, sedated Spaniard echoed down the stairs while Jo enlightened me. Apparently Juanita had lost interest in her exercise and had decided to try on her new bikini. This led her fertile imagination to fantasies of life as a model and she decided that the edge of the bath would make an excellent catwalk. Needless to say, she had slipped and Jo, responding to her shrieks, had found her lying in the bath, bleeding and squealing like a stuck pig. She patched her up as well as she could and took her off to the surgery to have the cut stitched up.

Omar and Abdul were in a state of high excitement. In two days' time their father had promised to visit with all arrangements made for their future. More to our interest, he had promised to pay all that he owed us. On Thursday evening, as we were preparing for bed, the telephone rang. It was Mr Fahadi. He apologised, but he would be unable to visit us next day. He had to go to Scotland. Jo remonstrated. He repeated that he could not come and rang off.

'I don't believe he ever intended to come, blast him,' cursed Jo. 'And what does he suppose I'm going to tell the boys?'

I phoned the Hilton and asked for Mr Fahadi. We held a short and acrimonious conversation, which ended with my telling him that his sons would arrive at Paddington next morning and that he could meet them there. I also assured him that their passports would follow when we had been paid in full and not before.

'I felt awful,' Jo told me when I reached home next evening. 'I promised them they were going to London to meet their father, but when we were packing their clothes they seemed as though they would rather stay here. When I put them on the train they were both in tears and flung their arms round my neck.' She wiped an eye.

'I rather got the impression their father would like to get me by the neck, but not with affection,' I assured her.

At lunchtime on Tuesday a taxi drew up outside the house and Azari alighted. She too hugged Jo before explaining her mission. From her handbag she produced eleven hundred pounds: payment in full of all her father owed us. Jo handed over the boys' passports and she set off back to London and her family.

'I didn't think he would ever pay up,' said Jo that evening. 'Never mind. We made a profit in the end though I could have done without all the hassle.'

'It's worth celebrating,' I told her, heading for the drinks cupboard.

****

'Do you realise it's snowing like mad?' demanded Jo.

'Don't worry, Darling. It won't last long. It certainly wasn't forecast.'

I had been called from my class by Peter French, who told me that a worried Jo was on the phone.

'Blow the forecast,' exclaimed Jo. 'I had to go into Exeter for a meeting of Managers' Chairmen with the Education Authority. By the time I left I was skidding all over the place. I picked up the two little ones and now I'm at the Convent. Sister Edwina let me use her phone. We ought to get home as soon as possible and you know how I hate driving in snow.'

I glanced at the staff room clock. It was almost four o'clock; time I was collecting my students' work.

'I'll be with you in fifteen minutes,' I promised.

Jo was right. It was coming down heavily and settling fast. A few huddled figures shuffled along the pavements in the January dusk as I turned into the Convent gates. We abandoned Jo's car and packed into the Peugeot, The two youngest with Alessandra at the back and our three older girls in the middle row of seats. The road wasn't too bad as far as Wydshiel but once we turned off for Shiel St Peters the going was decidedly hairy. At Oakshiel Bridge I nearly skidded into the ditch, producing squeals of alarm from the back and an expression from Jo that I assumed she must have learned from me; nurses would, I was sure, never be so forthright.

'Stupid I may be,' I replied, 'but my parents' marriage certificate is in the bottom drawer of my desk.'

At the foot of the hill I stopped.

'Why are you stopping now?' demanded Jo.

I pointed. Near the top of the hill was the school bus, stationary.

'I don't want to have to stop on the hill because of him,' I replied. 'Where are the binoculars?'

Jo reached under her seat and through the glasses I saw the bus driver disembarking his unruly passengers and mustering them behind the vehicle. He climbed back in, smoke poured from the exhausts and the children pushed like mad. Slowly the bus reached the crest and disappeared. The sound of cheering children drifted down to us.

'Right,' I said. 'Here we go.'

In the tracks left by the bus we negotiated the hill without difficulty and, coasting down the other side, turned safely into our drive. No other vehicle passed that way for five days.

After tea the children commandeered all Jo's tea trays and tobogganed down from the paddock, across the lawn and crashed down onto the drive. I made the mistake of going out to call them in for supper. Before I could protest, I found myself flying over the lawn on a tea tray and rolling in the snow till I met a painful tree stump.

Jo gave the children hot chocolate before bed. I gave myself a strong whisky.

Next morning the children were up and snowballing before I had time to call them. The local radio gave a long list of closed schools and impassable roads. After breakfast we walked up the hill. The snow had drifted till it filled the roadway. Where once we had been between hedges ten feet over our heads we were now level with the hedge tops. From the crest of the hill we looked over a black and white world. The Shiel was a black line down a white valley. The trunks of the trees in Oakshiel Forest were jet black beneath a canopy of white. To the west there were some gaps in the clouds and a patch of sunlight illuminated the summit of Haytor. Far, far away down the valley was a speck of yellow. Kevin Wills was clearing the road with his JCB. We needn't expect to see him for a few days yet. And nothing else would be on the road.

'That's an idea,' exclaimed Anne. 'We could toboggan all the way down the hill.'

By dusk there was a track the width of a tea tray and rivalling the Cresta Run for speed.

The weekend passed in a welter of flushed and soggy children. Jo could not get to Mass and the Vicar could not reach us from Shiel Lowdon for Evensong. Kevin's JCB inched toward us. Bob Merlin gave us milk; the tanker couldn't reach any of the farms. We phoned Cormac.

'It's OK,' he assured me, 'but I threw a snowball at Ginger Smith and hit Brother Davis.'

'I bet you can't sit down now,' I sympathized.

'Oh, he didn't whack me. I've got to learn five new first declension nouns by Monday,' he grumbled.

'And the best of Latin luck,' I told him. 'Before you meet Ginger again I suggest you learn the third conjugation verb "collineo" - to aim straight.'

By Monday the local farmers had constructed a sledge and hitched it to the giant tractor belonging to the swede harvester. With this device loaded with milk tanks Bob set off across the fields, where the snow was only a few inches deep, to intercept the tanker on the main road.

On Tuesday Kevin reached the far side of the hill and at noon on Wednesday, to the disgust of the children who saw their toboggan run demolished, the JCB rolled triumphantly into the village. I started out for college but the road to Wydshiel was so difficult that by the time I arrived John Peterson could only suggest that I went home again. On Thursday the unexpected holiday was over and everyone was back at school. On Friday the thaw came and the Shiel burst its banks.

****

'Would you be having any guns with you?' asked the customs official.

I indicated that we were importing nothing more lethal than six children into the Emerald Isle and he waved us on our way.

Having counted our pennies very carefully, we had decided that we could afford to take the family on holiday. After much debate we had settled on a boat trip up the Shannon from Athlone and Maundy Thursday found us crammed into the heavily loaded Peugeot on the road to Fishguard. We stopped for a meal in Neath and drove on through pouring rain and increasing gale to meet our embarkation time of nine o'clock.

'Not a chance,' said the man on the jetty. 'She's delayed in Rosslare by the weather and Heaven knows when the next sailing will be.'

We took our place at the end of the queue, exchanged a few grumbles with other disgruntled travellers, inserted the children into their sleeping bags and settled down to wait. In the small hours I awoke to see the ferry arrive and disembark its vehicles. We drove aboard and had cups of hot tea in the lounge. It seemed only a short time till she sailed again and breakfast was served. We dozed for most of the crossing and soon Rosslare was in sight.

'We'd better think about an early lunch,' said Jo as we sped along the empty road. 'That will give us plenty of time to find somewhere to spend the night.'

'Have you noticed anything?' I asked, some miles further on. 'Every café and pub has a sign saying "Closed".'

We drove on for another hour. Indications of traditional Irish hospitality were conspicuous by their absence. We were driving through a small town, the streets devoid of citizens and full of shuttered shops. An idea struck me.

'You realize where we are?' I asked.

'Well, yes,' replied Jo, puzzled. 'We're in Ireland.'

'And you know what day it is?' I persisted.

'Of course I do,' she snapped, tired of these riddles. 'It's - oh Lord!'

'Precisely,' I remarked. 'Good Friday. There's not a shop or a restaurant or a pub that's open all day.'

At that moment two figures appeared from an imposing building just ahead of us. It was an hotel. I stopped in front of the doors and dashed in.

'Can we have lunch here?' I asked the young waitress in the dining room.

'Indeed you can,' she assented.

We enjoyed an excellent lunch, served by the friendly girl. She might have cooked it too, for we saw not another human being in the whole place. Replete, we continued on our journey. It grew late. At last we spotted a sign - 'Bed & Breakfast'.

'She isn't allowed to take so many people,' Jo reported, 'but I told her of our problem and she says we can stay if we don't tell the Tourist Board!'

Another excellent meal, another night in strange surroundings, and a breakfast as good as I could have cooked myself. Then we were on our way towards Athlone.

'We didn't expect you so early,' the man in the boat yard told us when we eventually located him drinking tea in a little hut. 'Most people come by air and the airport bus doesn't arrive for a while yet.'

We were shown around the boat, bunks were allotted and we had a trial run out of the harbour. Then we were away, up the Shannon and into Lough Ree where we found a sheltered spot to tie up for the night.

'Hell and damnation!' exclaimed Jo.

'Pas devant les enfants,' chanted Phyllis and Anne.

Jo had been filling the kettle, not noticing that the water was squirting out of three holes in the bottom and soaking her slacks. We made tea with water boiled in a saucepan. We supped off the chicken that we had brought with us, frozen in an insulated box, and were early to bed.

'I'm all wet,' announced Jo next morning, in an aggrieved tone.

Her pillow was indeed soaked. I looked around. The after cabin was not well ventilated and condensation was dripping from a deadlight over our heads.

'Well, you have to expect a bit of water when you're afloat,' I told her.

'Maybe,' she groaned. 'But I'd rather it stayed outside. So far I've got wetter in the boat than if I'd jumped overboard.'

We could see a small town in the distance and I headed for it while Jo fried the bacon. After breakfast we tied up at the jetty and she led her brood up the road to Mass at the church. Afterwards we anchored near a small island, launched the dinghy and the children spent the rest of the day exploring while we dozed peacefully in the sunshine. Well, almost peacefully.

'Cormac caught a fish and fell in,' announced Phyllis. 'But I rescued him,' she added proudly.

Cormac had indeed caught a small pike and was duly photographed for posterity, holding his trophy against a nautical background. John, meanwhile, rowed the dinghy so far away that we had to pull up the anchor and recover him. Jo prepared supper. The fridge door fell off. Once more we settled for an early night.

'Mummy,' called Anne from the cabin door. 'Mary's been sick.' And so she had. With a vengeance. By morning John had joined her. We landed at Lanesborough and obtained kaolin and morphia, but one after the other the children succumbed to a short-lived but violent upset. The boat was fitted with central heating but each time I tried to make it work it only produced clouds of evil smelling smoke, which made the patients feel worse. Jo and I attributed our immunity to prophylactic doses of the duty free gin I had obtained on the ferry.

We proceeded upstream towards Carrick while the sufferers recovered. On Wednesday morning Jo was waiting to pay our dues to the lock keeper who was conversing with another lady.

'I can tell you come from Cork,' he told her.

'My parents came from Cork,' said Jo.

A long conversation ensued during which it transpired that the lady's family were patients of Jo's uncle, a dentist in Monkstown.

'Why!' she exclaimed. 'My husband is seeing your uncle this very afternoon.'

After that there was no holding them. The lock keeper raised his eyes in sympathy. He nodded towards the weir.

'A boat like yours went over there last week,' he remarked lugubriously. 'Three drowned.'

I prised Jo away from her fellow townswoman and we got under way.

'Come and see us if you're in Devon,' Jo shouted from the stern.

'How would she know our address?' I enquired sarcastically.

'She'd ask my uncle of course,' Jo sneered.

The return downstream was bliss. Jo bought a new kettle in Carrick and we managed to prop the fridge door shut with one of the dinghy oars. The sun shone and the children had recovered. We nosed into every inviting looking spot and the dinghy investigated each narrow creek. We were sorry to arrive back in the boatyard on Saturday.

We had another rough crossing and there was small welcome in the wet dawn of a Welsh Sabbath. Thanking Heaven for the motorway, we reached The Huers in time for Jo to take the children to the midday Mass while I thawed a shoulder of lamb from the freezer. It was good to be home.

Chapter 12

'I understand you're about to throw the girl out of your establishment with nowhere to go,' said Sir Digby.

I was beginning to wonder whether I was being made the victim of one of those hoax programmes that the children listened to on Saturday mornings. Only the fact that it was ten o'clock on a Thursday evening when the phone rang suggested otherwise. I had answered it in the bedroom and Jo was too far away in the kitchen for me to get her to listen in to the conversation.

'This is Sir Digby Vane-Trumpington,' he introduced himself in an angry tone. 'I have heard from my friend, Luiz Piñeiro, that his daughter - Juanita is it? - is a pupil of yours.'

'She is indeed,' I assured him. 'Do you want to speak to her?'

'No, I want to speak to you,' he replied. 'He tells me that he owes you this term's fees and that you are threatening him if he doesn't pay up immediately. Is this true?'

This was like being asked whether I had stopped beating my wife. I admitted that the term's fees had not been paid but assured him that I accepted that punctuality was not a notorious trait of the Spanish and that we were not in the habit of casting widows, orphans or young Spaniards out onto the streets.

Sir Digby seemed determined not to listen. 'Do you realize,' he interrupted, 'that Señor Piñeiro is one of the richest men in Spain? Just how much does he owe you?'

I told him, still protesting that we had never doubted that we would be paid.

'I shall post you a cheque in the morning,' he told me brusquely. 'And in future kindly refrain from threatening influential businessmen.' He rang off.

Three weeks later we began the half-term holiday. Juanita's parents were staying in London and came down to collect her. Leaving Jo, Juanita and her mother exchanging notes, I took her father to the White Lion.

'Now Luiz,' I demanded, once we were ensconced comfortably in a corner, demolishing a couple of pints, 'what the hell was all that nonsense with Sir Whatshisname and our fees?'

'Oh ho!' he chuckled. 'I thought that would be a good joke. Did he pay you?'

'He paid all right,' I assured him, 'but I certainly didn't enjoy the joke. You knew you'd be down this weekend and that we were perfectly happy to wait till then. Never mind. It's your round and, just for a joke, you can buy me a double whisky.'

****

'Mr Peters, Mr Peters, Shammy is in the back garden with Butch!' Marlene's voice rang up the stairs.

Tiggy was growing old and blind. Mind you, he could still spot a black cat on a black night and he could still create havoc every time Shammy was in season. Shammy, however, continued to sit virtuously on her bottom under a table and preserve her maidenly honour. On this occasion he had been locked in the shed while she was in the house but, as Marlene had so gleefully observed, she had found her way into the kitchen garden and succumbed willingly to the blandishments of Butch. Butch was the result of a long ago liaison between Tiggy and a village lady of the most dubious antecedents. There wasn't a lot we could do about the situation now and Shammy returned to the house later, a satisfied smirk on her face.

Marlene was the first of our summer visitors. As the German holidays were much earlier than ours she had arrived before St Peter's Tutorials had dispersed its pupils to their homes. An only child, she had grown up in mainly adult company and was somewhat scornful of her fellow teenagers. On the Saturday following her arrival a party from The Huers had arranged to go riding at the stables a couple of miles away. Jo had transported the main body but Marlene wanted to cycle and Mary agreed to accompany her and show her the way. On reaching the top of the hill Marlene announced that she didn't need a guide and had sped off, leaving Mary far behind.

When Mary arrived at the stables there was no sign of Marlene. The class saddled up. Then they saddled a horse for Marlene. Still no sign. At last, after waiting vainly for half an hour, they set off under the eye of a now indignant instructress. By the time they returned and Jo arrived to take them back for lunch the errant cyclist had not turned up.

'I think you'd better go and look for her,' said Jo. 'I can't imagine where she could have got to.'

I had spent the morning dealing with the problems of the tenants in King's Close and was looking forward to a pint or two of home brew. Instead I drove off in some dudgeon to search the Devon lanes for a wandering adolescent. I covered every possible lane and side road between us and Wydshiel without success. Then I took a tour of Oakshiel Forest, but in vain. I was heading for home, feeling distinctly perturbed, when, at the foot of the hill leading to the village, I saw a disconsolate Marlene. She looked up with delight, obviously expecting a lift home with the bike in the back of the Peugeot. Her smile was not returned.

'Where do you think you've been and what do you think you've been up to?' I demanded.

She opened her mouth to reply.

'You,' I continued before she could speak, 'you have caused everyone a great deal of worry. You have booked a riding lesson and not turned up for it. You have made six other children lose half an hour of the riding they had paid for. Now get yourself and your bicycle over the hill and when you get home you can sit down and write a letter to the instructress, apologizing for your behaviour and saying that you enclose three pounds to pay for your lesson.'

Her expression as she wearily pushed her bike up the hill was distinctly crestfallen and her welcome home decidedly muted.

From that time on she was a model visitor, joining in and usually taking a leading part in all the children's activities. We found her quite charming. At the end of a month her parents came to collect her and left for a fortnight's tour of Devon and Cornwall. On their way back they paid us a short visit.

'How did you do it?' cried her mother. 'And in only a month! She is our old sweet, happy daughter again.'

'I can't be sure,' remarked Jo when they had gone, 'but I do get the impression that most parents send their children abroad because they can't stand them at home any more. Perhaps we are doing some good in this world after all. I'd certainly like to think so.'

****

'For sheer impertinence it really takes the biscuit!' exclaimed Jo. 'After all that happened last year! Can you believe it?'

It was nearing the end of term. Thoughts of holidays predominated. I parked outside the house and the children leaped out and rushed to join the foreign pupils at the pool. Tiggy and Shammy, tails wagging, came to greet us. Shammy was showing signs of more than middle age spread. Through the window, Jo called me into the kitchen.

At the end of their afternoon classes the pupils had rushed to fetch their swimming gear and headed for the pool. Suddenly there was a piercing scream from Juanita, which sent Jo scurrying up the stairs. Half way up she met Juanita.

'I went to my room to undress,' she spluttered, her voice an octave higher than normal, 'and there was someone there by my bed! I don't know who he is.'

Pushing past her, Jo stalked indignantly into the room. Kneeling by the fireplace was Ernst.

'What are you doing here?' she demanded. 'How did you get here and who let you in?'

'I came on my bicycle,' he explained as though it was the most normal thing in the world. 'I thought I might have left the plug of my radio in this room last year. The door was open so I just came up to see. Then that girl,' he paused and pointed at Juanita, 'she came in and started screaming.'

'I don't blame her,' said Jo. She interrogated him as she escorted him down the stairs, through the hall and back to the gate where his bicycle was parked.

'Apparently he's staying with a family the other side of Shiel Lowdon,' she told me. 'I hope the agency did warn them. But the cheek of it! I wonder what he was really looking for. I thought we accounted for all that was missing.'

'You say he was kneeling by the fireplace?' I muttered. 'That's boarded up. Perhaps we had better have a look.'

We made our way to the room Juanita shared with Mary. The board in front of the grate was loose and I lifted it out without difficulty. Behind it we found a stack of 'girlie' magazines.

'Now we know why Omar, Juan and Ernst spent so much time in their room last summer,' I chuckled.

'Let me have a look,' said Jo.

I shook my head. 'Not fit for your innocent eyes,' I told her.

'How do you know?' she demanded.

I shrugged and went to water the chickens.

****

'Daddy! Daddy! There's eight of them now!'

Anne was beside herself with excitement. She had appointed herself midwife in charge of the delivery ward that morning when Shammy had first gone into labour. Her eyes were so round it was a wonder she didn't lose her contact lenses.

July was proving to be a busy month. As well as our usual crop of holiday making children there was a constant flow of parents, all wanting to discuss their offspring's futures. And now there were eight blind, squirming little creatures whimpering round their proud mother. All the children were enraptured; this beat watching chicks emerging from eggs any day. I suspected that their enthusiasm would not be so great in a few days' time when shovels, mops and disinfectant would be the order of the day.

Alessandra and Juanita were not present to add their Latin exuberance to the celebrations. Both had been collected by their parents at the end of term. Alessandra was now sixteen and beginning to tire of these unaccustomed rural surroundings. We had found a family in Exeter who would take her during the term and who had a daughter of the same age to accompany her to school and in sampling the delights of city life. On the other hand, the Piñeiros had asked us to enrol Juanita at the convent and to continue to accommodate her at The Huers. Sister Edwina had agreed to this arrangement and we looked forward with some trepidation to Juanita's ebullient return in September.

Hardly had the two girls left when there arrived an Iranian businessman and his fourteen-year-old son. He had flown to London with the intention of arranging his son's education and the agency had sent him to see us. Knowing nothing of the normal terms and holidays practised in this country he had intended to leave the boy at school. And this is what he did: he departed leaving us in charge of the shy and handsome Mamuhd. As they bade each other an affectionate farewell Jo became quite emotional at the thought of leaving ones youngest son in a strange country and not knowing when you would meet again. Mamuhd rapidly settled in and became one of the family and the puppies overcame his fear of dogs; in his part of the world they were carriers of rabies.

As the weeks passed, the pups grew in size, appetite and mischief. They soon learned to waddle away from their mother and then inquisitiveness took charge and they were everywhere they shouldn't be. One morning the door of the dishwasher was inadvertently left open and the kitchen door ajar. I walked in to find six puppies inside the dishwasher greedily polishing the plates stacked ready for washing. By day we spread a rug on the lawn for Shammy and there was usually someone willing to make sure they didn't stray too far. Cormac and John were appointed Guardians of the Gate to keep it shut at all times. On the outside we hung a notice:

PLEASE DO NOT
SQUASH THE
DUPPY POGS.

Across the road we could hear the couple who had bought the cottage after Mr Roberts's death calling each other.

'John, John,' shouted Mary. 'The Peterses are putting up a notice. They must be selling something. What can it be?'

'Children, if they've got any sense!' replied her husband.

****

'Of course,' suggested Sister Josephina, 'for such a family you would offer a substantial discount?'

We could hardly believe what we had been told. The charming couple from Genoa looked hardly old enough to be married, yet, according to Sister Josephina, Signor and Signora Rico had asked her to accompany them to England and to act as interpreter and adviser in selecting a school for their four children, aged ten, nine, eight and six.

Jo, as ever, had excelled herself in preparing a salad lunch. The table had been re-polished, as had the silver. Even the wine came from Peter Dominic's rather than my rhubarb patch.

'I suspect,' I told the nun as we sat down, 'that we have here a case of a dashing young student who eloped with his schoolgirl sweetheart.'

She repeated my remark in Italian. Signor Rico chuckled; his wife blushed. They helped themselves from Jo's lavish spread to a morsel of chicken and a lettuce leaf apiece, refusing wine and requesting cold water. Sister Josephina made up for both of them. Having tasted a sip of the fresh fruit salad over which my wife had laboured most of the morning, they made their departure, promising to return at the beginning of term bringing their children with them. I managed to have a few words with Sister Josephina in private.

'Kidnappers,' she explained. 'In Italy there are many kidnappers. Although they have guards at the house - they are very rich - already there has been one attempt to steal the youngest. They believe the children will be safe here. When they have learned the language they will go to an English school in Switzerland. There is not so much danger in Switzerland.'

'Why can't we keep them all?' demanded Jane, her arms full of struggling puppies.

We had inserted an advertisement in the local paper, offering puppies for sale. We were still suffering stiff opposition from the children, each of whom had a favourite. In the end we had agreed to keep a beautifully coloured bitch. There was an immediate fight over naming it.

'She's such a lovely gold colour,' said Anne. 'She must be called Golden Girl or Gigi for short.'

'There is one thing,' remarked Jo next day. 'Tiggy is going downhill so fast that I don't think he will be with us much longer. Living so far out in the country we are going to need a big dog around. The bitches bark at strangers but Tiggy frightens them off.'

By this time we had sold two of the three male puppies. The remaining one wore a permanently worried expression and resembled nothing so much as a picture of a seal cub waiting to be clubbed on a Canadian ice floe.

'I don't think he looks very threatening,' I said. 'If we keep him we'd have to give him a ferocious name like Attila.'

'Jaws,' suggested Cormac.

'That'll do nicely,' I told him. 'Baskerville Jaws of St Peters.'

'And Golden Girl of St Peters,' added Anne.

And so Jaws and Gigi were added to the family.

****

'Can you tell me?' demanded Belinda, 'just how are we to communicate with four Italian children who haven't a word of English between them?'

'Oh, that's all right,' I assured her. 'I had an aunt who always insisted that you could get along in Italy by speaking English and adding "o" to the end of every other word. She got us all thrown out of a restaurant in Soho by telling the proprietor that his daughter was a perfect little nymph!'

'Oh, do be quiet, Jeffrey,' laughed Jo. 'I asked you here to be helpful, not for your low sense of humour.'

Jo had invited her stalwart team of teachers to coffee in order to discuss the coming term. In addition to the four Ricos and Mamuhd there would be two more Iranians: Darush, a fourteen year old boy whose father lived in Germany and fifteen year old Mischa who flew with her mother from Teheran.

Olive, Belinda and Jill were relieved that they would no longer be responsible for supervising Juanita but a little perturbed by the thought of four such young children being thrust upon them. The basic rule of nothing but English at any time had worked well up to now but they agreed that they might have to make an exception and accept a translation from Paulo, the oldest, on behalf of his brother and sisters. I left them to it and carried on with preparations for my term, which began next day.

As it turned out, the main preoccupation in the staff room next morning was not the characteristics of our new intake but a demand from the Deputy Principal, who believed in planning well in advance, that we should suggest some suitable 'personality' for him to invite to open our Summer Fête next year. As far as I was concerned one TV or Pop star was much like any other and I retired to a corner chair with the *Times Educational Supplement.*

'I don't suppose for one moment,' proclaimed Heather, 'that Jeffrey has the slightest idea what Elton John looks like.'

'That's just where you're wrong,' I told her. 'I know exactly what he looks like. He's six feet tall, beginning to put on a little weight, dark hair which, like his moustache, he keeps clipped short and, in spite of his advancing years, devastatingly attractive to women.'

'What makes you think that, Jeffrey?' enquired Peter French.

'Oh, I don't just think so,' I assured him. 'I have it on the very best authority. Remember that little red headed girl we had last year; always happy and laughing. Went off to train as a telephonist. Elizabeth something.'

'Williamson,' suggested Heather.

'That's right. Elizabeth Williamson,' I concurred. 'Now she knew everything about every Pop star that ever was. One day last March I drove in and parked. It was one of those days when the morning sun comes out after rain and you know how you get both sun and reflection in your eyes as you drive to College. I remember it very well. My car was in for servicing and I was driving Jo's. When the dazzle hit me I groped around in the pocket for some dark glasses. All I could find was a pair the girls had given their Mum; you know, fancy shaped frames and bits of coloured glass stuck all over them. Wearing them made me feel a right idiot. Anyway, Elizabeth Williamson rushed across the car park and shouted, "Oh, Mr Peters. You look just like Elton John!" '

A groan ran round the staff room.

'I suppose I asked for it,' muttered Heather.

Chapter 13

'They'll be here on Sunday evening,' Jo told me. 'They are flying into Exeter Airport in their own 'plane.'

The term had started on Monday, but no Italian family had appeared. At last Jo had had a telephone call from Signor Rico's secretary in Genoa, giving details of their arrival.

A few weeks earlier Jo had returned from Mass to tell me the news that the Bishop had given permission for Saturday evening Mass to count as Sunday's. We were still enjoying the new pleasure of a lie in on Sunday morning. Of course, this did not mean the end of my cookery duties, only that I had to become a more versatile chef and produce succulent suppers instead of breakfasts. This Sunday morning we were up betimes and all the children's beds were made ready for the influx. At half past four in the afternoon we set off for the airport, leaving Phyllis in charge at home.

At the airport we could obtain information about every flight except a private one from Genoa. No one seemed to have heard of it and there was an air of confusion as preparations were under way for the arrival of an Aer Lingus flight which should have landed at Plymouth but had to be diverted because of fog. Suddenly, motoring onto the apron, there appeared a small, private jet. From it disembarked two adults and four children. We waited at the door marked 'Customs'.

When they emerged Signora Rico was holding the hand of an elfin six year old. Three other beautiful children clustered around her while her husband struggled with a small mountain of suitcases. He was quite able to converse without the help of an interpreter and told us that they could not accompany the children back home with us as they were flying on immediately to Paris. The children were introduced in order of age; Paulo, the oldest boy, as handsome as his father, then the beautiful Maria, the mischievous Angelo and the minute Angela. I sat down at a table with him to discuss business; leaving Jo to cope as best she could with mother and children.

In the past we had experienced difficulties with parents who had tried to evade paying our fees until the last possible moment. This was not the situation now. Signor Rico was perfectly happy to pay us; the Italian government was most unwilling to allow him to transfer money abroad. He had brought us the money in almost every currency imaginable. Luckily I spotted a copy of the previous day's *Times* sticking out of a waste bin. With the aid of its financial pages we settled down to count out three thousand pounds in Italian lira, Dutch guilders, German marks, US dollars, pounds sterling, AMEX travellers cheques and a few others.

As we began our task, the door flew open. The Dublin plane had arrived and the lounge filled with what appeared to be a hundred or so IRA supporters, each determined to drink the bar dry before the coaches arrived to carry them on to Plymouth. Our table was surrounded.

'Will ye just look at these two fellas, Mick?' A Guinness laden voice wafted over us. 'Sure, they must have a foin racket going for them.'

As quickly as possible I finished counting and stuffed my pockets with assorted notes. Warily eyeing the Hibernian horde, I separated the children from a tearful Mama, pushed the Ricos towards their 'plane, bundled little ones, luggage and Jo indiscriminately into the Peugeot and sped off into the night, mightily relieved to make our escape.

The Italians seemed in no way put out by this transition from familiar, sunny Mediterranean to alien rain-swept Devon. They joined in with the rest of our extended family, enjoyed their supper and settled peacefully to sleep in their unaccustomed beds.

Next day I spent the whole of my lunch hour passing bundles of assorted moneys over the counter of the bank. I returned to find a decidedly harassed wife trying to establish good manners at the tea table.

'I've had a hell of a day,' she told me. 'I went to call them for breakfast. Paulo decided to slide down the stair rail and, when I shouted at him, fell off, grabbed one of our newly painted banisters and broke it. Then I looked in the loo and found that one of them had let off the fire extinguisher and flooded the place with foam. At lunchtime I heard them shouting and looked out to see the two boys hanging Angela out of the bedroom window by her ankles.'

'Great Scot! What did you do?' I asked.

'What could I do? If I shouted at them they might let go. I phoned the insurance broker. "David," I asked him, "am I insured for everything that could possibly happen? Like pupils falling out of windows, for example." He promised me I was, so I went upstairs making enough noise so that they could hear me, and they pulled her in. I tried to explain the iniquity of their ways but I'm not sure they understood. As long as they're together they speak in Italian and we can't keep them apart all the time.'

'It sounds like time to put my aunt's theory to the test,' I told her.

Rounding up the four little problems, I led them into the living room, sat down in the middle of the settee and invited them to sit, two on each side of me. In my left hand I held a calendar. With my right I pointed to October.

'October,' I said loudly.

They nodded. I turned over the pages and pointed once more.

'November,' I said.

They nodded again. With my forefinger I tapped the space marked 30th November.

'Finito November - Finito polare Italiano,' I roared.

Four pairs of eyes widened in horror. Four jaws dropped open. A gasp exploded from four mouths.

'Comprendo?' I demanded

Four little heads nodded in unison.

On Wednesday Jo came running out to meet us as we returned home.

'What do you think?' she asked. 'The bank manager phoned. "Jo," he said, "congratulations. Your account's in the black." "Don't worry, Eric," I told him. "I'll soon have it back in the red so you can show a profit." '

On Friday evening she looked worried when we drove up the drive.

'What's up?' I asked her.

'It's the Ricos,' she told me. 'The teachers are finding them terribly trying. Belinda said she didn't think she could go on. I'd hate to lose her. We've got such a marvellous team.'

'What did you say to her?' I wondered.

'I told her that whatever happened, that was the worst week we would have. From now on it will be getting better all the way.'

Jo was right. They were not just mischievous little devils; they were intelligent little devils. Each week their English improved. Every so often we drew their attention to the approaching end of November.

On the first of December Angelo exploded into the kitchen.

'Meesis Peters, Meesis Peters,' he gloated. 'Paulo is speaking in Italian.'

Jo read him a lecture on the sin of sneaking.

Two weeks later I made my way upstairs to investigate the uproar that drifted down to us. Paulo and Angelo were having a slanging match - in English.

We had won.

****

'He's dead,' exclaimed Jo.

For some weeks Tiggy had been growing weaker and weaker. He still accompanied me to college but a short stroll round the car park was all he could manage instead of hunting rabbits to the far extremities of the sports fields. He ignored the puppies when they pawed him, eager for a game and I had to help him into the back of the car. This

Saturday afternoon he had fallen asleep on the lawn in the autumn sunshine. The four newly arrived Italian children looked as though they would dearly love to play some trick on him but I had threatened them with death and destruction if they pestered him so they set off for the paddock, probably to throw stones at the chickens. Jo looked out of the window and called me.

I buried him quietly in a corner of the rose bed. The ground was heavy clay and it took a long time to finish the job. As I finished, Simon and Corenne drove up to the house. I explained my toil stained appearance and they sympathised as I poured home brew.

'What will you plant there?' enquired Corenne.

'Well, it won't be a dog rose,' I assured her.

'I might have known you'd say something like that,' she groaned.

Death had always had the same effect on Jo as a Sports Minister on a drought and she was still wiping her eyes as she set off for Mass. Our visitors left soon after and I set about the task of preparing Chicken Maryland for fifteen. I came to the conclusion that life was easier in the old days when a frying pan was all I needed, even if it did mean getting up earlier on Sunday.

Next morning I returned to the bedroom having been listening to the wireless in my bath. Jo was lying in bed awake.

'Anything on the news?' she asked.

'The Pope is dead,' I told her.

'That's not news,' she exclaimed. 'That was a month ago.'

'Not that Pope,' I said. 'Your new Pope.'

She was silent for a moment. 'I always said that Tiggy kept good company,' she murmured.

That afternoon I was peacefully digesting my lunch when I was disturbed by Mamuhd.

'Mister Peters, Mister Peters,' he cried. 'The dogs. They have got the meat.'

Foolishly we had left the remains of a joint of beef in the dining room. The puppies, now big enough to reach the sideboard, had gone exploring and had been delighted at what they found. I thought back over the years of Tiggy's life. He would have been proud of his grandchildren.

****

'How about the Association of Residential Schools of English?' came a voice from the back of the hall.

'It wouldn't make a very elegant acronym,' replied the chairman after a moment's thought.

We had been surprised to hear how many little establishments like ours were catering for the ever-growing demand for an English education. We were one of the smallest, said the girl from the agency, but there were forty or fifty altogether and, she went on, there had been calls for us to get together and exchange views and information. The agency was sponsoring a meeting in London, chaired by one of the directors and would we like to be included?

It wasn't very convenient. For one thing it would be in the middle of term and, for another, neither of us was that keen on a day in London with its un-swept streets and crowds of self-centred pedestrians. In the end we decided to go. I obtained a day's unpaid leave, Jo persuaded Jill, one of her teachers, to remain on duty till our return and Corenne was enlisted to recover the family from their schools and bring them home. Mary opted to stay with a friend overnight. We hoped the meeting would be of value.

As it turned out, we learned a lot, not least that we were far from unique in the problems we had had.

'Anyone having problems getting Libyans to settle up?' asked a tall man in the second row.

The groan that ran round the hall was sufficient answer.

'Keep in touch with me,' he went on. 'My contact over there is Gadaffi's hit man. I always get paid.'

Others had similar offers of advice or help and we felt that an association had much to offer. A steering committee was elected to draw up a charter and we departed, hopeful of better things to come.

It was getting late by the time we reached Exeter and collected our car from the station car park and when we arrived home the younger children were in bed and the older ones on their way. Jill went on her way with our grateful blessings. We were sitting by the fire, going over the day's events, when Jo gave a start.

'Did you hear something?' she demanded.

'No,' I admitted.

'Well I did,' she insisted and headed for the stairs. She was away for some time and then her angry voice echoed down the stairs. She returned escorting a shame-faced Juanita.

'Where do you suppose I found Madam here?' Jo was as furious as I had ever seen her. 'I looked into her and Mary's room. Of course,

Mary's away, and so, I discovered, was she. I went on up to the boy's room where the light was still on. I asked if they had seen her and Darush said no but Mamuhd is too honest to lie and said nothing so I opened the cupboard door and there she was. And what do you suppose she was doing there? Looking for a book, she told me!'

A tearful Juanita was escorted back to her room. 'We'll have to tell her mother,' said Jo. 'We don't know what she'll be up to next and her parents should be warned. I'll have to phone them in the morning.'

Jo greeted us at the door on our return next evening. 'Your mother is going to telephone at six o'clock,' she told Juanita.

We wouldn't have understood the conversation even if we had listened in, but for at least a fortnight we had an unnaturally well-behaved young lady in the house.

****

'Girls!' exclaimed Cliff. 'What girls?'

It was a dark, wet and windy night when they arrived. Cliff was an old friend of Jo's brother, McCormac, and ran a taxi service in Oxford. We had engaged him to meet the flight from Rome with the four little Ricos and their father on their return from the Christmas holiday. He had paraded at Heathrow carrying a placard bearing the legend: 'RICO - CLIFF'. Contact had been made and Signor Rico had handed over his brood together with an envelope containing their term's fees.

They rushed into the living room in a wave of excitement, all identically dressed in the most expensive sheepskin jackets and high boots. Jo gasped as they removed their hoods and revealed close cropped heads.

'Oh Maria!' she cried. 'What has happened to your lovely hair? And yours, Angela?'

It appeared that they had spent a week of their holiday with cousins and returned infested with nits. Their mother had sent an abundance of special shampoo with them and a message to wash their hair daily until all danger had passed.

'Mama was very worried about what you would think of such a thing but I told her you were very nice and wouldn't mind,' Maria explained.

We sent them off to unpack their bags. Their excited chatter filled the house as they detailed their adventures to the other children. We turned our attention to Cliff who had been refuelled in the kitchen by Phyllis and Anne.

'Don't you think the two girls are beautiful, in spite of the haircuts?' asked Jo.

Cliff's jaw dropped. 'I thought they were four boys,' he exclaimed. 'That explains it.'

He had stopped at a service area on the motorway and happily led his little band into the 'Gents'.

'I just couldn't understand why two of them refused to use the urinals and insisted on going into one of the WC compartments together,' he chuckled.

****

'The present whereabouts of the Shah are unknown,' announced the newsreader on 'The World at One'.

'Is that going to affect us?' asked Jo.

'Bound to,' I told her. 'Think how many of our pupils have been Iranians. No knowing what will happen to them now.'

Our little school had seemed to be on its way to making enough profit to pay our children's school fees. We needed it. In September John was due to join Cormac at St Dominic's while Jane would move on to the convent with her sisters or at least, two of them. Phyllis was determined that she had had enough of school and proposed to enrol for a secretarial course at the local college which had a long and grandiose title but was known throughout the neighbourhood as 'Tivvy Tech'.

Our pupils were divided in their opinions.

'A very good thing,' pronounced Darush. 'The Shah was a very bad man. My father had to live in Germany.'

'Come off it,' exclaimed Jo. 'Your father lives in Germany because he makes a lot of money importing Persian carpets there.'

'He is a good man,' declared Mamuhd. 'He was doing his best to make our country important in the world.'

'What do you think, Mischa?' I asked.

'Me, I do not know,' she replied shyly.

'There you are,' I said to Jo later. 'We ought to set up business as an opinion poll. One-third in favour, one-third against, one-third undecided. Gallup couldn't do better.'

'What do you suppose Junko would have said?' she asked.

'I'd rather pretend she wasn't here,' I replied

Junko had arrived from Yokohama at short notice just after the Christmas holidays. This raised the number of our pupils to eight, even not counting Juanita who was, strictly speaking, some one else's pupil. By all the rules of bureaucracy we should now obtain permission from everyone, ranging from the district council to Old Uncle Tom Cobleigh. We decided that ignorance was bliss. The agency prognosis was gloomy and we foresaw a drastic reduction in the demand for what we were offering.

Junko had been well taught in Japan but still had difficulties with pronunciation. That Sunday we sat down to our lunch. Phyllis, Anne and Mary were trying to teach her the names of the various dishes but some she found impossible.

Phyllis looked at her two sisters and nodded.

'Junko,' they chorused. 'Say "crotted cleam".'

'Clotted cream!' said Junko, beaming happily at the applause that rang out round the table.

****

'Señora Peres is an old friend of my mother and she is staying in Exeter,' said Juanita. 'Please may I phone my mother and ask if I can visit her on Friday evening?'

Jo was up to her ears in work. Everything had been running smoothly for a change and she had volunteered to help her sister, 'Aunty Eff', who was moving into a house a few yards up the village on the other side of the river. Their sister, Marie, had also promised to come down from Hampshire and help with the move. This had brought the unexpected request from Marie's son, Charles, that he might celebrate his twenty-first birthday on Saturday at The Huers.

'Not on your nelly,' was my immediate reaction. 'You've got enough to do as it is.'

'Oh, I don't know,' said Jo in her usual insouciant manner. 'We're already feeding fifteen. Another dozen or so shouldn't make much difference.'

As it turned out, our family and pupils outnumbered the members of Jo's relations who would be in the area that night. Jo had prepared one of her famous cold buffets and spent Friday evening working in Eff's new home, secure in the knowledge that Juanita was safe with a family friend. On Saturday morning no one appeared to help with the final preparations and Jo was under pressure. We attributed the fact that Señora Peres dropped her charge at Shiel Lowdon, to walk home across the field, to strange Spanish customs and got on with the work.

The party was a great success. Toasts were drunk with increasing frequency. 'Happy Birthday to You' was sung off key. Six-year-old Angela fell asleep before the cake was cut and was carried off to bed by Phyllis. The others gradually drifted away and it was not long after midnight when Jo carried out her patrol round the bedrooms while I let the dogs out for the last time before locking up.

I was trying to make myself useful in the kitchen next morning when the phone rang.

'You take it,' I told Jo. 'I'll keep an eye on the breakfast.'

'Who is it?' she demanded, obviously not comprehending the opening conversation. 'Otto? I don't know any Otto. I think you must have the wrong number. You want to speak to who? Juanita? Why do you want to speak to her?' Suddenly her eyes narrowed in suspicion. 'Was it you who brought her home yesterday morning?' Her face grew red with fury. 'And was it you she was visiting on Friday? No you cannot speak to her, not now or ever.' She slammed the receiver down.

'That little ....!' she spluttered. 'She lied to us and she lied to her mother. There never was any family friend in Exeter. She's been with this Otto, whoever he may be.'

It was getting on for noon before we succeeded in making contact with Juanita's parents. By this time Jo had extracted the whole story from a sorrowful Juanita. Otto was a Turkish student whom she had met while shopping. Jo explained the situation at length to Señor Piñeiro and then to his wife who demanded to speak to her daughter. By the end of that conversation Juanita was in tears.

'She called me a - what do you call it? - a tart,' she sobbed.

We discussed matters over the phone for a long time. In the end we agreed that Sister Edwina must be informed and that if she were willing, Juanita would remain at the convent and live with us until the end of term. Under no circumstances was she to visit anyone unless accompanied by an adult.

'We deserve a drink,' I told her, heading for the cupboard. 'What the hell is this?'

An enormous black saloon, bearing a CD plate was coming up the drive. It stopped at the door and the driver eased himself from behind the wheel. He was quite the biggest and ugliest man I had ever seen while the bulge under his left armpit suggested that he was carrying a small howitzer. From the back seat alighted a boy of about fourteen.

'Oh no!' cried Jo. 'He's not due until tomorrow. We haven't a spare bed until Charles leaves.'

'He' was Carlos, the son of a South American diplomat of immense importance and, as ever, in imminent danger of being kidnapped. He made friends with everyone and proved adept at everything. He turned a treble summersault into the pool and swam three lengths before surfacing. He spoke the language of each of our pupils and won every game of cards or backgammon that was played. The others christened him 'Einstein' and followed him everywhere. At the end of his month's stay everyone turned out to wish him goodbye. Even his gargoyle of a chauffeur smiled on seeing him again.

'That lad will go far,' said Jo. 'I'd like to meet him in about fifteen years' time.'

'Juanita looks as though she will go far,' I replied. 'Will you want to meet her too?'

'Oh, I do hope so.' she replied. 'I just hope they can find her a reputable girls' school well out in the country somewhere. With her looks and proclivities I'd hate to be responsible for her once she's sixteen.'

'I think they'd do better to find her a husband,' I replied.

Chapter 14

'What do you think?' called Jo from the doorway, her smile stretching from ear to ear.

'I think you look as though you've had a drink so I needn't pour you another,' I replied.

'Don't be such a meany.' she retorted. 'I'm no longer on the Board of Managers. We had our usual meeting and I pointed out that as the two youngest were leaving at the end of term, I would no longer be eligible to be the Parent's Representative. Canon looked mightily relieved but Roger and David tried to talk me into remaining anyway.

' "No," I said. "I think I've done my stunt."

' "I think you mean "your stint"," suggested David.

' "Leave it in the minutes as it is," said Roger. "I think "stunt" adequately describes Jo's efforts!"

'So,' she went on, 'we elected a new chairman, Roger, and you can pour me a drink after all, to celebrate one less chore.'

For the next few days the phone rang incessantly. Jo had made herself very popular as a manager and she was urged time, and time again, to stay on in the job but as she pointed out each time, and I had to agree with her, she was unlikely to have the same enthusiasm as she had when our own children were among the pupils and, after a while, the protests died away.

Shortly after Jo's release from gubernatorial duties John was confirmed. As happened every year, Monsignor seized hold of me as we made our way out of the church.

'Come on, Jeffrey,' he insisted. 'You must come and meet the bishop,' and, for the fifth time in five years, whole rows of devout Catholics were shouldered aside so that the Bishop could meet the only protestant in the congregation.

'Only one more to go, Your Grace,' I assured him.

Outside, a collection of the local priests was standing. I joined in their conversation. There was an infants' school attached to the little convent in the church grounds with a small gate leading onto the road. Beside it was propped the lollypop lady's pole.

'Look at that,' I exclaimed. 'I'm surprised you allow such a thing.'

'What are you talking about, Jeffrey?' demanded Father Patterson.

'I didn't expect,' I replied, 'to see in a place like this, and on a day when no less a person than the bishop himself is visiting, a sign saying "STOP CHILDREN".'

'Do take him home, Jo,' pleaded Father Patterson.

****

'I'm sorry,' said the girl from the agency. 'You're far from being alone. Remember all those people you met at the meeting last autumn? You all swore to be associates and to co-operate. Now you are bitter rivals for the last few hundred French, Italian or Japanese children coming over and, as far as we can see, it's going to be even more cut-throat in the future.'

'We're going to have to think of something else,' Jo told me.

'I think you're right,' I replied, 'but summer is upon us and we shall have enough problems with our visitors to keep us going for a while.'

Summer visitors came and went and September arrived. Junko was the only pupil in the house. The girls were in their element with a room apiece and no brothers to torment them, but our four teachers were massively underemployed.

'I've had an idea,' said Jo.

I hastened to the larder for home brew.

'Go on then,' I told her, handing her a glass.

'Well,' she said, 'in Exeter there is a college running English courses for specialists: engineers, surgeons, scientists, people like that, fairly senior in their professions suddenly put in a job where English is essential. We could offer them first class accommodation, *cordon bleu* food and reasonably intelligent conversation.'

'Can't make the situation any worse than it is now,' I admitted.

'I'll give them a ring in the morning,' said Jo.

'We're going to have to redecorate,' she told me next evening. 'The Director of the Language College likes the idea. I got on to Eric at the bank and persuaded him to let us employ the painters. They start next week.'

By the time the decorators had finished, The Huers had never looked so elegant. Also it was almost Christmas and we need expect no foreign businessmen till the New Year when there would be six more lots of school fees to be paid. The overdraft looked like getting out of hand, as if there were anything unusual about that.

'Let's enjoy Christmas,' said Jo. 'Then we can start worrying.'

It was in mid-January that Jo acquired her first businessman, an Italian engineer called Fredrico. She went to town on her cooking. First she submitted for my approval a twenty-eight day menu and instructed me to consider a suitable wine list. Then the evening routine was ordained. Heaven knows how she managed but by seven o'clock the children were fed, the dining table laid with the best silver and dinner ready in the 'hostess' trolley. At seven thirty I offered our guest an aperitif and five minutes later Jo, looking elegant, joined us. At eight she led us into the dining room. By the time coffee and cigars were finished it was usually well past eleven.

'You certainly impressed Fredrico,' said the Director. 'He hasn't stopped praising English cooking since his first week. He tells me that none of his six wives could cook like you, Jo.'

'He never told us he'd had six wives,' exclaimed Jo.

'Oh yes. I think he's a bit of a lad with the ladies,' the Director told her. 'You'd better look out, Jeffrey, if he comes over from Italy again. I think he fancies Jo.'

'Oh dear!' she exclaimed. 'To think I used to sit chatting to him after breakfast in my negligee!'

'Man mad! Never change, do you?' I chuckled. This was a mistake. One should not make remarks like that when ones wife is standing behind ones chair with a jug of water. I went upstairs for a towel and a dry shirt.

Fredrico was followed by Marcel, from Paris, and then by a Belgian named, incredibly, Hercule. He had never heard of Agatha Christie and was puzzled at the references to detectives until we explained.

'You'll have to give this caper up,' I told Jo. 'My waistline is expanding so much I shall need a new suit every time you have a new guest.'

Jo and I had a digestive holiday over Easter but towards the end of April we were joined by Emil, a physicist from Poitiers. He was equally impressed by Jo's cooking. On the Friday before he was due to leave he invited us out to dinner at a restaurant we knew well. The proprietors' daughter was in the same class as Jane at the convent.

We entered the restaurant and were made welcome and served drinks in the foyer. As we entered the dining room there was a chorus of greeting from one corner where sat Jack and Terry Turnbull and Simon and Corenne Flint-Jones. We introduced Emil and chatted for a while. Hardly had we started our meal when another greeting rang out from the doorway. More old friends had arrived, this time our solicitor and his wife.

'*Ma foi*!' exclaimed Emil. 'Is there no one in Devon you do not know? At the Golf Club I tell my opponent that I am living in Shiel St Peters.

' "Oh," says he. "You must be staying with Jo and Jeffrey Peters."

'Then we come to a little restaurant in a place I never heard of and everybody knows you. Perhaps one day I shall mention your name to some one and he will say, "Jo who?" '

On the following Tuesday Phyllis failed her driving test. We sympathised but she was very down in the mouth. On Thursday Jo was looking distinctly off colour and we were relieved when Emil told us he would have to leave early next morning instead of staying over the weekend. I phoned Jo at lunchtime and she sounded awful. By the time I had collected the three girls and reached home she was in bed struggling to breathe. I phoned the surgery. Jack was on duty and promised to come and see her.

'I don't like the look of you one bit,' he told her.

'You always were so flattering!' she croaked.

He left her with various medicaments and promised to call again next day. This time he was even less happy.

'I'm going to send you in to the hospital,' he said. 'This needs investigating further. I'll arrange for an ambulance to collect you. It'll be here in about an hour.'

Jo dressed but it was three hours later that the ambulance arrived and carried her away. I took the girls to Mass at six o'clock and carried on to visit her. She looked terrible and I left her trying to get some sleep. Next morning she looked and sounded even worse.

'They just won't believe that because the pillows are encased in plastic it doesn't mean my allergy to feathers isn't there,' she whispered. 'They say they haven't any foam pillows and even if they did it wouldn't make any difference.'

I drove home, collected two non-allergenic pillows, drove back to the hospital and, in spite of an indignant nurse, swapped them for the feather variety. She lay back and I stayed till she fell asleep.

Next day we, the girls and I, visited her after school. She looked a little better but was still struggling for breath. By the time we reached home, so was I. Phyllis proved that she was her mother's daughter by ordering me to bed and phoning Simon.

'You've got the same bug as Jo,' he told me, 'and you won't be out of bed for a week.'

If only Phyllis had passed her test life would have been simple. As it was, the three youngest phoned their various chums and sympathetic mums invited them to stay. Corenne drove them to school next day and went on to explain the situation to Jo in hospital. Phyllis stayed home from college and kept house for Junko and me.

The next few days are a painful memory. In the end Jo returned from hospital, restored to health and beauty.

'My God!' she exclaimed as she listened to my wheezing groans. 'You're worse than I was. I'm going to ask Simon to get you into hospital at once.'

I managed to dissuade her and she awaited Simon's visit next day with no patience whatsoever.

'Ah,' he said, removing his stethoscope. 'That's much better.'

'Better!' exclaimed Jo. 'What on earth was he like to start with?'

We spent our convalescence going through the books.

'You'll have to stop this scheme,' I said. 'Apart from my figure, you're spending more on food and wine than you're getting from your guests.'

****

'Mrs Peters,' said Junko, 'what happens at an auction sale?'

'We ought to take you to one,' replied Jo. 'I'll ask my sister if she would like to come with us one day.'

On the following Thursday Olive had a day off from teaching her solitary charge and Jo, Eff and Junko set off in Jo's little car to a sale at an old manor house near Cullompton. They were waiting for us when I returned with the girls from school.

'How did it go?' I enquired.

'It was great fun,' Junko assured me. 'We fell off our seat.'

I raised a questioning eyebrow at Jo.

'The best news,' she told me, 'is that I got you a roller for the lawn. You know you've been complaining of the lack of one for years.'

'What's it like?'

'Oh, I didn't see it. There was too big a crowd in the barn for me to get in, but I saw "Lot 76 - grass roller" so I bid for it and got it for a quid. I've been waiting for you so we can go and collect it in the Peugeot. Then we wandered round the house and Eff saw a couple of items she liked. When it was lunchtime we took our sandwiches into the garden and there was a garden seat, Lot five hundred and something, so we sat on it. There was a little puppy chasing its tail and we were all laughing so much at it that the seat collapsed under us leaving us rolling on the grass. Well, we managed to prop it up again so it looked OK and then we thought we had better not be around when they auctioned it so we came home. Now we ought to go back for the roller.'

I edged the car through the crowd, which was still milling round the barn and parked near the doors. We went in to find Lot 76.

'Oh!' exclaimed Jo, pointing.

There, in all its glory, stood the roller. The cylinder consisted of about a ton and a half of solid Dartmoor granite while the axle was attached to a cast iron frame designed to be harnessed to four sturdy Percherons and towed about the meadow.

'I don't think it will quite fit into the Peugeot,' I told her.

'Thinking of opening an agricultural museum are we?' came a voice from behind us.

Peter and Peggy Mountjoy owned a substantial farm less than a mile away. As with many of our friends, we had met when collecting girls from the Convent School. We explained our predicament.

'I'll get a tractor and tow it up to our place. It can stay in a corner of the yard till you can make arrangements to collect it,' offered Peter.

We were profuse in our thanks. As far as I know it's still there to this day.

****

'Stop fussing,' I demanded. 'I'm perfectly all right. I'm just feeling tired and want to go to bed, that's all.'

All this Sunday I had been feeling more and more feeble. I could hardly be bothered to get out of my chair to see our visiting relatives off and now I was on my way to the bedroom. I felt exhausted. Jo came in and extracted a description of my symptoms.

Simon arrived. He and Jo talked. He prodded me about in the normal way of doctors.

'You, Old Lad, have a bleeding ulcer,' he pronounced.

'Just watch your language in front of a lady,' I ordered him.

'Shut up and listen,' he riposted. 'I ought to send you straight into hospital. I would too if it weren't for Jo here. She's perfectly competent to nurse you, but it's strict bed from now on and no nonsense about it. I'll leave some pills with her and bring some more when I come and see you tomorrow.'

'A right little harbinger of happiness and cheer today, aren't you?' I remarked. 'OK. I'll be good. Now, how about a drink?'

'A drink!' he exploded. 'Now look here Jeffrey, if you are very good and make real progress you may be allowed a glass of sherry before your Christmas turkey. But nothing from now on till I give you permission.'

'Christmas!' I expostulated. 'But that's more than two months away.' I lay back on my pillows. Life seemed to have lost its savour somehow.

About a month later Simon made one of his regular calls.

'Morning Jeffrey,' he greeted me. 'How is it today? Not black and tarry, I hope.'

'More the colour of plain chocolate,' I assured him.

'That's a good sign, anyway,' he responded. 'In fact you're making excellent progress. I've brought Corenne over to see Jo. Think you can face a visit?'

Jo poured the visitors a drink and I glowered at them as I sipped my tea.

'I want to know,' started Corenne, 'what you are going to do next. You've no school and there was no profit in your businessmen proposition.'

Jo sat down on the bed. 'As a matter of fact,' she smiled, 'I've had an idea.'

'Simon!' I cried. 'I think I'm about to have a relapse.'

'Oh, never mind him,' said Corenne. 'Come on Jo. Let's hear it.'

'Well,' Jo started, 'you remember Eff and I went to fetch the boys home at half term. We spent the day going round the town and we found, in an old warehouse, a marvellous craft centre. It really was fabulous. And, I thought, there's nothing like that for miles round here. What do you think?' She turned towards me.

I could think of a dozen objections without even trying. I began to list them.

'Never mind all that,' she interrupted me. 'I've had a word with Eric. He's our bank manager,' she explained to the others. 'And he thinks we could finance it by selling the King's Close property. Now we've got to find a warehouse.'

'I don't believe what I'm hearing,' I told Simon. 'Can't you prescribe a sedative for her to bring her down to earth?'

I was allowed to get up for a few hours each day. I seldom saw Jo who was employed in strange goings on with the local Council.

'They have an old warehouse by the river,' she told me. 'It's a superb building and it's empty. I've asked Nugent and Frogmore to negotiate a lease.'

The weeks flew by. I was allowed to go back to work, much to the relief of the members of the staff who had been saddled with my collection of students as well as their own. Jo reported each day on her progress. Christmas came and went. Paul Nugent assured us that all was going swimmingly. Just before the monthly meeting of the council's planning committee in February we discovered that the agents had omitted to include any catering facilities in their plan; delay number one.

'We shall never be open by Easter at this rate,' complained Jo.

She was right. It was the middle of April before we were able to sign the lease and let Gary Gibson, our builder, loose on the old warehouse. Then came the unkindest blow of all. Nugent and Frogmore had not registered the plans with the building standards office, who had a backlog of planning applications running into months. We implored Paul Nugent to do something about it.

'Not a chance,' he told us. 'I'd need a magic wand, and I haven't got one.'

'Oh, I do like that,' said the little man in the building standards office. His job, obviously, was to frustrate honest citizens in their endeavours to improve their lives and he was protected by a wall of solid timber and armoured glass from their ire when he succeeded. I had indicated the dimensions of the coffee bar counter on the plans. 'And I suppose,' he went on, 'then we insert the scale: "One thumb-joint to the yard." Anyway, we need a cheque for forty pounds before we can accept the application. Make it payable to the council. Thank you. You should hear from us in about six weeks.'

Jo was almost in tears of rage and I dragged her out before she could attack his fortress. In the end we told Gary to go ahead and start work with or without approval.

'No problem,' he assured Jo when she told him she wanted to open in time for the spring bank holiday and the half term.

An article on the proposed 'Riverside Crafts' appeared in the local press, shortly followed by an interview on local radio. In answer to the question, 'Why are you in such a hurry?' Jo replied that when she wanted something she had always wanted it yesterday.

A few days later someone showed us a copy of the local fascist weekly rag. 'Mrs "Flash" Peters' it described her.

Jo had assembled a gathering of assorted craftspeople and women and promised them we would be ready for business on the Friday before the holiday. At four o'clock on Thursday the workmen were still hard at their labours.

'We shall never do it,' she wailed.

'Go home,' said Gary. 'Come back at nine o'clock tomorrow.'

We obeyed him. Next morning the only sign of building work was a few implements and a sack of cement hidden under the stairs. The phone rang. 'We finished at four this morning,' said Gary. The stall-holders arrived and began to arrange their wares. The coffee urn boiled. An adventurous visitor poked her nose through the doorway. Jo was in business.

Chapter 15

'Oh no!' gasped Olive. 'It's enormous. How are you going to fill it, Jo?'

Olive had decided to abandon teaching and to follow Jo's adventures in the world of commerce by serving, on three days each week, in the coffee bar. She had assumed, on viewing the place from the outside, that Jo was leasing the small extension on the side of the warehouse. In fact this housed only the old wooden staircase and, on successive floors, the ladies', the gents', the pantry and the staff loo. The rest of the establishment consisted of, as Olive described it, four enormous areas which echoed our footsteps as we entered.

The first two soon began to fill with various stalls as Jo enticed more and more people to rent a space from which to sell the products of their skilful fingers. On the third floor tables and chairs stood ready for the anticipated rush of hungry customers. On the bar stood containers filled with genuinely home-made comestibles while the urn bubbled merrily in the corner. Olive made up in energy what she lacked in inches and neither empty teapot nor filled ashtray lasted many seconds without being dealt with.

'It looks crowded,' I told Jo on Bank Holiday Monday.

'There are a lot of people here,' she agreed, 'but most of them are my stallholders. Only a few genuine customers so far but those all seem to like the place.'

A child's voice drifted up the stairs. 'Mum, it's only an old jumble sale.'

'I hope too many people didn't hear him,' muttered Jo. 'After all our efforts to make the place attractive!'

'It looks jolly good, Mrs Peters,' said someone behind her.

She introduced Mr Swivel, the Head of the Council Department responsible for the warehouse, to all intents and purposes our landlord.

'What are you going to do on the fourth floor?' he asked.

'We have one or two ideas,' Jo told him, 'but at present we can't do anything until we build a fire escape.'

Jo had satisfied all the fire and health authorities as far as the third floor but the fourth sat empty for a year while she concentrated her efforts on filling the first two with crafts-folk. I was lost in wonderment at the variety of skills displayed on her stalls. I was gazing at a collection of bits of driftwood, which had somehow been turned into paper rests, door-stops and the like when a voice straight from the banks of the Spey asked if I liked what I saw. This was Annie who came, as I thought, from Aviemore. We reminisced for a while over the ski slopes and the changes that had taken place. She had married a Devonian and now lived on the edge of Dartmoor.

'I found that,' she informed me, pointing at a tangled mass of old roots now cleaned and varnished, 'on the beach at Budleigh Salterton. D'ye like it?'

'If I'd found it,' I told her, 'I'd have taken it home for firewood.'

'Aye,' she said. 'That's because you're a Philistine, and a Sassenach Philistine to boot.'

****

'We're going to miss you, Mr Peters,' said Sister Edwina. 'I've never laughed so much as I have at your committee meetings.'

I had cunningly introduced a motion that no member of the PTA should serve for more than three years on the committee. Once it had been passed I pointed out that I had already served for four and was therefore ineligible for further service.

'That's fine,' said Jo when I told her. 'So there's no reason why you shouldn't chair a meeting of all our crafts people next week. We are going to discuss how to improve our sales and you know how I hate doing anything like speaking in public.'

I appealed to the children. 'What's your mother's favourite pastime?'

'Talking,' they replied.

'But not in public,' Jo insisted.

'Not much fun talking when you're all alone,' said Anne.

The following Tuesday evening found me facing a crowded coffee room. I explained the object of the meeting and invited suggestions. In particular I pointed out the absurdity of each stall holder remaining on duty throughout each day when only two or three could easily man each floor, freeing the others to carry on potting, painting, sculpting or whatever comprised their various crafts. Most of the people present were amateurs hoping to make a small profit out of their hobbies and grateful for the chance to meet like-minded others but there were enough professionals to ensure that the debate was restricted to business matters and the conclusions likely to improve efficiency.

By the end of the evening a committee had been elected. I insisted that Jo was to be the ex officio President with powers of veto over matters affecting either finance or the conditions of our lease. To my relief, Fred Barron volunteered to take the chair and was unanimously elected, together with Secretary and Treasurer and representatives from each floor to organise the rosters of those who would man the stalls on each day. Jo was to open a bank account on behalf of the members and to work with the Treasurer in ensuring that the takings of members were properly accounted for.

'I would na' wish to be rude,' called Annie from the back of the room, 'but can we please be sure that we have a different bank from yours. If anything should happen that caused your bank to freeze all your accounts we'd prefer that we could still get our money.'

'There speaks the canny Scot,' I told her. 'Always a careful eye on the bawbees.'

'Aye,' replied Annie. 'Do that and there'll never be sorrow in your hoose.'

'Let's hope there's never sorrow in this hoose,' said Jo as she laid the supper table when we reached home.

'I'll drink to that,' I replied, suiting my actions to the words.

****

'I've had a complaint about your fire precautions,' said the fire officer.

I had driven up river from the college to lunch in the coffee room with Jo. The officer's unheralded arrival took us by surprise.

'I can't think why, Mr Mortimer,' said Jo indignantly. 'Nothing has changed since your last visit. You can see for yourself that the fire escape doors are unlocked and you must have seen the extinguishers on your way upstairs. Come and sit down and have a cup of coffee while I fetch the receipts showing that they are brand new and a copy of the contract with the suppliers to service them regularly.'

'No need, Mrs Peters,' he assured her. 'I was here when they were delivered, remember?'

'Who has been complaining?' I asked.

'Couldn't tell you that,' he replied, 'but we are legally bound to investigate when somebody complains.'

'Who on earth are these people who keep doing things like that?' demanded Jo when he had gone.

'Not "people",' I replied. ' "Person" I suspect is the word. We'll have a look at all the little nuisances we've had, this evening when you get home.'

From the beginning we had been pestered by odd pin-pricks, insignificant in themselves but irritating collectively. Someone had objected to our original planning application and from then on everything Jo started seemed to raise somebody's ire. When we applied for a licence to serve wine with our lunches there had been an objection, though the objector failed to turn up at the magistrates' hearing. Some of the crafts-folk were nervous when letters containing innuendoes of malpractice appeared in the local paper. I had written a blistering riposte but the editor knew more about the laws of libel than I did and would only suggest a watered down version, which I did not accept.

'I'll bet you a pound to a penny it's the same bloke,' I told Jo that evening. 'I'll write him a letter inviting him to come to the Riverside and discuss his complaints openly.'

'What have you written?' she demanded later on. 'Nothing too rude, I hope.'

'Me, rude?' I exploded. 'I'll have you know that I've written a charming letter and called him nothing stronger than a fascisto-communist and a paper tiger. Nothing you could describe as rude.'

I posted my letter next day and on the following evening the phone rang. Mary answered it.

'Daddy,' she exclaimed. 'It's him!'

'It is he,' I corrected her pedantically. 'Anyway, who is he?'

'The man you wrote your not rude letter to,' she replied.

We conversed at length. Of course I was mistaken. I had misread his letters in the paper. His objections had all been the result of a misunderstanding and establishing a craft centre in the old warehouse was quite the best idea since sliced bread. He wished us well and would bring his family to the coffee room next time he treated them to a cream tea.

We were never bothered again.

****

'Mrs Peters, Mrs Peters. Please can we spend our summer holiday with you? Papa says we may if you are willing and I told him you would love to have us for a month.'

Jo stood aghast, holding the telephone with her hand over the mouthpiece. 'It's Maria Rico,' she told me. 'I can't cope with all of them and run the Riverside as well.'

The three sided conversation continued for some time as Jo asked after the various members of the Rico family with one side of her mouth and discussed the pros and cons with the other. With a sinking heart I agreed that we couldn't turn them down but that I should have to look after them while they were here.

Jo was busier than she had ever been. Not only had she a business to run and a family to feed, but Phyllis, her senior helper, was both engrossed in the affairs of the local Young Farmers' Club and had enrolled as a student nurse at Taunton. We had bought her an old banger for her eighteenth birthday and she roared up the drive on evenings off to regale us over supper with grisly tales of bedpans and laying out corpses before vanishing again to a rabbit shoot or some other agricultural pursuit. I was not best pleased to see a notice on the rear window advising me to 'Wake up with a young farmer'.

Anne was engrossed in her 'A' level studies and had little time to spare for the likes of us, spending most of her holiday in Exeter at the library. Sister Edwina had arranged for her Chemistry sixth formers to attend the neighbouring boys' school where the laboratory facilities were superior. Anne returned from her first session in delight.

'We learned how to make guncotton!' she told us.

Fortunately Mary had succumbed to the lure of money and not only enlisted as one of Jo's waitresses for the holidays but had recruited some of her fellow fifth formers as well. Even Cormac and John were occasionally pressed into service as salesmen or washers up and even Jane, still too young to be employed, earned some illicit pocket money from time to time.

I need not have worried about the Ricos. Only three of them arrived; Angelo had stayed in Switzerland with a school friend. Paulo discovered boats being hired out on the river near the warehouse and talked the proprietor into giving him a job as a boatman. Jane introduced the two girls to riding and they were hooked. Each morning I delivered the three of them to the stables and they were happy for the day.

'It's a question of weather,' said Jo.

'Whether what?' I asked.

'Whether the weather is wet or fine,' she told me. 'If it's fine all the grockles go off to the beaches and the moors. If it's wet they explore, looking for indoor entertainment.'

'And what could be more entertaining than a craft centre in the heart of Devon?' I suggested. 'With a glass of cider to wash down your pasty and a cream tea to follow.'

'Exactly,' replied Jo.

By September she was more fervent at praying for rain than any farmer I ever met.

****

'Romeo and Juliet,' suggested someone.

'Romantic but they don't sound like a couple of Devonians,' said Ernie.

'William and Mary, then.'

'Too regal.'

'Napoleon and Josephine?'

'Not tonight.'

'Scarlett and Rhett?'

'We don't want to burn the place down.'

It was late on a damp, autumnal evening and a group of crafts people had gathered in the coffee room to discuss our pre-Christmas advertising campaign. Ernie Hoofe, the toy maker, had suggested a series of letters by a young couple, published in the classified columns of the local paper. Jo had persuaded the young lady in their advertising department that this was unobjectionable from their point of view and we were now trying to find a suitable pair of correspondents.

'Why not Adam and Eve?' asked Ernie's wife, Catherine.

'Why not indeed?' I echoed. 'Adam, the horny handed son of toil, being lured to the delights of Riverside Crafts by the temptress, Eve.'

We settled for Adam and Eve and agreed to a letter appearing in each Friday's edition for the next few weeks. Research had shown that even those who seldom read the paper were most likely to see it on Friday. Jo set about compiling the letters.

The first letter appeared the following week. It read: 'Adam. Thank you so much for that lunch at "Riverside Crafts". The meal was delicious and the wine superb. Let's meet there again soon. Eve.'

As the weeks went by the letters praised more aspects of the establishment. Adam thanked Eve for the gift of a leather belt and she thanked him for a pair of earrings. Adam told Eve that the paintings she had admired in the coffee room were equalled by those on the second floor. Eve told Adam that the handmade Christmas candles would make suitable presents for anyone. The tone of the letters grew noticeably warmer.

'If you keep this up much longer,' I told Jo, 'you'll have Adam buying the engagement ring from Susan and an Easter wedding with Samantha dressing the bride, and the reception in the coffee room.'

'Not a bad idea,' she said, 'but in fact the last one is due the week before Christmas.'

On Friday, the eighteenth of December, newspaper readers read: 'Darling Adam. Thank you, thank you, thank you for the gorgeous mohair jumper from "Riverside Crafts". They really do have everything one could want. I shall wear it constantly. Love. Eve.'

On the following Tuesday a determined looking lady stalked into the coffee room where Jo was presiding.

'Where is he? I want to meet this fellow. What does he look like and what does he do? That's what I want to know.'

In her gentlest tones Jo asked some pertinent questions.

'This fellow Adam who's been messing about with my daughter Eve, that's who. I knew she was up to no good and thought she was seeing someone behind my back, but it was when she came home wearing a mohair jumper and I saw that letter in the paper that I put two and two together. Now, where is he?'

'It took me more than half an hour to convince her that Adam and Eve were figments of our imaginations,' Jo told me that evening.

'She was a farmer's wife from near Crediton and she only half believed me then. She wouldn't even stop for a cup of tea and still went off in a huff.'

****

'It's Fred here, Jo,' said Fred. 'The rain is coming in through the roof and running down the walls as far as your coffee room.'

Fred Barron was half of the firm 'Tots and Toddlers' and made wooden toys, mainly of the pull-along variety. His wife, Betty, complemented this with soft, cuddly toys and infants' garments. We had met them for lunch in a pub during January when the craft centre was closed for the winter, and had discussed possible improvements to the layout. Fred had offered to put his skills to work and refurbish the second floor, in return for which 'T&T' were allotted half the first floor at a peppercorn rent. His voice on the phone sounded worried.

We had been enjoying a peaceful Saturday morning but now we leaped into the car and made our way to the Riverside. As we had been warned, the rain was trickling down from the leaky roof and penetrating down the walls as far as the third floor. Thanks to Fred we were in time to rescue the paintings that hung on the walls and to mop up the puddles which were forming on the floor. The sun came out and we threw open the windows for ventilation.

'What are we going to do?' asked Jo.

'Not a lot we can do at the moment,' I replied. 'The terms of our lease make our landlords responsible for maintaining the roof, but the chances of getting any reply from the Council offices an a Saturday morning are nil. You'll have to pray it doesn't rain again over the weekend and ring them first thing on Monday. We have paid the quarter's rent, I hope?'

'Oh yes,' Jo assured me. 'It's the one bill I always pay on time.'

Jo rang me in the staff room at lunchtime on Monday.

'How did you get on with the Council?' I asked her.

Her voice seethed with indignation. 'I asked to speak to Mr Swivel and was put through to him and what do you suppose he said?'

'Nothing helpful, I take it,' I replied.

'He told me there was nothing he could do and suggested that I stood under the hole with an umbrella,' she raged.

'What on earth did you reply to that?' I wanted to know.

'I told him he'd better think again and slammed the phone down. Then I phoned David, the insurance broker, and told him about it. He's just rung back. He phoned Swivel and explained to him that the insurance company would be prepared to sue for any claims resulting from the Council's neglect to maintain the property in a proper condition. He's been promised prompt action.'

'Good for you,' I told her.

It was a cold February and we sympathised with the workmen scaling the scaffolding and replacing slates. Inside the thick walls it was warm and dry and Fred, in his spare time, transformed the second floor from a haphazard collection of stalls to a well laid out sales area. Jo reopened for business a week before Easter and the customers flocked in.

'We really must start thinking about how to utilize the top floor now,' insisted Jo. 'It really is a pity to waste all that space. But what can we use it for?'

'Couldn't you attract enough crafts people to fill another floor?' I suggested.

'I'm very doubtful. Besides, the coffee room's being on the third floor means that people are tempted to buy all the goodies they see on their way up. Once they've had their ploughman's or whatever they probably wouldn't go on upstairs. It's got to be an attraction in itself.'

A couple of weeks later I drove to the Riverside for my lunch. I took my copy of '*The Times*'.

'Look at this,' I told Jo, holding the paper open so she could see a photograph on the back page. 'Look at all the expressions on their faces: envy, longing, covetousness.'

'What. No lust?' she asked. 'If you're going to start listing all the deadly sins you must have lust.'

'Perhaps the chap in the middle of the back row, if you insist. But don't you see what they are looking at? It's a model railway.'

'So?' She looked puzzled.

'It needs a large area and it's an attraction in itself,' I told her. And they are all grown men except this poor little chap in the school cap who's nearly being trodden under foot in the crush. That's what you want for your fourth floor. And it would give the women more time on the sales floors. You're always saying that Mum and little Flossie would buy more if only Dad and little Willy weren't hurrying them up. If Dad and Willy were paying to see the trains instead of going down to the river bank to throw stones at the ducks they wouldn't be so impatient to get the girls out of the place.'

'And where do we find a model railway?' demanded Jo.

'That's our next problem,' I replied.

Chapter 16

'No really,' cried Olive, 'it's too much. I can't possibly be a party to this sort of thing.'

'Whatever are you talking about,' asked Jo, running up the stairs to the fourth floor.

'There's a dead pigeon up here,' shuddered Olive. 'It's all wrong. The place is a bird trap. The poor thing must have flown up the stair well and couldn't get out again. I can't be associated with somewhere like this.'

'Oh, don't be ridiculous, Olive,' Jo remonstrated. 'The whole of this floor is open house to pigeons. There are all sorts of places where they can fly in and out. What do you think all these white blobs are on the floor? That's one of the reasons why we can't use it yet. It's got to be made bird-proof.'

To prove her point a pair of pigeons flew down from the gloom of the rafters and out of a window.

'There you are, you see. That window has a pane missing so that they can escape. Now stop fussing and come back to the coffee room; there's someone down there, I'm sure.'

'And sure enough,' Jo told me that evening, 'there was a haughty looking lady rapping imperiously with her knuckles on the counter and holding a lead, on the other end of which was the fattest and shaggiest dog I've ever seen.'

'I'd like a cream tea,' said the lady. 'Are you sure the cream is fresh?'

Jo assured her that the cream was fresh from the dairy that morning and Olive prepared her a tray. She then proceeded to the far corner of the room and sat sipping cups of tea and feeding scones, thickly spread with Devonshire cream and strawberry jam, to the dog.

'It broke my heart,' Jo said later. 'All that lovely cream being scoffed by a dog whose most urgent need was a strict diet. I suppose she derived some vicarious pleasure from the process but I was glad Olive had gone out to the pantry. I'm sure she would have started a protest movement on the spot.'

Both the customer's and the dog's appetites having been satisfied, she left the coffee room and made her way downstairs. A few minutes later Jo heard an irate voice from the riverbank below: 'Trixie, Trixie. Come back here this instant.'

Peering from their third floor vantage point, Jo and Olive looked down at a flustered lady on the bank bellowing angrily at the dog, which had managed to fall into the river and was being swept downstream towards the weir. As the bank stood three feet above the water level there was little chance of the poor beast's being able to follow its mistress's instructions and she was forced to canter down the path alongside it.

'Oh my God!' shrieked Olive and rushed full speed down the stairs, closely followed by Jo. There was, of course, nothing either of them could do.

'The silly woman kept shouting, "Look out. She'll bite you," but I was too busy restraining Olive. I was sure she was going to jump in to save the dog,' said Jo. 'Luckily Ivor heard us and ran after us.'

Ivor was an aesthetic young man who covered pieces of unoffending canvas in daubs of paint reminiscent of the infants' art lessons of my teaching practice when I was at St Lawrence's. His golden hair hung plaited down his back and he smoked Turkish cigarettes in a long, ebony holder. He was as tall as Olive was minute, though only a fraction more around the waist. Racing along the path, he overtook the group of gesticulating women and hurled himself down on the bank with his torso hanging vertically towards the water.

'I was sure he would go in, and we were getting terribly close to the weir,' Jo told me. 'I grabbed his ankles and hung on for dear life. Olive stood astride him, pulling hard on his pigtail, which only made his eyes water, he told me later, so that he couldn't see anything, but he managed to grab the dog by its collar and somehow get it up onto the bank, soaking himself and both of us in the process.'

'You silly little dog,' said the lady and, seizing hold of the lead, stalked away along the path without another word.

****

'Who the blazes,' I asked, 'is Chicken George?'

'He's a funny old man who uses naughty words,' said Jane.

'And why was he in the coffee room this morning? Come to that, how do you know he uses naughty words?'

'Oh,' she replied airily. 'He mutters to himself all the time and he wouldn't do that if he wasn't swearing, would he?'

'Perhaps not,' I replied. 'How about helping your aging parent and mashing those spuds.'

It was an evening during half term and Jane and Mary had been working with their mother at the Riverside while John had been manning one of the sales floors. They had been joined by Anne and Cormac from the library in time to attend the six o'clock Mass. I had prepared a mountain of fried chicken, fried bananas and sweet corn ready for their return. They pounced eagerly on the food and a steady chomping took the place of their chatter. I left them to it and led Jo into the living room where I poured a drink apiece.

'Thanks,' she said. 'I was ready for that. We've had a frantically busy day. The kids were great. The two girls must be whacked. They've hardly had a break from serving and washing up since we opened.'

'What about this customer who mutters swear words all the time?' I wanted to know. 'And why "Chicken George"?'

'Olive called him that, the first time he came in,' Jo replied. 'I don't know why. He's a funny old boy, a tramp I suppose, but he seems harmless and he only turns up soon after we've opened when there aren't many customers about. Could have done without him this week though, when we really are busy.'

'What does he do?' I asked.

'He orders a scone and a pot of tea. Then he takes them into a corner and sits muttering to himself as he eats. When he has eaten the entire scone and drunk all the tea and emptied the hot water jug and the milk jug he eats all the sugar in the bowl. Then he puts the saucer on the plate and the sugar bowl on the saucer and the cup in the bowl and the milk jug in the cup.' She paused for breath. 'Then he walks off down the stairs and away up the river bank.'

'You haven't asked him if he knows anything about model railways, I suppose?'

'He's about the only person I haven't,' she replied 'I can't find anyone capable of even advising us.'

'Nor I,' I told her. 'Never mind. Something will turn up when you least expect it. At least you ought to be making a profit at present.'

'This week's been OK,' she said, 'but remember, it is the holidays and lots of people are around. Last year we had rotten sales in June and I had to struggle to hang on to the crafts people we already had. Talking of which, a couple of awfully nice girls came in today. They want somewhere to sell naturally based skin tonics and suchlike. Do you think it could be called "Craft"?'

'If you've got space, let it to them,' I advised her. 'What do they call themselves?'

'They say they've got a franchise from someone called "Body Shop" who specialize in that sort of thing.'

'Let them have a booth but don't invest any money in it,' I told her. 'It'll never catch on.'

****

'Cheer up, Jo,' said Catherine. 'With all this crowd you must be making a profit.'

The weather all summer had been about right, from our point of view: sufficiently good to attract visitors to the South West but sufficiently bad to drive them off the moors and beaches. Craft ware was selling well and Jo's tenants were paying their rents on time without too much grumbling. In the coffee room Mary and Jane, under the eagle eye of their Aunty Eff, were serving food and drinks as fast as clean crockery arrived from the pantry. Jo had purchased an ancient commercial dish-washer, which Gary Gibson had plumbed in with great difficulty. Every so often it would fall silent, as though it had completed its full circuit. Then, when one of our intrepid waitresses lifted the lid to extract the contents, it would burst into life again, drenching the poor operator in hot suds and creating slippery puddles all over the lino, which had to be mopped up. Nevertheless, the two girls were happy, and showing a substantial profit from the tips left by grateful customers.

'We'll need a lot of profit to cope with this invoice,' muttered Jo. 'Betty Barron said she was giving it to me because their accountant wanted to recover the VAT, but somehow I don't trust them. It's supposed to be for Fred's work last winter on the second floor but two thousand and forty five pounds seems a lot of money.'

'Never mind,' said Catherine. 'It'll all work out in the end. Come and see Ernie's latest.'

Ernie produced some of the most fantastic toys and Catherine's corner was always surrounded by children gazing at the display. Their parents, brought up in an age of plastic, were not so impressed but any child accompanied by Granny was a guaranteed cash customer. Ernie's speciality was a wooden articulated doll that came in various sizes down to a minute half-inch version. Catherine carefully opened a small box. On a bed of cotton wool lay a doll only a quarter of an inch long. With a needle Catherine moved the arms and legs into various positions.

'You really must get her to show you when you next drop in,' Jo told me that evening. 'Any way, she did cheer me up a lot. I still don't like this invoice though.'

'If it is only an accountant's device for recovering VAT, that's up to them,' I assured her. 'If they demand payment then we send them a bill for an economical rent for the space they occupy. Let's see.' I sat down with a piece of paper and switched on my calculator. ' That area, I think, should let for two hundred and twenty pounds a month. They are paying ten. For the ten months of the year you are open they would owe us two thousand, one hundred. We send them a bill in return and they owe us fifty five!'

'I do hope you're right,' said Jo.

****

'I've got a job as a secretary in Exeter,' Phyllis announced.

'What do you mean?' exclaimed Jo. 'We thought you were happily settled, nursing.'

'I was at first,' Phyllis explained, 'but I hate people dying and when I got onto the geriatric ward I hated it even more, so I've got a new job and given my notice to the hospital.'

'Well at least I shall be spared having three bossy nurses in the family, telling me what to do,' I remarked.

Anne, whose 'A' level results had not been good enough to support her ambition to be a doctor, had decided to enrol at her mother's old hospital, as a student nurse and I had been pulling all their legs about the standard of nursing care I could look forward to in my old age. Anne was now working flat out in Jo's coffee room with the intention of saving enough to visit her godparents in South Africa before starting her training. She walked into the room.

'Did you hear on the news,' she asked, 'that the Prime Minister was in trouble with the Police? Apparently she was in a hurry to get to a meeting and her chauffeur was too slow for her liking so she ordered him into the back seat and took over the wheel herself. These two speed cops saw this Daimler doing ninety down the road so they flagged it down and one of them got out and looked into the car. Then he stepped back, saluted and waved it on. "Who was that?" asked his companion.

' "I don't know," said the first speed cop, "But he must have been hellish important. Margaret Thatcher was his driver." '

'If you start telling your patients stories like that,' said Phyllis, 'you'll make their illnesses worse than they were to start with.'

'What I really had to say, Mum,' continued Anne, 'was that Aunty Eff took a phone call from someone in Wales asking if we would sell her pottery. I've got her phone number here.' She held out a piece of paper.

'What do you think, Darling?' asked Jo.

'Well it would be stretching your proud boast of "West Country Crafts" a little,' I told her. 'I know Wales is in the West but so far all the crafts people have been from within the peninsula. So have all the things you sell upstairs.'

'What about tea and coffee?' demanded Phyllis.

'Your mother's clientele,' I assured them, 'are sufficiently erudite to realize that the tea and coffee harvest in Devon is insufficient to provide for their needs and appreciate that we must buy elsewhere. As far as her wool counter on the first floor is concerned, we assume that it all comes originally from Dartmoor sheep except that we decided some time ago that Icelanders and Falklanders should be classed, for Riverside Crafts purposes, as honorary Devonians.'

'You should put a sign up calling it "THE WOOL BAAA"!' said Anne.

****

'Mrs Peters, Mrs Peters!' shrieked Jean. 'Come and look what's happened in the Ladies'.'

Jean came in and cleaned the Riverside after leaving her children at school in the morning and dropped in again to check the lavatories on her way to fetch them in the afternoon. This afternoon something had obviously upset her. Jo ran downstairs to the first floor.

'It looks as though someone's had a wedding party,' she gasped. All the toilet rolls and paper towels had been methodically torn into small pieces and distributed like confetti until the floor was ankle deep.

'It must have been that funny woman,' called Catherine from the floor above. 'You know; the one who was writing poems for the Queen.'

Catherine was not only the craftspeople's Treasurer but also Jo's chief support when she was troubled. They had spent the earlier part of the afternoon, when the lunchtime rush was over, dealing with the accounts and Jo had been confiding her doubts about our dealings with the Barrons. She did not share my confidence that we owed them nothing and lay awake at night worrying. They were interrupted by Olive who pointed out a customer seated, out of sight from the coffee bar, behind the central pillar. She was middle-aged and wore a white turban, a long, blue, shapeless dress and scarlet sandals. This in itself was nothing unusual among the habitués of Riverside Crafts. What had attracted Olive's attention was the fact that, while consuming a single cup of coffee, she had emptied the vases of paper napkins from both her own and the two adjoining tables and was industriously scribbling on them with a felt pen. Jo strolled over to her table.

'You look busy,' she remarked.

'Yes,' replied the lady. 'I'm writing a poem in praise of the Queen. I shall send it to Buckingham Palace and they will write to tell me how much Her Majesty enjoyed it. They always do.'

'Wouldn't she enjoy it even more if you wrote on proper paper?' asked Jo.

'Oh, this is just a rough draft,' she was informed. 'When I've finished I shall copy it onto proper lined paper that I tore out of an old exercise book. Then I'll post it.'

'I think it would be better,' said Jo, 'if you were to write it on your own paper to start with, rather than using up all our napkins.'

'Why shouldn't I use them?' demanded the poetess. 'They're put out for use by the public. I'm a member of the public.'

'That may be so,' explained Jo, 'but they are put out for use on the basis of one napkin for each customer. You have helped yourself to three dozen and that becomes rather expensive.'

'Oh!' screamed the poetess leaping to her feet. 'You're all the same, you people. No respect for genius.'

Snatching the results of her labours from the table, she proceeded to tear the whole lot into small pieces, tossing each handful into the air.

'That's what you can do with your paper!' she exclaimed and, seizing her handbag, stalked out of the room and down the stairs.

'I was too busy clearing up bits of napkin to follow her,' said Jo that evening when relating the story to me. 'Obviously she felt that once she'd started on a paper tearing spree she should follow it to its logical conclusion.'

****

'Five A's, three B's and a C,' announced Cormac.

'What was the C for?' enquired Anne.

'That's the first thing everyone has been asking,' Cormac expostulated dismally. 'It was for Latin, if you must know.'

'Never mind,' I consoled him, 'it was a jolly good result and you needn't take any notice of your sisters. In a family like ours we blokes must stick together. You'll never know what a relief your birth was. Up till then all the relations I had in the world were a wife, three daughters, a mother, a sister and a niece. When the sister phoned from the hospital to say I had a son I dashed straight into town and bought a rugger ball for you so that you'd start life with the right ideas. Now, what are you going to do for your 'A' levels?'

'Maths, Further Maths and Physics,' he told me.

'Well,' I said, 'the best of British luck. Those are subjects I know nothing at all about so I'm not likely to offer any ridiculous advice. Now you can come and apply the laws of physics in helping me to stack some logs at the side of the house so that they will be nice and dry when we want them.'

We spent an hour stacking logs and he retired to his room with a glass of home brew to contemplate the unfairness of life in awarding him only a C for Latin.

'Catherine has a secret admirer,' Jo told me that evening.

'If it's a secret how do you know?' I asked.

'Well,' she replied, 'she thinks Tom Ernley, you know him: the miniature landscape painter, she thinks he fancies her. Apparently he's always trying to make body-contact, like hands meeting in the till or when he holds the door open for her he stands so she can only just squeeze past. We have a little joke about it whenever they are both in on the same day.'

'What does Ernie have to say about it?' I asked, wondering whether a blood feud was about to break out between soft toys and miniatures.

'He says it's all in her imagination. "Man mad" he calls her. "Was I mad to marry you?" she replies.'

'I can see you having more problems to worry about than running out of coffee filters,' I told her.

'Oh, you don't know half the things that go on when you get a crowd of artists all mixed up together,' she chuckled.

'Such as?' I enquired.

'Never you mind,' she told me enigmatically.

I wondered if I ought to mind, then fetched myself a drink to help the wondering.

Chapter 17

'Sell The Huers!' I exploded. 'You must be crazy, Eric.'

'Look,' said the bank manager in his usual calming tone, 'you have a steady cashflow from Jo's craft centre but your loan is mounting every month and you just can't keep it going like that. Your kids are about to leave home and you're not using half the rooms here. Now, if you sold this house and bought somewhere smaller you could pay off the loan and get yourselves on a sound footing again.'

There wasn't much we could say in reply to this logic and we returned home in a state of depression. At suppertime the whole family was affected and bad tempers were the order of the day. The half-term break was proving to be less than revivifying. It had started with a letter from the Barrons' solicitor demanding immediate payment of two thousand and forty-five pounds. I had written to them inviting them to pack their goods and never darken our doors again. Then we had had a long interview with a partner of our own solicitor who had countered their demands with one for rent owing to us. Now the children were mutinous at the thought of leaving the only home any of them remembered.

'Never mind,' said Jo in a desperate attempt to introduce a little cheer into the proceedings. 'On Sunday morning the clocks go back and we can have a long lie in.'

The children looked even more morose and, having loaded the dishwasher, filed silently out of the kitchen.

The gloom continued to spread. Every weekend seemed to be spent in showing prospective purchasers around the Huers. In vain I explained that an eight hundred year old house might be expected to contain a few defects. All they asked to see was our woodworm guarantee which, we discovered, had expired the year before. The children delighted in drawing attention to anything that might deter the ogre who threatened to steal their home. At the Riverside, war existed between the stall holders on the first floor, who had been brainwashed into believing that we were throwing 'Tots and Toddlers' out onto the streets having robbed them of their just dues, and those on the second floor to whom Catherine had explained the true facts of the case. The advertising campaign was a mere shadow of the previous year's 'Adam and Eve' success.

'You really ought to look at Grange Cottage,' said Christine. 'It's got everything you really need including an Aga and room for the dogs.'

Grange Cottage was a few miles down river from The Huers at Shiel St Michael. The owners, friends of Christine, wanted to move nearer their children's school. Christine was right. It had everything we needed in half the number of rooms. There was room for all our treasured furniture and a huge kitchen with room for family meals. The only problem was finding a purchaser for The Huers.

One evening in November a couple arrived to view the house. Mr and Mrs Robinson were quietly delighted with everything they saw. They made an appointment to return on the Saturday with their family. The whole family, Mr and Mrs, their daughter, her husband and two small children and their son, his wife and their three. We offered various forms of refreshment but all were politely refused though one little girl who claimed to be thirsty was permitted a glass of water. In the end they made us an acceptable offer. Then they explained that they had three houses to sell before setting up a family commune in Shiel St Peters. We agreed to exchange contracts before Christmas and, in turn, made our offer for Grange Cottage, which was accepted.

Our solicitor wrote to confirm that 'Tots and Toddlers' had abandoned any idea of suing us. Fred Barron glared at me as he handed over the keys. I waved goodbye as they drove off but neither of them reciprocated.

'But you can't show it to anyone else,' exclaimed Mr Robinson. 'Do you realize that you would make three families homeless if you decided not to sell it to us? We are Mormons and wouldn't break our promise to buy it.'

Jo promised that we would not sell the place to anyone else and encouraged them to exchange contracts as soon as possible. Life held some promise after all.

We enjoyed a happy Christmas and started the New Year as I hoped it would continue: with ham and eggs for breakfast washed down with Buck's Fizz.

'The Robinsons still haven't exchanged contracts,' remarked Jo a week later.

'Try ringing them.' I suggested. 'We can't exchange on Grange Cottage until we know it's OK.'

There was no reply.

'I'm beginning to get suspicious,' said Jo.

'You heard what he said,' I replied. 'They couldn't possibly let us down now.'

The weeks went by. At the end of January our solicitor rang. The Robinsons had backed out of the deal.

'And they didn't even have the guts to tell us themselves,' raged Jo. 'Now what do we do?'

We went back to the agents.

'Mrs Hill is still very interested,' we were told.

The Hills' offer was five thousand pounds lower than we had hoped for but we were in a hurry. The deal was struck. Both contracts were exchanged. We were on the move.

****

'But that's my birthday,' protested Mary.

'I know,' I replied. 'Moving house is no way to celebrate your eighteenth, but there is no other date that will satisfy everyone concerned. We'll try to arrange some sort of a party in the evening.'

'Oh, this is absolutely ridiculous!' Jo burst into the kitchen.

'I know,' wailed Mary. 'It's not fair. The others had parties on their eighteenths.'

'I wasn't talking about that,' said Jo. 'I've just been on the telephone to the solicitor. We're all stuck. The building societies won't release any money until the keys have been handed over and no one will hand over their keys until the money has been paid. It all starts with the people in Budleigh Salterton whose house the Patricks are buying. They're going to France and want to be paid before they sail on the thirtieth. The Patricks can't pay them before we pay for Grange Cottage. We can't pay for the Cottage till the Hills pay us. The Hills can't pay us till we hand over the keys and in any case, they are in a house they've rented till the end of March and they have to get out by the thirty-first.'

'Say that again,' I suggested.

'The people in Budleigh....... Oh shut up, you idiot,' she exclaimed as Mary and I burst out laughing. 'What are we going to do about it?'

'I'll need a pint while I think about that one,' I told her and set off for the pantry.

That weekend I needed a lot of pints and spent most of my time on the phone. There didn't seem to be any solution. There were only a couple of weeks left and no one had a clue how we were to unblock the system. Jo was up to her ears in preparations for re-opening the Riverside in time for Easter. I had an idea.

'How much would it cost to borrow seventy thousand pounds for twenty-four hours?' I asked the solicitor. 'I make it about forty quid.'

'In that region,' she agreed.

'Problem solved,' I told Jo. 'For twenty-four hours we own two houses. The Patricks pay the couple in Budleigh. They move out on the twenty-eighth while the Patricks pack. They move out on the morning of the twenty-ninth and we move in. The Hills move in here on the thirtieth. QED.'

'What about me?' demanded Mary.

'You can help us move,' I replied. 'Then we'll take you out to dinner.'

'Big deal!' she sneered.

Anne had returned from her trip to South Africa, very sunburnt and bearing gifts of exotic origins. John, though described by his sports master as 'a useful scrum half', was not yet very tall. We would have welcomed the help of a six-foot, seventeen-year-old sergeant in the CCF but Cormac informed us, with barely concealed glee, that our move coincided with a visit, laid on by the Army Schools Liaison Team, to Sandhurst. John Peterson had agreed to my absenting myself on what was the last day of the college term. The craft centre had reopened the previous week and was to be left in the capable hands of Olive assisted by Jane with Catherine keeping an eye on things. Simon and Corenne had volunteered to help. All was ready for the great move.

****

'Do we want what?' exclaimed Jo. She listened carefully to the caller while her eyes widened. 'I'll have to ask Jeffrey,' she said and, covering the mouthpiece with her hand, turned to me.

'It's Mary Patrick,' she explained. 'Do we want four sheep? She was going to give them to someone but they can't have them after all.'

I knew the Patricks' paddock was far more neatly kept than ours. They had four ewes who clipped the grass with enthusiasm. Did we want them? I knew nothing of the habits of sheep but then, I knew nothing about cows before we acquired Susie.

'Oh, let's give it a try,' I said. At least, I thought, it would save me hours of driving the lawn mower round the paddock.

The house was in chaos. In every room lay packing cases filled with everything except our vital requirements for the next two days.

Tomorrow, Monday, afternoon the removals men would arrive to load their pantechnicon, all ready to be delivered to Grange Cottage the next morning. The dogs sniffed their way suspiciously through the jungle of boxes, unable to understand what was happening to their domain.

'I don't think the dogs have ever met a sheep,' remarked Jo.

'I wonder if the sheep have ever met a dog,' I retorted.

'Oh yes,' she replied. 'The Patricks have a large Alsatian.'

I ruminated on the probability that theirs was a well-trained and highly disciplined hound whereas Jaws and Gigi were inclined to follow their own inclinations. Shammy was getting too old to do anything but set up an hysterical barking at the approach of strangers. This alerted her offspring who put the fear of God into unsuspecting visitors. How they would react to strange woolly objects was a matter for speculation.

The move went remarkably smoothly. Our pantechnicon pulled up at Grange Cottage as the Patricks' pulled out, both sets of removals men hurling cheerful invective at each other. Jo and her helpers were not far behind and soon our furniture was settling into its new position. By noon all had been unloaded and the men returned for a second load. I remained at The Huers to see all was in a fit state to hand over to its new owners next day. I shall always be grateful to one of Jo's friends who hurtled, broom in hand, into each room as it emptied and, in no time at all, had it clear of dust, cobwebs and the general detritus of sixteen years of occupation.

No sooner had the men returned to The Huers than a van arrived at the Cottage with the new bed that Jo and I had ordered to celebrate the occasion. The deliverymen took one look at the stairs, sucked their teeth and pronounced the impossibility of transporting their load to the first floor.

'Why ever not?' demanded Jo.

'We might damage it getting it up there,' replied the older of the two.

'And then you'd claim it wasn't in good condition,' added the other.

No amount of cajoling on Jo's part could persuade them and they departed, having dumped the bed on the kitchen floor. Simon sized up the job, fetched the towrope from his car and with much straining by everyone the securely bound bed ascended to the landing and into our bedroom.

The second load left for Shiel St Michael and I made a farewell check on the old home. Then I drove off to the new, detouring to drop the keys at the estate agents' on the way. That evening we enjoyed a slap up meal at a neighbouring restaurant and Mary was somewhat mollified after we had drunk to her newly gained freedom.

Early next morning Jo and I walked the dogs to the paddock. The sheep galloped to greet us, or at least, the bucket of sheep's' supplement, a sort of muesli, which smelled deliciously of molasses. They stuck their noses through the wire fence. The dogs inspected them from the other side. There was no animosity on either side. We let ourselves into the paddock and emptied the bucket into a trough. The sheep jostled each other to get at it. The dogs ignored them and then, suddenly, took off after a foolhardy rabbit. We were at home.

****

'We put them to a ram in late autumn,' said Mary Patrick. 'They should lamb about the end of April. Samantha is probably too old now but Lucy, Lambkins and Redcurrant all produced twins last year.'

Jo's eyes gleamed at the idea of putting her midwifery skills to use again. My thoughts were more of gratitude that we had an old freezer in my workshop, which would be filled with succulent joints of hogget in due course. Not to mention kidneys for breakfast six times over!

The sun shone, the cherry trees were a mass of blossom and it was Easter. Jo and her helpers were rushed off their feet as the first tourists of the year filled her coffee room.

'I think we may have found him,' she told me one evening on her return home.

'Who?' I wanted to know.

'The man we've been looking for,' she replied. 'The man with a lifelong passion for running model railways. He came in for a coffee and we started talking. You'd like him. An ex-sapper. That's what started us talking. I asked what tie he was wearing.'

'Is he mad, Methodist or married?' I asked.

'All three probably. Why?'

'All sappers are one or another,' I told her. 'He must be mad if he wants to run a railway at the Riverside. What's he called?'

'Peregrine Jones. Have you ever come across him in your travels?'

'Doesn't ring a bell,' I said. 'What have you arranged?'

'He's coming to see us on Saturday. With his wife. I would like you to come and meet them.'

Saturday came and by eleven thirty we were ensconced in one corner of the coffee room talking railways for all we were worth. Peggy

Jones sold lace and would be happy to have a stall on our first floor. Perry had run a model railway before but the rent of his seaside showroom had proved too much of a burden. We agreed on a fifty-fifty share of expenses and profits.

'Could you do it in three months?' asked Jo. 'That would mean you would be open for the summer holidays.'

'I could try,' said Perry, ' but it will be damned hard work. Still, we'll give it a go.'

'I don't like the look of Lambkins,' I told Jo on the following evening. 'She reminds me of the time Susie had milk fever after calving. The vet injected calcium and she was all right after that.'

Jo accompanied me to the paddock where Lambkins lay looking miserable.

'You're right,' she said. 'I'll phone the vet first thing in the morning. Thank heavens it's Monday and the Riverside is closed.'

'Well?' I demanded next evening. 'What did the vet say?'

'Stupid old man,' she exclaimed.

'Who? Me?' I asked.

'No, you fathead,' she laughed. 'The vet. According to the neighbours he's the best in the area but he seemed to think I knew exactly what was wrong with her and kept asking whether I wanted to save Lambkins or the lambs. I kept on saying I wanted both but he wouldn't explain what the trouble was. In the end he gave her an injection and said he'd call tomorrow. I don't think he's done her any good at all.'

Lambkins certainly looked as miserable as ever and not even the sheep's' muesli tempted her appetite. Next morning she was dead.

I phoned the knacker who had dealt with Susie. He didn't want to know.

'A dead sheep's not worth the petrol,' he explained.

'Try the local hunt,' suggested our farming neighbour.

The huntsman was delighted and by the time I returned home that evening the corpse had vanished.

'Twin lamb fever,' said the farmer's wife. 'You've got to watch out for that.'

The vet's bill was enormous.

****

'Oh, aren't they gorgeous,' drooled Olive, staring at the photograph. 'What are you going to do with them?'

'Eat them,' I replied gleefully.

Her eyes widened; her jaw dropped. 'You beast!' she shrieked and then, to my horror, burst into tears and fled into the kitchen.

We had spent a sleepless night. Jo never had subscribed to my theory that animals were perfectly capable of getting on without human assistance and had diagnosed a breech delivery in Redcurrant. As a result I had found myself, at one thirty in the morning, squatting in an old stable and, by the light of a couple of hurricane lamps, assisting at the birth of a small, black-faced, ewe lamb. Jo sat glowing at the result of a job well done while I brewed hot chocolate, liberally laced with whisky. It seemed about five minutes after we finally got to bed when the wireless switched on to wake me up again.

Having put the kettle on the Aga and let the dogs loose, I strolled down the paddock to the old stable. Redcurrant's offspring was enthusiastically nudging her mother. So, to my surprise was Lucy's: another ewe. I returned to the house and called Jo with the news. She fled down the garden path with shining eyes and followed by the girls. I retired to the bathroom.

Jo was convinced that Lucy would have another, and I promised to rush home at lunchtime to see that all was well. When I did so I found she was right and a third addition, this time a ram, had arrived. I fetched the Polaroid camera and photographed the trio lying in the spring sunshine. Then I drove to the Riverside. Jo was not in the coffee room and I handed the photograph to Olive. This was a mistake. I shouted down the stairs to Jo and, when she arrived, explained what I had done and fled through the fire exit to my car and back to college, just in time to greet my class as they filed in.

'What shall we call them?' I asked Jane that evening when we arrived home.

'The twins are Adam and Eve,' she replied, 'so that if you want to resurrect your advertisements you can claim to know them personally. The other is Hecta.'

'Why Hecta?' I wanted to know.

'I like Hecta,' she said.

'A fair enough reason, I suppose,' I agreed. 'But you'll have to be duty shepherdess and keep an eye on them.'

The farmer's son gave me a lesson in the use of the diabolical looking tool that the Patricks had left us.

'Just fit the rubber ring over the prongs,' he instructed me. 'Then grip the handles tight and slide the ring up her tail as far as there - that's it - just leaving enough for her to keep the flies away. Now, slacken your grip so the ring is tight round her tail, slide out the prongs and Bob's your uncle.'

I repeated the operation on the other two and then once more, much less pleasantly, on the ram. I supposed I would get used to it just as I had become accustomed to using the hypodermic injector to caponise the cockerels.

'We ought to keep Eve and Hecta to replace Lambkins,' Jo told me.

'O.K.,' I replied. 'But no arguments, please, when Adam is ready for the pot.'

'I heard that,' shouted Jane from the next room.

****

'I'm sorry to tell you,' said John Peterson in the staff room on the first morning back from the half-term break, 'that Sharon will not be with us any more. You remember Richard Williams who left us last term? Apparently they had been seeing rather too much of each other, doing what comes naturally it seems, and Sharon is expecting a baby in November. She has gone home to her parents till then.'

I had always thought that the house parents had the most difficult job in the college, running a home for fifty or so lively teenagers on lines that would be approved by responsible parents. As teachers we gave what support we could but the brunt fell on their shoulders. I had had a taste of their problems with our foreign pupils and realized that, no matter how careful they were, there would always be little lapses such as the case of Sharon and Richard.

The break had gone well at the Riverside. Jo had been inundated with customers and glad to have Anne, Mary and Jane to work in the coffee room. Perry and Peggy were hard at work on the floor above but the noise did not put off the hungry horde. Now all was quiet again and would remain so throughout the whole of June until the first flush of summer visitors arrived in the West Country. The model railway was taking shape behind tall glass barriers and Perry was proving to be a most enterprising artist. His network ran from the city, with its underground line visible through the glass, across the moors, alive with sheep and hikers, down the riverbank, passing our warehouse and weir, and ending in the busy docks with cross-channel ferry and working cranes.

'Mr Peters,' said Mandy one morning. 'Do you think that we could select our own essay subjects one day?'

Mandy was a bright and cheerful sixteen-year-old and, it seemed to me, unlikely to present the house parents with many problems. Only one thought filled her mind. Her tee-shirt sported a proclamation: BOTHAM BOWLED THIS MAIDEN OVER, and she was never without her current copy of Wisden. The other students complained good-heartedly that they were unable to watch anything other than cricket on the television as long as she was around. The last one I considered likely to have to return home to an irate Mum.

'I don't see why not, Mandy,' I replied. 'Is there any particular reason for your sudden conversion to literary ambition?'

'Oh yes,' she said. 'You see, on Saturday something happened to me which had never ever happened before.'

A nagging doubt crept into my mind. Could I have been wrong in my assessment of her character?

'In fact,' she went on, 'I was beginning to think it never would happen.'

My heart descended slowly towards my hush puppies.

'And,' she continued, 'it was so wonderful that I wanted to tell you all about it.'

'Are you quite sure, Mandy,' I enquired in a hoarse voice, 'that you really want me to be the confidante of your secrets?'

'Oh yes,' she said again. 'You see, it was like this.'

My heart reached the floor.

'On Saturday morning,' she began, 'the house parents told me they had organised a coach trip and they wanted me to come on it. Well, I got on the coach and everyone kept talking to me and asking me questions so that I didn't really see where we were going. It wasn't until we stopped that I realized we were in Taunton at the county ground and....Oh Mr Peters, I met Ian Botham!'

Chapter 18

'Mr Swivel came to see me today,' said Jo. 'Guess what they're going to do.'

'Not a clue,' I replied. 'Nothing to our advantage, I suppose?'

'I'm not sure,' she said. 'They want to make a pub out of the cellars on the ground floor.'

Our warehouse stood on massive walls at ground level. The spaces between the walls had been lengthened by tunnelling into the hillside at the back and were used for various purposes, mainly as storerooms, garages or small workshops. The first and second floors, where Jo's craftspeople sold their wares, were built into the hillside which levelled off outside the third floor so that we were able to satisfy the fire authorities by having a doorway through which one could walk along a pathway to a car-park at the top of the hill. In winter, when the river rose high up its banks, I always expected the tunnels to flood, but even when the water flowed over the road it never quite reached their doors. Those old merchants who built the warehouse two centuries ago knew how to keep their goods safe and dry.

'I suppose a pub there would take some of your coffee room trade,' I opined. 'On the other hand, anything which attracts customers to the area can't be bad for business.'

We agreed that as there was nothing we could do to influence the outcome we might as well support the project. At the next meeting of our craftspeople's committee we reported the potential development, which was received with enthusiasm. The reaction of the tenants of the cellars was less enthusiastic. Many of them were regular visitors to the coffee room for refreshment and poured out their complaints to Jo's ever-sympathetic ear. She usually managed to cheer them up before they left.

Meanwhile, Peregrine Jones had almost completed his masterpiece. Occasional curses rang down the stairs as a faulty connection led to two trains colliding in the least accessible section of the track but he was rapidly getting these under control and all seemed set for the exhibition to be open in time for the school holidays. By the time they were over we were threatened with having the smallest family we had had since Anne was born. Phyllis and Anne were both off to London, Phyllis to work as a nanny and Anne to start training as a student nurse. Mary was looking for a job and muttering about a flat of her own. If that came about, when the boys went back for the autumn term we would be left with only Jane in residence at Grange Cottage.

'Won't that be blissful?' I asked. 'Already, since Phyllis's birthday, we've reduced the number of those awful teenagers in the house from six to five. Now we shall only have one for most of the time and I'm sure she will be anxious to make her ancient parents happy and keep the volume of her horrible noise machine turned right down.'

'It's going to cost you!' came Jane's voice from the top of the stairs.

'John and I were thinking you might like us to be weekly boarders,' volunteered Cormac. 'Then we'd be home at the weekends and you wouldn't have that lonely feeling all the time. And you'd have someone to keep Jane in order. She'd become insufferable if she were the only one here.'

A pillow flew from the landing with remarkable accuracy and the conversation ended with the sounds of battle from upstairs.

'I'm not sure I don't agree with your theory that it'll be heaven when they're all grown up,' said Jo.

****

'What about the Mayor?' volunteered Ernie.

'We tried him,' replied Jo. 'Not available.'

'There ought to be someone who would draw a crowd,' said Catherine.

'There would be if we could afford it,' Jo told us, 'but any sort of celebrity seems to charge the Earth and we've spent most of our advertising budget already.'

'Well, we will just have to do without the opening ceremony,' said Peregrine. 'But we must advertise it well even if there's not much money available. Any ideas on that, anybody?'

A baffled silence ensued. Ideas were not much in evidence that evening and a feeling of gloom spread over us all. 'The Riverside Model Railway' had steam up and was ready to go. Opening day was on Saturday week when the schools had just broken up but suggestions as to how to draw the crowds were decidedly lacking.

'How about a sandwich man?' cried Catherine. 'My nephew did that for his school fete once. I think he's still got the boards and I'm sure he would walk around town for a small amount. Then you might persuade the local paper to publish an article on the railway. With a picture of Perry dressed as 'The Fat Controller'. That should really wow them!'

'I don't think I could possibly run the place if it weren't for Catherine and Ernie,' Jo told me as we drove home. 'One or the other always has an idea at the right time and if anything is going wrong they'll find some way of turning it into a laugh.'

The week passed. Jo had persuaded the paper to publish a few lines. A photographer appeared and recorded Perry in his stationmaster's cap, standing beside his model. The term neared its end.

'Mr Peters,' whined a voice from the back of the class. 'Why do you make us work today?'

'Is there any reason why I shouldn't, Sharon?' I wanted to know.

'But today is the last day of term,' the whine continued.

'Well, that's the answer to your question then, isn't it?' I replied.

'Huh?'

'In the term we work. In the holidays we don't. Today is the last day of term. We work. Tomorrow is the first day of the holidays. We don't work. Seems pretty obvious to me.'

A sullen muttering rumbled along the back row and I heaved a sigh of relief when the bell rang and I could send them on their way. Introducing students to the harsh realities of life was never popular with them.

On Saturday mornings, come term or hols or model railways, I set off in the Peugeot with Jo to collect the following week's supplies from the cash and carry. On our way we passed our sandwich man extolling the virtues of the Riverside. We loaded gross after gross of cola cans, crates of coffee filters and all the other items for the delectation of her customers. Then we returned to the coffee room. We made our way in through the fire escape and found Anne, together with Jane and one of her school friends, serving drinks and cakes as though they were going out of fashion. A queue of railway enthusiasts stretched down the stairs and onto the road outside.

The railway looked as though it would be a success.

****

'There's something wrong with Redcurrant's foot,' reported Jane one morning. 'She's limping badly.'

I went down to the paddock. Sure enough the ewe was lame and trailed behind the others as they hastened towards me in the hope of some titbit.

'Her hoof needs paring,' said a voice from the other side of the hedge. One of the farm hands was repairing the fence. 'You'll need a sharp knife and trim off all that excess growth.'

For a couple of years now my hip had been stiffening up and I doubted whether I could bring down a full-grown sheep with a rugger tackle, let alone keep it subdued while I operated on its foot. I decided to call on Cormac for help, but he was leaving for the Riverside with Jo. He was to have instruction in running the railway in order to give Peregrine an occasional day off. During the summer holidays the craft centre was open seven days a week instead of closing on Mondays, which was the normal routine. This meant that Jo worked seven days a week but she tried to ensure that no one else did. I decided to issue a 'warning order' and deal with Redcurrant that evening.

I settled down for a couple of hours with Jo's books. My experience of book keeping was limited to those excruciating hours each quarter when the adjutant selected one to be a member of the board auditing the Sergeants' Mess accounts. Invariably the whole thing had to be explained by the Mess Steward whose probity one was investigating. Jo had invented her own system which was as complicated as her address book which consisted of an old diary in which were listed, starting from the back, all the names, addresses and telephone numbers she might need, in the order in which she had first met or made contact with them. This worked splendidly for her because of her infallible memory of events but I could never find anything in it that I needed. However, between us we produced a set of figures that our long-suffering accountant translated into something acceptable to the Inland Revenue.

I was still at work when the phone rang. It was Jo. Peggy, it seemed, was the heroine of the hour. She had spotted a couple of young women removing one of Camilla Smith's hand-knitted jumpers from its stand and sneaking off down the stairs. With cries of 'Stop thief! Police!' she pursued the pair up the road until they vanished into a public toilet outside which she was joined by other craftswomen who laid siege to the refuge until the arrival of the police. The miscreants emerged empty handed and denying any knowledge of a jumper but a search revealed it hidden behind a cistern and they were taken off in a Panda car to durance vile. Every one was delighted except Camilla whose jumper was retained by the constabulary as evidence.

The family returned that evening, eager to relate the story of Peggy's pursuit of the villains but I seized Cormac and led him off to the paddock where he successfully pinned Redcurrant to the ground. I set about paring the unwanted portions of hoof and had almost finished when she gave an extra heave and pulled her leg from my grasp. Cormac grabbed at it and received a vicious slash from the Stanley knife in my right hand. He released the ewe while I toppled sideways and fell against her. She took a nasty kick at a part of my anatomy I did not wish to have kicked. I took avoiding action. As a result of all this I discovered that I had Redcurrant jammed against a fence post with her leg locked between my knees and was able to finish the operation unaided. Cormac was already halfway back to Mother who cleaned his wound, then pushed him into the car and set off for the surgery, stitches and anti-tetanus jabs. On their return I made some amends by giving him a generous whisky. His attitude towards veterinary duties became slightly less hostile.

Arriving at the breakfast table a couple of days later I found a present from the children resting against my chair: a shepherd's crook and a first aid outfit!

****

'They can't do that,' cried Peregrine. 'Just think what builder's dust would do to my railway.'

Mr Swivel had been to call. If there were to be a pub below us they would need to put ventilators up through our floors to roof level. Jo had arranged a meeting with the brewery's engineers during the half term break. She canvassed the craftspeople who would be affected and all were happy except Perry. He certainly had a point; keeping his display clear of dust and condensation was his daylong occupation.

In the end we included Perry in the team we assembled to discuss the matter with the brewery. After much talk we reached agreement. They would complete their work after the New Year, when we would be closed. Perry was more or less mollified by their promise to place a protective cover over the railway while they worked and to provide giant vacuum cleaners to clean up any dust that might penetrate this defence. Most of the craftspeople removed their goods each winter anyway and so would not be inconvenienced by the work. The engineer who was to carry out the work was a friendly soul and Jo felt she could trust him to see that we did not suffer any harm. She agreed that she would meet him on the second Monday in January to give him a set of keys to the building.

It was the first Christmas the two youngest had ever spent anywhere but at The Huers and Jo was determined to let it be no less enjoyable. Our advertisements were not as entertaining as the 'Adam and Eve' campaign but we had a good influx of customers seeking suitable gifts. Jo and Catherine had had an idea, which they proceeded to put into practice. They loaded trays with small articles from each of the stalls and set off in Jo's car for a day visiting local old people's homes. I met them on their return.

'We've had such a day,' laughed Jo. 'The very first place we went to we found everyone waiting for us in their dining room. We put our trays on the table and there was one old lady who picked up everything we had brought and shouted, "Rubbish, rubbish. Throw it on the fire." '

'Yes,' agreed Catherine. 'And she would have, too, if the staff hadn't been there to save it.'

'But then,' said Jo, 'she looked at my dress and started off again, shouting, "What's she wearing? Rubbish, rubbish. Throw it on the fire!" Still, we sold quite a lot. Especially Catherine who was making up to one old man.'

'That sounds like my missis,' Ernie grinned.

'I sold him all sorts of things,' Catherine told us. 'But he kept on saying his money was in his bedroom so I had to go with him to collect it,'

'Man mad; that's her,' chuckled Ernie.

We closed our doors on Friday night, the day before Christmas Eve, and held a party in the coffee room at which some of our craftspeople displayed unexpected talents. Ernie led a most harmonious Barbers' Shop Quartet but Ivor, after an impressive intake of white wine, came to grief trying to juggle eight scones simultaneously. Annie, who had cooked the scones, took umbrage in incomprehensible Gaelic.

There wasn't room at Grange Cottage for the eighteen-foot tree that had stood in the hall at The Huers, but the festivities were just as lively. Uncle McCormac arrived with a giant turkey and associated bottles, Phyllis and Anne travelled down together from Paddington and I ignited not only the brandy on the pudding but also Cormac who was holding it. Christmas was voted a success.

A fortnight later Jo was making up a spare set of keys to give to the engineer next morning when the phone rang. I heard her involved in a lively conversation in my study.

'Would you believe it?' she snorted, walking into the kitchen. 'They've changed their plans and never bothered to tell me. It was only because the engineer still had the meeting in his diary that he phoned to check that they had told me it was off. If it hadn't been for him I'd have spent tomorrow hanging around in the warehouse waiting for someone to turn up. Just wait till I see them again. I'll give them ventilators all right!'

'Never mind,' I told her, pouring her a consoling drink. 'Come and sit by the fire thinking beautiful thoughts and be grateful you don't have to go out in this weather after all.'

'There's nothing beautiful about my thoughts of those brewers,' she assured me.

****

'Will you just look at this?' stormed Jo. 'Who the blazes are they and what do they think they are playing at?' She thrust an envelope into my hands.

'It looks to me as though you've ordered an advert to be inserted in a booklet about the conference facilities in a hotel in Skegness,' I told her. 'Why on earth did you do that?'

'Don't be an idiot,' she fumed. 'Can you imagine me doing that?'

'Of course I can't,' I assured her, 'but where did they get it from. It's a copy of one of our old leaflets. Have you done any advertising with this firm?'

'Not that I can remember,' she told me, 'but then, I get so many people wanting us to advertise through whatever it is they publish. If I accepted every offer we'd spend all our profits on advertising. But this is a bill for one hundred pounds. I can't afford that.'

'One hundred plus VAT,' I agreed. 'Don't worry. I'll sort it out.'

This, I realized, was a try on by a firm of dodgy publishers but Jo was not convinced that somehow she would not have to pay, even though she had not authorised the advertisement in the first place. In the end I took the offending booklet and its accompanying bill back home with me and settled down to enjoy myself.

As all our sales were over the counter we had no need of printed forms other than our standard agreement with the craftspeople. On the computer that Jo had given me some time before I constructed an invoice for one thousand pounds plus VAT and, with my tongue firmly in my cheek, wrote a strong letter pointing out that they had used our leaflet without our permission, that we retained the copyright of any item produced in the craft centre and that we would be grateful for the early settlement of the enclosed bill for our copyright fee.

A few days later Jo was once again infuriated. 'They've replied to your letter. I had ordered some advertising from them. Here's a photocopy of my signature. But it was two years ago for a booklet they were going to place in the bedrooms of all the best hotels in Exeter. Not Skegness, of all places. And they never did publish the booklet.'

Once more I retired to my study and composed a reply to their somewhat ungrammatical letter, pointing out the absurdity of their claim and enjoining them to settle our bill forthwith.

We heard nothing more for a fortnight and then, to our immense glee, received a letter from their solicitors telling us that they did not believe we had a claim against their clients and would be prepared to receive any writ we might issue against them.

'Solicitors don't come cheap,' chuckled Jo. 'That'll teach them.'

****

'I can count, you know!' Jane stormed into the kitchen.

The previous day Jane's class at the convent had visited London in order to see a performance of 'Twelfth Night'. They left at crack of dawn and returned late in the evening. I had seized the opportunity to take our ram lamb, now a well fattened hogget, to the butcher and he now reposed in the depths of the freezer. This morning had seen the usual rush to get ready in time for school and it was not till now, after tea on Friday, that she had visited the paddock.

In the autumn I had borrowed a ram from the farmer who, very obligingly, dipped my sheep at the same time as his. I collected it with its harness, which held a bag of dye on its chest. I had hardly had time to return to the house before Samantha trotted proudly across the paddock with a dye mark on her back. At her age we were pretty certain that she was well past lambing but Mary Patrick had assured us that she was always first to greet a new 'toy boy'. It looked as though she was living up to her reputation. I phoned the Riverside. Olive answered.

'Tell Jo that Samantha has a satisfied smile on her face,' I told her.

'Will she know what that means?' asked Olive innocently.

'I'm sure she'll get the message,' I replied and rang off.

Now it was spring. Only Lucy and Redcurrant showed signs of a successful liaison with the ram but Adam had to go. I tried to explain that the sheep were no different in my scheme of things from tomatoes or onions. They were all grown for the table.

'But tomatoes don't come running and lick your fingers,' sniffed Jane. A look of horror crossed her face. 'Those chops we had for supper last night! Were they......?'

I nodded.

'You're horrible!' she sobbed, running up the stairs.

'But they were jolly nice chops,' I called after her.

'I agree with her,' said Jo, 'but we have business to discuss. Mr Swivel phoned me this afternoon. The brewery want to put the ventilators in again. Of course they had to wait till we had re-opened. I told him there wasn't a chance but he assured me they would make an offer we couldn't refuse. We are meeting them on Tuesday and I'd like you to be there. I've invited some of the members of the Craftspeople's Committee as well. If we do close for a month it will affect them all.'

I agreed to attend the meeting although Tuesday was the day before the summer term started. Educationally I was finding life busy. Jane had sailed happily through her mock 'O' levels but John's results had been disappointing in the extreme. We had accepted Cormac's suggestion of weekly boarding and each Friday evening I collected the boys and, over the weekend, John sat in my study and completed three 'O' level papers, Maths, Physics and English. Cormac and I then discussed his efforts with him and hoped that we could improve his eventual results. I still had my normal marking to complete and had not been helping Jo as much as I might. She coped as cheerfully as ever.

The brewery's representatives arrived, together with Mr Swivel. They were obviously not used to business meetings held with a motley throng of painters, potters and railway enthusiasts and with customers being served their cream teas on the other side of the coffee room. They outlined their proposals. There was a massive gasp of horror.

'We can't close in May,' exclaimed Catherine.

'I should think not,' Jo confirmed. 'Look,' she explained to the brewers, 'In May there are two Bank Holidays and the half term. It's the first time in the year when we really get to make any profit. Then there's a dead period till the visitors start arriving at the end of June. We couldn't close in May.'

The brewers were adamant that May was the only time that would fit into their schedule. We were equally determined that we wouldn't close.

'We would, of course, compensate you,' their leader assured us.

'You'd have to,' replied Jo. 'We have about fifty craftspeople with stalls here and they'd all have to close. To some of them it's only a paying hobby but to many it's their living and they can't afford to lose all that business.'

'Oh, we'd be generous,' He assured her. 'We could offer you five thousand pounds.'

'Five thousand!' exploded Jo. 'That, distributed among all our people would amount to a hundred each and leave nothing for all the things like our profit and,' she looked at Mr Swivel, 'you'd still expect us to pay our rent, wouldn't you?'

He nodded.

'So what would you consider an acceptable offer?' demanded the spokesman.

'Try fifty thousand,' suggested Jo.

He stood up and picked up his papers.

'If that's your attitude, Mrs Peters, I can only say that you will never see one of our public houses here on the riverside.'

'I do hope you find somewhere as nice,' Jo told him as they made their way out.

Chapter 19

'Any of your students giving problems?' asked John Peterson.

We were sitting in the staff room for our weekly meeting. None of the others raised any points.

'I'm worried,' I said, 'about Ivor. I can't cure him of this ridiculous habit of his. When he writes a word with an "r" followed by an "n" he runs the two together to make it look like "m".'

'Is there anything very terrible in that?' asked Peter French. 'We've got him down to train in Electronic Servicing. It's unlikely to affect his chances of employment.'

'That's just were I disagree,' I told him. 'When a prospective employer looks at the signature "Ivor Redburn" he's going to think someone is taking the micky out of him.'

'You're right,' chuckled John. 'Keep hammering at him and any of the rest of you who deal with him keep an eye on that.'

I was marking some essays that evening and had just composed another rude remark to add to Ivor's signature when Jo returned from the Riverside.

'Darling,' she cried from the doorway. 'I'm going to be an awful nuisance.'

'Impossible,' I replied with affected gallantry. 'What's the matter?'

'It's this order form,' she said, picking an envelope out of its pigeonhole. I've promised to get some special wool for one of our customers by the weekend. I've phoned the suppliers and they promised to send it as soon as they received my order. But it must catch the last post this evening.'

'That's OK,' I told her. 'You fill it in and I'll drive into Exeter and post it at the sorting office by the station. The last collection from there is very late.'

A little while later I set off bearing a large envelope containing not only the order form but cards of samples and other materials. At the sorting office I found a mass of cars parked all over the place while their owners, most of the office managers in the city, queued to post their evening mail. At last I reached the head of the queue and inserted the envelope into the mailbox let into the side of the building.

'Thanks very much,' said a voice from the box, and the letter was snatched from my hand.

'Not a lot of those left,' said the man behind me.

'What's that?' I asked.

'Talking letter boxes,' he replied.

****

'I'll go,' said Jane.

It was a Saturday evening and Jo, Terry Turnbull and I were finishing the bottle that had accompanied our supper. Jane was sitting with us when the doorbell rang.

'I've escaped from Exminster Hospital,' said the man at the door. 'I want to get to Exeter.'

I leaped to my feet in spite of my stiffening joints. Exminster was the local mental hospital and I didn't think they wanted patients to escape.

'You're a bit out of your way,' I told him. 'Exeter's the other way from here. You'd better come in and have a cup of tea.'

He made himself comfortable at the kitchen table and Jo and Terry engaged him in conversation.

'My name is Ken Ford,' he told them.

Jo and I exchanged glances. Kenford was the next village along the road from Exminster.

'I'm very hungry,' he said.

'Go and carve some ham, Jeffrey,' said Jo and set about buttering slices of bread. I took the carving knife into the utility room, removed the ham from the refrigerator and proceeded to carve some generous slices. After a few minutes Jo joined me. We looked at each other and erupted into a fit of the giggles. For a few moments we were helpless, struggling not to allow the sounds of our mirth to be heard in the kitchen, then we regained self-control and returned to the kitchen where Terry, while pouring a mug of tea, had removed every knife in sight and was just hiding them in a drawer, rolling her eyes alternatively towards heaven and our visitor. She grimaced at the carving knife in my hand, snatched it away and consigned it to the drawer with its brothers.

Not wishing to use the telephone in the kitchen I left them chatting while he wolfed his sandwiches. Opening the door I found Cormac and John poised to charge in should help be required. Leaving them on guard I picked up the phone and dialled 999. The sergeant was very helpful, promising immediate action, and I returned to the kitchen where I found Jo, Terry and Jane listening to our visitor.

'Oh yes,' he was telling them, 'I've got a nice girl friend. Mary Ward she's called. She'll be eighty seven next month.'

We strangled another outbreak of giggling. Jane looked as though she would explode. For the next half hour we listened as he related the history of twenty years in the hospital while chain-smoking Terry's cigarettes. The phone rang. I went to the study and answered it.

'I'm sorry,' said the sergeant. 'The patrol car can't find Grange Cottage. Where exactly are you?'

I described our home, adding, 'There's a grey Peugeot estate parked outside the door.'

'Got it,' said another voice on the phone. 'We passed the Peugeot five minutes ago.'

I returned to the kitchen and went out of the back door. A police car pulled up at the gate. Two large officers climbed out and joined the party in the kitchen. More mugs of tea were poured. Terry produced her last packet of fags. 'Ken Ford' explained how he had arrived.

'The only thing is,' said one of the policemen, 'we've been on to Exminster and they say they haven't got any one missing.'

'You take him back there,' I said. 'We can't afford to keep him.'

He climbed into the back of the police car, still chatting happily, and they vanished into the night.

'Did you see his eyes?' asked Terry. 'Merciless they were. If I hadn't hidden all the knives there's no knowing what would have happened. Why does something happen every time I visit the Peterses? Just wait till I tell Jack about it. He'll never believe me. My hands are still shaking.'

'Have a drop of Scotch,' I suggested.

'Oh no. Well just a very small one then,' she acquiesced.

****

'Sit down, Jeffrey,' said John Peterson.

I lowered myself into the comfortable armchair facing his desk.

'I've a letter here for you. It's from the Principal. I'll leave you to read it in peace while I look after your class.' He left me alone in his study.

I rapidly reviewed my conduct over the last few weeks. I did not normally see eye-to-eye with the authorities and seldom conformed to the introduction of fashionable follies. However, I could think of nothing I had done lately which would merit a written instruction to mend my ways and opened the envelope with some perplexity.

'Dear Jeffrey' it began in the Principal's hand. Sufficiently informal, I thought, to preclude it's being notice of impending dismissal. I read on.

St Jude's, it appeared, was anticipating smaller numbers of students, not only because of the end of the baby boom of the sixties, but also the fact that as the LEA's became strapped for cash they were looking for cheaper alternatives for their youngsters. I was nearing sixty, when I could draw my pension, and was thus the logical member of the staff to be offered generous terms of redundancy.

I found the idea appealing. For years I had been growing more and more deaf and was now reduced to working on the theory that there were only half a dozen possible answers to any question. Thus, as long as I picked up one or two key words, I knew which one I had been given and could respond accordingly. The theory would have worked well had my students not been adept at producing impossible answers and so leaving me in helpless bewilderment. In addition, I was finding just walking had become less and less enjoyable and at home employed a stick to help me exercise the dogs.

That evening I showed the letter to Jo. As she read it, a broad smile spread over her face.

'That's the best news you could have given me,' she exclaimed. 'You've no idea how you change from the first day of term. If you don't believe me just ask the kids. They all know how unapproachable you are compared with your holiday self.'

I could believe her. John Peterson had had comforting words on the old tale that teachers who waited to retire at sixty-five always died within the year. I began to look forward to Christmas with even greater enthusiasm.

****

'This pub's doing us a lot of good after all,' said Jo.

The brewery had decided to go ahead with their project in spite of their departure from our meeting. They had discovered that they could just as easily build their ventilators through the other end of the building, which was used only for the storage of odd items belonging to various people.

'Why the blazes?' demanded Peregrine when he heard the news. 'Why couldn't they have worked that out in the first place instead of raising all that hassle with us?'

'Ah,' said Lucy. 'They're big business, you see.'

Lucy worked with leather. Sitting at her stall, one sandaled foot protruding beneath her ankle-length skirt, auburn hair hanging down to her waist and with the knives and punches of her trade around her, she might have been the original for one of those nineteenth century prints; 'Virtue and Industry' perhaps. Somehow she managed to scrape a living in the intervals of cheering everybody up on a dull day, helping out wherever help was needed and falling desperately in love with a series of young layabouts who, for my money, deserved the application of a sharp boot rather than the ministrations of Lucy. She was convinced that the evils of this world were due to 'Them', a gallimaufry of big business, governments, bureaucrats and sharp traders whose machinations combined to thwart her every effort. She was also convinced that the brewery's engineers had designed the entire plan in order to cause the maximum disruption to Riverside Crafts and it was only Jo's efforts that had defeated them. I couldn't entirely disagree.

The summer visitors had departed and business would normally have been slack in the coffee room but the workmen engaged on converting the cellars needed sustenance and Jo, Olive and the other helpers found themselves busy each lunchtime. Soup, pasty with a glass of beer and followed by treacle tart proved to be the favourite choice. The profits might be temporary but they were welcome.

'We've got a lovely crowd now,' Jo told me. ' Everyone joins in and they all want to make a success of the show.'

'Are you getting your rents on time?' I wanted to know.

'More or less,' she assured me. 'But next year we are due for our rent review. If it goes up a lot we shall have to increase the craftspeople's. And none of them make so much that they can afford a big rise.'

'Just as well the school fees are subsiding,' I replied.

Cormac had passed his A-levels and had been accepted by Southampton University. He and I were patting ourselves on the back as John had obtained B's in English, Maths and Physics, the three subjects in which we had coached him. He had achieved a C in History for which we took no credit and was to take A-levels two years hence on condition that he achieved at least one more O-level next year. Jane had collected eight O-levels and was remaining at the convent for another two years.

'Let's take a break,' said Jo. 'It's years since we had a holiday on our own.'

The last week in October provided a feast of colour on the banks of Loch Awe though we were glad we had brought our waterproof jackets. I discovered that Scotland has a craft centre roughly every half-mile, in each of which Jo held long discussions with the proprietor, exchanging cards and promising a welcome in Devon. I, meanwhile, creaked gently round the woods and burns and managed to visit the Commando Memorial while Jo inspected woollens in Fort William. As she wasn't there to tell me how daft I was, trying to take photographs with the lens cap on, I have no record of this visit.

Our trip to Edinburgh was a delight and the rain held off until we were almost home.

We were required to vacate our flat by ten on Saturday morning. In fact we were on the road by nine. There is dual carriageway all the way from Loch Lomond to Cornwall and we decided to try to reach home that evening. We took turns, driving for about two hours each. Somewhere near Taunton I told her we might just be home in time for the six o'clock Mass. And so we were. I drove straight past Grange Cottage and pulled up outside the church as Big Ben was striking six on the car radio. Dropping Jo, I turned round and, three minutes later, met the Peugeot coming the other way with Cormac at the wheel and the family inside, late for church. Their mother whispered some rude remarks about making it on time from Loch Lomond when they joined her in the pew.

****

'Is it true, Mr Peters?'

'Is what true, Tracey?'

'Is it true that you are retiring at the end of term?'

I had intended to announce the fact on the last day of term but someone had leaked the news and my students were demanding to know why I hadn't informed them earlier.

Tracey shook her dreadlocks at me. 'Why man,' she exclaimed, 'we could have organized a party for you. I'd have got my brother down.'

The prospect of an evening in the Students' Recreation Room with Tracey's brother's steel band pounding in the corner was reason enough for my reticence. I had offered no objections at all when the ear specialist had ordered me to refrain from attending discos or other places where I might be subjected to loud noises. As it was I escaped with a short meeting after the traditional Christmas Dinner when I was presented with a matching pen and pencil.

'And it's not filled with red ink like you usually use,' said Tracey.

My colleagues, too, were generous in their farewells and I left the college for the last time with the Peugeot loaded with shrubs for the garden and brandy for my cellar.

Christmas passed in its customary over abundance of alcohol and festive wrapping paper. I managed not to set fire to Cormac.

On the first day of term I rose at my usual hour and duly set off with Jane. Having deposited her at the Convent I drove straight past St Jude's with a broad beam on my face and returned home to more coffee and a prolonged study of the papers with my feet under the kitchen table. For the rest of the day I pottered about the place humming happily to myself.

I discovered that there was a lot to be said for a life of leisure. My time was my own and the only limiting factor on my activities was my increasingly arthritic hip. I took over all Jo's book keeping. The accountant was impressed.

'I think I can afford to reduce my fees,' he told us. 'I can understand these books.'

Jo was furious. 'What does he think he's talking about?' she demanded. 'Nothing could be simpler to understand than my accounts.'

I held my peace.

I made a nasty discovery.

'Look, darling,' I said. 'Last quarter you increased your turnover by a lot. I think you'll have to register for VAT.'

'What does that imply?' Jo wanted to know. 'Doesn't it mean we can claim back the tax we pay on what we buy?'

'That's true,' I told her. 'But ninety per cent of your purchases are food on which you don't pay any tax. But you have to charge VAT on all your coffee room sales willy-nilly. That means you have to increase your prices by fifteen per cent.'

'But if I do that,' she riposted, 'the customers will stop coming to me. We've always kept our prices as low as possible to attract them. Why can't we just go on as we are?'

'Because,' I replied, 'one day the Excise man will appear on the doorstep, demanding to look at your books. Then they will charge you VAT on all your past sales, whether you've charged it or not.'

The discussion continued intermittently for some weeks but in the end Jo agreed that there was no choice. We filled in the appropriate forms and received a parcel of pamphlets and instructions, which I studied with care.

The craft centre reopened in March. I began to learn some of the mysteries of catering and would spend my days on errands to collect *gateaux* from the confectioners' and cream from the dairy. I also learned how to make the homemade soups with which Jo had established her reputation. On the one occasion that there was a complaint I excused myself on the grounds that my eyes had been watering so much from peeling the onions that I could not see I was overdoing the garlic.

I began to wonder how I had found time for teaching.

****

'What about a Victorian weekend?' suggested Sam.

'What do you mean,' asked Jo.

Sam was chairman of the Craftspeople's Committee and we were discussing, under the heading on the agenda of 'Any Other Business', the eternal problem of attracting more visitors to the Riverside.

'I know just what Sam means.' The unmistakable Scottish accent rang from the back of the room. 'We all dress as Victorian craftspeople. As many as can bring in their tools and we show how our wares are produced.'

'That's just it, Annie,' said Sam. 'What do you all think about that?'

We discussed the idea for a while. It seemed a likely attraction for the Easter weekend and at first there were no objections. Jimmy, the wood turner, promised to set up a small lathe in the entrance lobby and Sam's wife, Lorna, gave up work on her knitting machine and undertook to bring a spinning wheel and spin one of the fleeces that were still sitting in my shed from the previous summer. The sandwich board was engaged once more and there was just time to get an announcement in the local paper.

'I don't think I can approve of this, as a matter of principle,' said Lucy. 'Dressing up as something we aren't just to attract customers seems wrong somehow.'

Lucy invariably looked as though she had stepped from the pages of a nineteenth century novel.

'Don't worry, Lucy,' replied Sam. 'Just be your normal self. There's no compulsion about this.'

He turned his head and winked craftily at me.

'I'll be home for Easter,' said Phyllis. 'My employers are taking the boys to Spain. Can I bring a friend? She comes from Finland and her employers are going away too. I'd hate to think of her all alone here for the holiday.'

The Young Farmers had trained Phyllis well. Within weeks of taking up her nannying duties she had met every other nanny in the area and organized them into a mutual support group known to the employers as the Hampstead Mafia. On the evening of Good Friday she arrived and introduced Greta who looked like every man's dream of a Scandinavian *au-pair.*

'Better keep an eye on the boys with her about the house,' I remarked.

'Don't be daft, Daddy,' she replied. 'Greta's almost the same age as me. Much too old to be interested in those two.'

'I was thinking more of what they might be interested in,' I told her.

Easter Sunday dawned bright and clear. Jo indulged in her first chocolate since the beginning of Lent. At the Riverside a crowd of Victorian citizens assembled and soon attracted the notice of the passers by. Jo, in her guise as Mrs Bridges of 'Upstairs, Downstairs' fame, led her team into action and they were rapidly inundated by hungry customers.

Soon after noon Perry, who looked every inch like the stationmaster who first welcomed the Puffing Billy into Darlington, reported that the steam train on a commemorative run down the old Great Western line had run out of steam in Exeter. Phyllis and Greta, looking for all the world like the stars of a period movie, leaped into Jo's car and, with Cormac and his camera to record the event, sped into town. Sure enough, there in St David's Station was a train with an admiring horde of railway buffs gathered round the engine. The two girls were able to climb unseen into one of the rear coaches, make their way to the front and emerge to the plaudits of the throng to whom they proceeded to distribute leaflets extolling the attractions of Riverside Crafts. By four o'clock, the steam engine having been towed away for repairs, the railway enthusiasts had joined the crowd at the Riverside and Jo's supplies of food were running short. Perry was running out of tickets and the crafts people were doing a roaring trade.

'First time today that I've actually seen a steam train running,' commented one of Perry's enthusiasts.

'Have you anything in your freezer?' demanded Jo that evening on the phone to her various producers of home made goodies. 'Jeffrey will pick it up first thing in the morning.'

And so I did. I was just in time with my delivery for the rush to start again. Although not as great as on the previous day, a respectable crowd took advantage of the bank holiday and came to see what we had to offer. Every one reported record takings for the weekend. The local paper was generous in its reporting with a picture of 'Mrs Jo Bridges' on its front page.

'I think you have much fun in England at Easter time,' said Greta.

Chapter 20

'Mr Peters, you haven't been doing your exercises,' admonished Molly.

The orthopaedic surgeon had been sympathetic. 'Yes,' he agreed, 'you have an arthritic hip but there's not a lot we can do at the moment. Perhaps in two or three years' time. In the meanwhile, go and see a good physiotherapist. I'll get my secretary to make an appointment for you.'

And so it was that I first presented myself at Molly's surgery. 'Mr Peters!' she exclaimed. 'Your back! Whatever have you been doing to it?'

In vain I pointed out that it was actually my hip that was hurting. With a couple of pencil strokes she produced two illustrations.

'That's what your spine should look like.' She pointed the pencil at a graceful curve. 'And that's yours.' She jabbed the lead at an erratic zigzag. 'Before we think of anything else we'll have to deal with that.'

A series of exercises followed, together with instructions as to how to sit, lie, sleep, stand and walk. After a few weeks I realized that the pain had diminished considerably. There was a short break from her ministrations while Molly went on holiday after which it was my turn to sympathize with her while she regaled me with tales of a month with her family under canvas in a sodden English summer. She rewarded my neglect with a series of minor tortures and sent me on my way. I relaxed as I closed the door behind me.

The surgery window flew open and Molly's head appeared. 'Posture, posture, posture,' she called.

I straightened up and made my way down the path and out of the gate. Her voice followed me across the road to my car. 'Mr Peters. Stop limping just because you think I can't see you!'

The wet weather may have flooded Molly's children out of their tent but it had also brought a flood of visitors to the Riverside. I made almost daily visits to the cash and carry store to replenish Jo's coffee room. Today was no exception and an hour after leaving the surgery I parked the loaded Peugeot as close as possible to the pathway leading to the fire exit. In spite of Molly's ministrations I still found myself limited in the amount I could carry and had to make many journeys to the coffee room door. On returning from one I found an irate looking man inspecting the car.

'Can't you read that this is a private car-park?' he demanded.

'Of course,' I agreed.

'Then why the devil are you parked here?' he continued.

'Who are you and what business is it of yours?' I wanted to know.

'I'm a doctor,' he began, 'and I ...'

'You're a what?' I interrupted him.

'I'm a doctor,' he repeated.

'Well all I can say to you, Doctor,' I sneered, 'is thank God you're not mine. All the doctors I know are decent, honourable people, devoting their lives to the relief of human suffering. But you, when you see what your professional eye immediately diagnoses as a chronically arthritic and asthmatic sexagenarian with a heavy load to carry, think to yourself, "Aha, I'll have some fun with this old beggar. I'll make him drive to the bottom of the hill and carry his load up four flights of stairs." Well I'm not bloody well going to and you can put that in your pipe and smoke it.'

I picked up my next load and set off along the path, ignoring Molly's instructions and limping heavily. On my return he had vanished.

****

'You shouldn't have included wages in your input totals,' the VAT Inspector admonished me.

'Don't you mean "output"?' I queried.

'No I don't,' he snapped. 'I do know what I'm talking about.'

I sighed. The language of accountancy had always baffled me. As far as I could see 'output' should mean money one had paid out and 'input' money one had taken in. Of course, the adoption of terms the layman could understand would put accountants, lawyers and many others queuing outside the employment exchange so no doubt there is a logical reason for the mysteries they practise.

'Why shouldn't I include it?' I asked.

'The simplest answer to that is because it tells you not to, here in the handbook, not to mention on the return itself,' he replied.

'So it does,' I agreed. 'Oh well, what else have I been doing wrong?'

'Not much that I can see,' he said. 'What do you think, Mike?'

His colleague ceased wandering around my study inspecting the assorted photographs on the wall, which recorded my military past from battle-dressed wartime recruit to my last appointment before retirement.

'Seems all right,' he concurred.

I made coffee in the kitchen and returned to the study.

'Look,' said the Inspector. 'You're making life very difficult for yourself. I'd get rid of those complicated record books and use a simple ledger entry like this.' He demonstrated.

'And what about telephones?' asked Mike. 'Don't you use your phone here on business?'

'Hardly used for anything else,' I told him.

'Well there you are then. If you use it for the business then you can claim back the VAT on your return.'

'Very generous of you,' I said.

'We're not here to break you,' he replied. 'As long as you don't try to fiddle your returns our attitude is that the better your business, the more tax you will contribute in the end.'

Jo rushed into the house on her return that evening. 'You poor darling,' she exclaimed. 'Was it awful? Let me pour you a drink.'

I did nothing to restrain her and we sat down by the fire.

'Tell me all about it,' she demanded.

I complied. 'And they agreed that most of our motoring was on business and we could include ninety per cent of our petrol bills,' I concluded.

'Well!' she gasped. 'And to think I've spent the whole day worrying about how you were getting on. Not helped by Perry telling me tales of people he knew who had been imprisoned for making wrong VAT returns. All that sympathy wasted. And I poured you an extra large gin!'

'That's something I'm going to input right now,' I assured her, suiting the action to the word.

****

'I must say, it's very generous of them,' remarked Jo.

We had been invited to dinner to celebrate the opening of 'The Waterside Inn', the new pub underneath Jo's craft centre.

'Well, we'll certainly accept,' I told her. 'It should be very interesting after all those months of work down there. I just hope it doesn't entice too many customers away from you.'

'We're bound to lose some,' she replied, 'but so many of our regulars come in for coffee or tea and a chat that I don't think we shall suffer too much. A lot of them bring their children too. They wouldn't be welcome in a pub.'

We enjoyed our meal and agreed that the pub might draw visitors who would visit the craft centre even if they didn't want refreshment. We chatted to a numbers of acquaintances who professed similar views. It was a most enjoyable evening and we returned late, replete and hopeful. The phone was ringing as we opened the door. I picked it up.

'Is Aunty Jo there?' I was asked. 'Can I speak to her?'

'Of course you can, Joanne,' I replied. 'Your Goddaughter sounds excited,' I told Jo as I handed her the receiver.

A torrent of superlatives flowed over the line.

'She's getting married next month,' Jo told me. 'Oh lor! I haven't a thing to wear.'

'If we're travelling up there next month why don't we go on for a few days?' I suggested. 'We've never visited the Lake District.'

The morning after the wedding saw us heading North up the motorway. John was in the back of the car. He had been included to distract him from the disappointment of the discovery that he was not likely to obtain any A levels and that a further year's fees would be wasted. He was due to start a YTS course at a bank in October. His distraction had been successfully completed the previous day when he had surrounded himself with a bevy of bridesmaids and only reluctantly embarked for the Lakes. The car was well loaded for, as well as our holiday clothing, we had all our wedding finery. On the rear window shelf rested a flowery confection of Jo's and my grey topper. The roof rack was proving a worthwhile investment. A number of cases were securely lashed to it. Or so I thought.

I had just overtaken a lorry and was pulling into the inside lane in front of it when the driver began flashing his headlights. Glancing in my door mirror I saw something bouncing in the road: a black grip. A familiar black grip. The black grip with all Jo's spare clothes in it.

I pulled onto the hard shoulder and stopped, hazard lights flashing. We all got out. The grip was lying unharmed on the white line between the middle and outside lanes, cars and lorries flashing by on either side, missing it by inches. I turned to John.

'That could cause an accident,' I told him. 'There's the nearest phone, about four hundred yards away. Nip along there and phone the police.'

I turned back to Jo. She was poised like the veteran basketball player that she was, ready to dash in to seize the ball and pass it to the shooter.

I grabbed her arm. 'What the hell do you think you're doing?' I demanded.

'I'm waiting for a break in the traffic so I can nip in and grab it,' she replied, struggling to release my grasp.

'For God's sake don't be so daft,' I shouted. 'Some of those cars are doing a ton. There's no chance you could get out there and back.'

'But my clothes,' she wailed.

'To hell with your blasted clothes. They're insured. If you got out there we'd never find enough of you to bury. Now you just get back into the car and stop this nonsense.'

There was a loud bang, like a bursting balloon. A car had hit the grip fair and square and it had exploded, spraying intimate items of Jo's underwear along the carriageway. Her new shoes, made for her only last week by Lucy, were struck by successive cars in the fast lane and were making rapid strides on their way to Scotland. We returned to the car.

John had just reached the telephone. He turned to look at us and I flashed the lights at him. He waited till we reached him and I explained what had happened. He had guessed as several items of clothing had already passed him. We agreed that there was no longer a danger to traffic and went on our way, Jo running through the list of belongings and explaining why each item was precious and could never be replaced.

We spent an entertaining week in Ambleside. David, our insurance broker, agreed on the phone that we were fully covered for Jo's losses and she replaced some of them. The more important items could wait till we returned to civilization in the form of Laura Ashley. Her prime delight, however, was the abundance of craftspeople and the woollen mills. Orders were liberally placed for the next season. On the Friday evening we phoned home. Jane answered and Jo spoke to her.

'Oh Heavens!' she gasped. 'How awful for you. They can't do that to you. Don't let them.'

I snatched the phone from her. 'What on Earth is the matter?' I demanded.

'Nothing,' replied Jane. 'Sister Edwina has made me Head Girl.'

'But that's marvellous,' I told her. 'Well done. What ever is your Mum making all the fuss about?'

'Well, you know how she hates standing up in front of a crowd and holding forth. I don't mind really but I expect you to write my speech for prize giving for me.'

'You shall have them rolling in the aisles,' I promised her.

****

'I hate working at the weekend,' said Jo.

'I'm not overjoyed at having to cook the Sunday dinner,' I told her.

It had been mutually decided by Jo and the craftspeople that Riverside Crafts ought not to close completely between Christmas and Easter. After much debate it was agreed that there would be little business during the week but that Friday, Saturday and Sunday should bring a small profit.

Christmas had seen Jo and Catherine of on their tour of local homes for the aged. From one they had returned with a tale of one old dear who had bought two-dozen pairs of baby's bootees, 'For my grandchildren, you know.'

'Has she really so many grandchildren?' asked Jo, unwilling to take advantage of the old soul.

'Oh yes,' replied the Matron. 'Mind you, they're all grown up now but she stays happy remembering them in their cots.'

Just before the holiday there was a phone call from the local paper. Would the craftsmen and women parade in the same Victorian clothes that they had worn at Easter, this time in the guise of carol singers for the benefit of the paper's photographers? Sure enough, on the front page of the Christmas Eve edition was a large picture of the Riverside Crafts Choir with songbooks in hands and lanterns held aloft on poles. Jo had insisted that they mention the winter weekend opening and the message got through: on the first Sunday of the New Year there was a record demand for coffee and cakes from families taking a stroll by the river between Church and dinner. One small boy produced the revolver that Santa Claus had left in his stocking.

'You're not going to shoot me, are you?' asked Jo.

'Oh no,' he replied. 'I wouldn't do that because you're a very old lady.'

'I thanked him very much,' Jo told me later, 'but I don't know whether genuinely or sarcastically. Anyway, the bank manager wants to see us.'

'Why?' I asked. 'I thought we were beginning to break even.'

'You're only just beginning to break even,' said the bank manager when we saw him on the following Thursday. 'Frankly, by now we had hoped you would be well on your way to repaying some of the loan.'

'But Eric,' replied Jo, 'at least we're on the up at last. Surely we can go on for a year or two.'

We talked for a long time as he pointed out that most of our success had been due to an exceptionally wet summer and the longer we carried on the shorter, and therefore the less valuable, the remainder of our lease became. He extolled the concept of building a business to maximum profitability and then selling it at the optimum moment. It was a dejected Jo who finally agreed that we should consider putting Riverside Crafts on the market.

'I'll send my assistant round tomorrow,' said the agent.

'I'd rather you came yourself,' replied Jo. 'We've known you a long time and this has all to be very confidential.'

It appeared that he was going on holiday but we were in no hurry and agreed to a date after his return.

'Mr Swivel wants to meet us,' Jo told me, putting down the telephone receiver. 'He sounded terribly secretive about it and doesn't want anyone else to know. I said we'd meet him at the Riverside tomorrow morning.'

'The Council have had an offer to turn the whole warehouse into a hotel,' Mr Swivel announced. 'Nothing definite yet but I've been told to ask you how you would feel if we wanted you to surrender your lease in return for the lease of another suitable Council property.'

We promised to give the matter due consideration, indicating that we had no objection in principle.'

'What are you grinning about,' demanded Jo as we drove home.

'Don't you see?' I chuckled. 'When we get home you just phone Eric and tell him about it. Turning all those old buildings into a modern hotel is a project running into millions. And in the way is Mrs Peters with a lease running into the next century. He'll laugh his head off.'

****

'Triplets!' gasped Jo, leaping out of bed.

I had crept out early to inspect the sheep, infuriating the dogs by leaving them in the garden so as not to disturb Lucy who had seemed likely to lamb any day now. Sure enough, nestling in the straw were two little ewes and a ram. I returned to the house at my speediest hobble and woke Jo with the news. She raced off, pausing only to call Jane on her way to the paddock, leaving me to enjoy my bath.

'We'll have to keep an eye on them,' she told me at breakfast. 'All three were trying to suck but Lucy kept butting the smallest one away, that's the ram lamb. We must make sure he's properly fed.'

For the rest of the day I paid frequent visits to the new arrivals and, sure enough, Jo was right; whenever the little ram tried to suckle, his dam butted him away. He bleated pathetically but received no nourishment. I phoned Jo that afternoon.

'What do you know about bottle-feeding lambs?' I asked her.

'I think Mary Patrick said not to give them cows' milk,' she replied.

'Well I'm not trying to catch Lucy and milk her,' I said.

'Don't be daft,' she told me. 'We need goats' milk. There's a place out along the Honiton road with a sign outside saying they have it for sale. You'd better go and get some and we'll try it when I get home.

Six o'clock that evening saw me pouring warm goats' milk into a bottle.

'I thought I'd finished doing this when the children were weaned,' I remonstrated, 'but then you had me doing it for piglets. Now, when I was sure there would be no more piglets, I'm doing it for sheep. It only needs one of the kids to marry and I'll have gone full circle with grandchildren. If your daughters follow in Mother's footsteps they needn't think I'm going to take on their piglets.'

'And I can put that in my pipe and smoke it, I suppose,' said Jane. 'Never mind. I'll get some practice in with Larry here.'

Larry waxed as fat on goats' milk as his two sisters did on mother's and soon learned that he could squeeze under the gate into the garden at feeding time. From there it took no time at all for him to appear in the courtyard, bleating to be let into the kitchen where he was presented with his bottle and sent gambolling back to the paddock.

'He's a very intelligent lamb,' Jane informed me.

'He jolly well isn't,' I assured her. 'Just see what he has done.'

'What's that?' she demanded.

'He's the stupidest lamb that ever was. Remember John's story about the Irish turkey? The one who was looking forward to Christmas? Well Larry beats that hollow. He's just scoffed the whole of my mint bed. That'll be a new taste sensation; mint fed lamb.'

'Don't be horrible,' exploded Jane. 'This is one lamb I'm going to protect from you, whatever happens.'

'I wouldn't bet on it,' I told her.

****

'What's all this about, Jo?' demanded Peregrine. 'I was just talking to Catherine when Mr Swivel wandered in with three other men; businessmen they looked like. They walked around for a while and then Swivel says in one of his loud whispers, "Mrs Peters doesn't want her craftspeople to know what's going on." So what is going on?'

'Honestly Perry, I don't know,' Jo told him. 'You had Jeffrey's letter and then you saw the papers where it said that there were plans to convert the place into a hotel. I just don't know any more than that. As soon as I do, you will be the first to know. And I won't agree to anything which doesn't give everyone fair notice to make whatever alternative arrangements they wish.'

'I'm so fed up with this,' she told me that evening. 'Everyone wants to know what is going to happen and I've nothing to tell them. But it's making them all so touchy. It's not a bit like it used to be when we started. Then everyone was looking forward to something good and it was fun. Now everything is uncertain. We had a woman today who made jewellery from seashells and wanted to take a space but I couldn't give her any promise beyond next year. In the end she agreed to come, but she'd lost the enthusiasm she had arrived with. The Committee never meets and they leave it to me to run all their matters as well as my own. One of our new tenants came up to me yesterday and said she didn't see why they should pay the bank charges on the craftspeople's bank account. I asked if she thought I ought to and she said yes, she did!'

I sat her down by the fire, poured a large Dry Martini apiece and set about cheering her up. 'What does Catherine say about it?' I asked.

'Oh, she's always the same: always has something cheerful to say and we always finish with a good giggle. And she comes in every week without fail to check the craftspeople's accounts. They don't know what they owe to her. If she and Ernie weren't there I think I'd have chucked the whole thing in by now.'

'Well, as long as we have friends like them we ought to be all right,' I said. 'Think of the fun you're going to have doing battle with the Council when the time does arrive.'

'Yes,' she replied gleefully. 'I can't wait to see Mr Swivel's face when I tell him what I have in mind.'

There was a mild explosion at the back door; Jane had arrived.

'Sister Edwina wants me to go to France and teach tadpoles,' she announced, spreading outer garments, shopping bags and papers over the furniture.

Jane's A Level results had not been as good as she had hoped and she had abandoned thoughts of University. She had settled for a secretarial course at the local college but decided to take a year off education first. That evening she had had an appointment at the convent to discuss matters.

'What on earth do you mean, "Teach tadpoles"?' asked Jo.

'She asked if I would like to go to their sister convent in the South of France and teach English to infant frogs,' Jane explained. 'I rather like the idea. I think I'll go.'

'You do that,' I told her. 'And while you're at it see what you can learn about the local wines. It's in convents and monasteries that you find the real experts.'

'Trust you to know that,' she replied.

Chapter 21

'Goodbye Darling. Do look after yourself,' cried Jo.

'She'll be all right,' I assured her.

Anne waved as the train started to move and then, shouldering her rucksack, made her way towards an empty seat. This was the moment Jo had been dreading ever since the day, almost a year ago now, when Anne had phoned to announce exultantly, 'I passed'. There followed, in harrowing detail, the tale of the weekend she had spent undergoing the selection procedures to be accepted as a venturer in one of Operation Raleigh's expeditions. Now she was on her way to Gatwick, en route to Chile and high adventure.

For months Anne had laboured to collect the sponsorship money that she had to produce. Riverside Crafts had played its part with a collecting box in the coffee room, entreating customers to 'Send Anne to Chile'. Luckily I had banked most of the contents at the beginning of September leaving only some small change for our burglar to find when he called a couple of weeks later.

I had just settled down with the books and the VAT form when Jo phoned to tell me of the event. I drove down to see for myself what had happened. With great difficulty I climbed the three flights of stairs to the coffee room where I found Jo hoovering up the mess left by our visitor, who had jemmied away almost the whole of the fire door to obtain entry. He had left with a few cans of beer and the contents of Anne's collecting box, leaving behind him his jemmy, which must have been worth more that his loot.

'He does this a lot,' said the Detective Constable. 'Just helps himself to stuff which can't be identified. We'll catch him one day, though.'

The local paper told the story of a mean thief robbing a nurse of her sponsorship money and Jo's generous customers refilled the collecting box.

'Are we ever going to hear any more about this move?' demanded Peregrine when the police had departed and Bill Brewer, the carpenter, was working to restore the door. 'It'll take months to shift our railway.'

'I know,' replied Jo. 'I've made it clear to Mr Swivel that we must have sufficient time to plan our move and that it's too late now to contemplate anything before next autumn. As soon as I know any more I'll tell you and everyone else at once.'

'I'm absolutely fed up,' Jo told me that evening. 'I'd like to sell the whole bang shoot. All the fun has gone out of it and it's impossible for anyone to plan anything. Even getting people in on time when they're supposed to be manning the floors is getting more difficult.'

'Why not try selling it to the Council if you feel like that?' I suggested.

'I'll talk to Mr Swivel. It's certainly an idea,' she replied.

For a few weeks after this there was some serious discussion but in the end the council was only prepared to make a derisory offer and then only on condition that Jo stayed on as paid manageress.

'I'm not doing that,' she assured me. 'I'd rather be my own boss any time.'

'I'd rather have you for a boss than anyone I know,' I promised.

'You've been practising your flattery again,' she purred. 'But I like it!'

****

'Can't fit you in for another five months,' said the surgeon. 'Say about mid-June. With a new hip you should be gambolling around like a young lamb by autumn.'

It couldn't come too soon as far as I was concerned. For the last two years I had creaked around the place, struggling to get up the Riverside stairs and spending sleepless nights unless I resorted to painkillers. Now I had some hope of relief.

In spite of my grumbling we had spent a happy Christmas. Anne had returned with tales of derring-do, of sitting in a rubber boat overhanging a waterfall, of being lost in a blizzard on the rim of an active volcano and bubbling over with an obvious sense of achievement. Jane was glad of a break from convent cooking.

'They simply pour sugar into everything,' she told us. 'I'm sure they look upon God as a great big sugar daddy in the sky! I've told them I won't be back after next term. My figure wouldn't stand it. Yes, I'd love some more cream with my mince pies, please.'

Cormac, now at least four inches taller than I and much broader across the shoulders, was as unlikely a potential mugging victim as could be imagined. Why he should spend his spare time acquiring his black belt at the University Karate Club was a mystery to us.

Now the children had returned to their various pursuits and the February rain dripped steadily from the thatch onto my log pile. Jo was busily employed in encouraging her craftspeople to brighten up their stalls in preparation for the Easter holiday and I was, as usual, late with my VAT return. The surgeon's promise was the only bright spot on the horizon.

'Thank you for telling me, Mr Swivel.' Jo put the receiver down and turned to me. 'They have contracted with the developer subject to our vacating the building and surrendering our lease. I really don't want to start a new business all over again. I think I'd rather sell the lease back to them and see if any of our craftspeople would like to build it up again in a new place.'

'You'll need a good negotiator,' said our solicitor next day. 'The chap who does this sort of work for the Council is pretty tough. Leave it with me for a couple of days. I'll think of someone suitable.'

'I have a feeling that this is going to be a lively year,' said Jo.

****

'I'm afraid it's the end for her,' said the vet. 'She's very old for a Labrador.'

For days now Shammy's condition had been deteriorating. Her only activity had been to drag herself into the garden and try to dig a little hole in the rose bed.

'She knows,' said the farmer's wife. 'She's trying to dig her grave.'

Cormac had helped me lift Shammy into the car and we had taken her on her last journey, leaving Jo wiping her eyes with a tissue. My own sorrow was tempered by the knowledge that never again would

I have to apologise to the neighbours for their devastated dustbin. Jaws and Gigi had not inherited this trait of their mother's.

It was sorting out time in the Peters family. Jane had returned from France and enlisted as a maid of all work at a seaside hotel to earn some money before college in the autumn. Cormac was planning his favourite summer pastime: back-packing round Europe. Anne had promised to take some leave and help Jo when I came out of hospital. We had realized that the sheep would have to go; I couldn't deal with their shearing and dipping and there was no sign of agreement between our negotiators and the council's, so that Jo had little spare time from the Riverside.

'You see those woolly things in the paddock?' I pointed with my stick and our visitors, old friends of Jo's, nodded with puzzled expressions.

'You probably think they're sheep, don't you?' I went on. Their baffled looks increased.

'Well,' I continued, 'they are really self-operating lawn-mowers and jolly efficient at the job. What's more, instead of consuming expensive petrol, their by-products are lamb chops, which go into the deep freeze or fleeces which Jo sells to enthusiasts from her wool counter. You wouldn't like them, I suppose?'

My offer was declined on the grounds that a suburban lawn did not need such intense mowing. I promised myself that I would be even more persuasive next time.

'How are things going?' Jo was on the phone to the agents. 'Well, I'd expect them to make an unacceptably low offer. What have you suggested to them? Oh, why don't you want to tell me? Oh well, I suppose you have your reasons.' She put the receiver down and turned to me. 'They don't want to tell us what they are asking. It sounds a bit odd. Surely we ought to know.'

'I can only think that they have asked for some ridiculous, astronomical figure and don't want to tell you in case you begin to think that's what you might get.' I told her.

'Oh I do hope you're right,' she chuckled.

****

'Mr Peters. Mr Peters. Come along now Mr Peters.' The voice penetrated my muzzy mind. 'You can wake up now Mr Peters. The operation's all over.'

I opened my eyes. A blurred face hung over me, sandwiched between a blue dress and a white cap. Two pairs of hands lifted my shoulders and pillows were inserted behind me. Something was different but for a moment I couldn't think what. Then it dawned; my leg felt battered and bruised but the awful nagging pain of the last few years had gone. I tried to sit up.

'Now just lie back on these pillows and don't try anything silly.' admonished Sister Allen. 'Tomorrow is soon enough for you to be moving around.'

The next few days were among the least restful I can ever remember. Apart from a stream of visitors, nurses appeared every few minutes and took my temperature, made my bed, asked me what I would like for lunch, washed me, asked what I would like for supper, fed me pills, took my temperature, powdered my bottom, asked what I would like for breakfast, fed me pills, switched off my light and then at odd intervals shone a torch in my face until it was time to take my temperature again. I didn't mind a bit. I was feeling ten years younger already and fit for anything. The physio' exercised me on my crutches, the surgeon pronounced himself satisfied with my progress and, on the fourth day I was allowed to make my own way to the X-ray department for the necessary photographs.

Jo came in at least twice a day, grinning like a Cheshire cat, and bearing good wishes from everyone. The children sent 'get well' cards and arrived in time to watch 'Neighbours' on the television. Corenne gave me a hug and a kiss while Simon proffered a 'Sodastream' bottle, the contents of which he assured me would do me good. He was quite right, as I discovered when I sipped the contents and found it to contain more gin than tonic.

Meanwhile I was instructed to learn by heart the list of dos and don'ts that were to rule my life when I was released. 'No bath for three months.' I wrinkled my nose. 'No sex for three months.' Well, that made sense; who on earth would want to make love to someone who hadn't bathed for the last twelve weeks? The list seemed endless.

Seven days after my arrival at the hospital, with the approval of the surgeon, the physio' and the radiographers, Jo and Anne arrived to take me home. With the aid of Sister Allen they stretched me out on the back seat of Jo's car and drove away, homeward bound. I negotiated the stairs with my crutches and was soon tucked up in my own bed, with bolsters on either side to prevent my rolling over onto my hip, which was forbidden in the book of rules. Anne's news was good; she had succeeded where I had failed and had found a good home for our little flock including, to Jane's delight, Larry.

With my fingers crossed beneath the sheets I promised to obey every instruction of my two nurses.

****

'How's our hippy this evening?' demanded Corenne.

'Bright as a button,' Jo assured her. 'Heaven knows what he'll be like when he gets rid of his crutches. I had to prevent him from riding on the lawn-mower this afternoon.'

'Now you watch it, young Jeffrey,' Simon admonished me, following our two wives into the drawing room. 'There'll be plenty of grass to mow when that hip is completely healed. Just let it take its time.'

'Don't worry,' I replied. 'I'm behaving myself very well. Look, I can serve your drinks without falling over.'

The kitchen doorbell rang and the dogs ran barking to investigate. I followed more slowly and shooed the dogs away before opening the door.

'Hullo,' said the stranger, shifting his bucket from his right hand to his left. 'Oh, have you had an accident?'

I reassured him that all was well and asked how I could help him.

'I was wondering if you would mind,' he told me, 'if I went into your paddock and collected some sheep droppings for my onions.'

'Well,' I replied, 'I wouldn't normally have any objections but we got rid of our sheep last month.'

His jaw dropped. 'But I've just looked,' he exclaimed. 'There's a whole flock of them in there!'

We made our way across the lawn and, sure enough, there were two-dozen of what looked to my untrained eye to be purebred Southdowns, complete strangers to me.

'Help yourself,' I told the visitor. 'I don't know whose they are but you're welcome to anything they leave behind.'

'Do you often get people dropping in to ask for a supply of sheep muck?' enquired Corenne in an intrigued tone.

'Surprisingly often,' I told her. 'I gather it's the done thing to put a bucketful in a barrel of water and feed your prize onions with it. That's the way to win championships.'

'That may be so,' remarked Simon, 'but I've finished feeding my onions now. They're ripening in this sun. I've done what the book says and lifted them with a fork. So why should he be so anxious to make more feed at this time of year?'

'Not a clue,' I said, 'but I don't believe a burglar coming to case the joint would arm himself with a bucket and pretend to be an onion fanatic. Let alone ring the bell and make sure I'd recognise him in future. It'll have to remain a mystery.'

'Much more mysterious,' Jo pointed out, 'where did the sheep come from?'

'I don't know that either,' I replied, 'but I'm not going to spend the evening phoning round all the farmers in the area. It can wait till morning.'

Showering and dressing in the morning still took me a long time and Jo took the dogs for their morning constitutional. She returned to help me with my socks.

'What do you mean, sheep?' she demanded. 'There's not a sheep to be seen anywhere.'

After breakfast I strolled, if one can stroll on crutches, down to the paddock. Jo was right: not a sheep in sight. The grass, though, had been nibbled short and there were one or two other bits of evidence that the onion grower had missed.

We never discovered where they had come from.

****

'How much?' shouted Jo. 'But that's ridiculous.'

She had answered the phone in my study but her voice was clear, even to my deaf ears, in the kitchen and she was obviously not best pleased. The conversation continued for some time and then she stormed back.

'So much for your astronomical sum!' she raged. 'Would you believe, the negotiators started bargaining at the smallest sum we'd thought of as acceptable and they're well on their way to half that at the moment. What's more, everyone concerned is off this weekend for their summer holidays and we needn't expect any further action for three weeks. And whatever happens we must let those poor crafts people know what's happening in time for them to make their plans. Not to mention Perry and his railway. It's enough to make you spit!'

Jo set off for the Riverside in a black mood. She was not much happier when she returned that evening. 'Everyone wants to know what's happening and I don't blame them,' she complained. 'All I can do is promise to tell them as soon as something is decided, and that's little enough cheer for them.'

'Cheer up,' I told her. 'Something will turn up.'

'Fat chance!' she snorted but gracefully accepted my proffered drink.

It was a week before something did turn up. The phone rang and Jo answered it. 'No,' I heard her say, 'we never have met.' Her voice grew softer and she huddled over the phone in a conspiratorial manner. It was a good half hour later when she emerged from the study, an enigmatic smile on her face.

'One of your secret admirers?' I enquired. 'As Ernie would say: man mad!'

'Don't be daft,' she replied. 'Surely you realize that all my secret admirers are forbidden to phone me on this number. They only call me at work.'

'So who was it then?' I wanted to know. 'It sounded as though you were getting pretty close.'

'That, I'll have you know,' she told me, 'was no less a person than the chairman of the firm who want to develop the warehouse. He's as fed up as we are with all this shilly shallying and wants to get on with the job. We had a long talk and I told him what we wanted for the lease. In view of the negotiators' offer I felt couldn't ask for more than the minimum so I told him I wasn't prepared to bargain. In the end he agreed that it was a reasonable amount and we can expect to hear from the chairman of the Council committee in the near future. Now sit down at that word processor and write a letter to all the people at the Riverside. You can fill in the dates later but let's have a letter ready to go the moment we sign the agreement.'

'To hear is to obey,' I assured her. 'One letter coming up.'

I need not have hurried. The chairman of the committee concerned with our affairs was determined to beat us down in price but Jo was adamant and in the end he conceded. Then the lawyers on either side had their say and it was some time before we were ready to exchange contracts.

'Hold on a minute,' said our solicitor. 'This agreement has to be approved by the Court.'

'Pull the other one!' exclaimed Jo. 'What on earth has it to do with the courts what agreement I reach with the Council?'

'Ah!' came the reply. 'You are surrendering a valuable asset to the Council. For all the law knows you might be a pair of senile old dodderers and the wicked Council taking advantage of you. I know you're not and it isn't but this is for your protection.'

'I wish they'd protect us from burglars and phoney advertising firms,' said Jo.

****

'Look,' said Jo, 'we finally exchanged contracts at half past four last evening and here I am, first thing this morning, to give you this letter with all the details. We've been warning you for three years that it might happen and now it has. In three months' time we hand the warehouse back to the Council. That means we close at Christmas. I've spoken to Mr Swivel and he tells me that there is a smaller building just along the riverbank, which will be available in the New Year. If any of you like to continue business from there he says the Council would look very favourably on the idea. As far as I'm concerned, we've built up a lot of goodwill over the years and you'd be welcome to use the same name. But now that Jeffrey has retired I'd like to join him and not start a new project from scratch.'

There was another rumble of discontent but less strident than before.

'Good for you, Jo,' came Annie's unmistakable highland voice. 'I've been here as long as anybody and there's hardly been a day when you weren't here. You deserve a rest and jolly good luck to you.'

'I was very grateful to her,' Jo told me that evening. 'All the old hands agreed with her and we settled down to plan how those who wanted to could carry on the Riverside. Camilla and Susan and Tom Ernley went off to see Mr Swivel and everyone finished up cheerful.'

'And what are you planning?' I asked her. 'No more ideas for the moment I hope.'

'Nothing that I've really thought about,' she replied. 'The first thing is to get you out and about again.'

'I'll drink to that,' I assured her, almost tripping over my crutches as I hastened to the cupboard. 'Next week is my appointment with the surgeon. I shall drive in to see him, waving my crutches out of the window.'

'You'll do no such thing,' she informed me. 'You're not driving until he says you can. Nor giving up your crutches.'

'I bet he says I can. And I don't really need these to get around with. I shall take them back to the hospital with thanks. Then I shall drive home and then I'll have a proper bath instead of a shower. There are all sorts of things I haven't been allowed to do for the last three months that I propose to get on with.'

'Promises, promises,' muttered Jo on her way to the kitchen.

****

'This looks fine,' said the surgeon, putting down the X-ray photograph he had been studying. 'And the wound has healed nicely. I'd like to see another X-ray in a year's time but you can chuck away your crutches. Don't do anything foolish; no disco dancing or marathon running.'

I promised to behave sensibly for the next few months and returned to the car.

'Move over,' I told Jo. 'We're back to normal. I'll drive and you tell me to look out, the lights are red!'

'I only say that when you drive so fast I think you haven't seen them,' she remonstrated.

I drove happily home and suggested a celebratory drink.

'You've got work to do,' Jo protested. 'All the books to be up to date. Deregister for VAT from Christmas. And masses of letters to write; I'll give you a list of all my suppliers.'

'Tomorrow is time for that. Today we celebrate. "Painless Peters", that's me!'

I was feeling on top of the world and the days flew past. The books balanced, the letters were posted and I made the stairs at the Riverside with no effort.

'You're looking ten years younger,' Catherine told me.

'I feel it,' I assured her.

'Watch it, Jeffrey,' called Ernie. 'She'll have her eye on you next!'

'Not while I'm around, she won't,' Jo told him.

Camilla Smith appeared at the doorway. 'It's all agreed,' she laughed. 'There's a dozen of us all chipping in. We held a meeting last night and Tom and I went to see Mr Swivel this morning. The Council will give us a five-year lease. Isn't it exciting?'

'Ernie hasn't told you our news yet,' said Catherine.

'Come on Ernie,' cried Jo. 'What treat have you in store for us?'

'We've been invited to exhibit at a trade fair in New York in the New Year,' he told us. 'We fly on the twenty-fifth of January.'

'Well!' exclaimed Jo. 'Here I was expecting everyone to be miserable when we closed down the old home and now it's just like when we started. Everybody has something to look forward to. Isn't it lovely?'

'And it is lovely,' she assured me that evening. 'I'm so glad for everyone. A really happy ending to the Riverside story!'

'What about you?' I asked. 'No craftspeople's quarrels to arbitrate. No youngsters pouring out their troubles. Come summer, not even any of our own kids around. Just me to put up with all the time. Won't you miss it all?'

'Not really,' she replied. 'Remember all those years ago, when there were just the two of us and all the plans we made then? None of them worked out as we expected but it's all been fun and now we can start all over again. The only difference is that we're a bit older and our bank account is out of the red.'

'If I remember,' I told her, 'I promised that you should sit on a cushion and sew a fine seam, and feed upon strawberries, sugar and cream. There hasn't been a lot of that in your life. You really ought to have married a millionaire.'

She put her arms around my neck. 'Don't you believe it.' she said. 'I don't envy anyone. Nobody's grass has ever been greener.'

EPILOGUE

The phone rang. It was Phyllis.

'I'm all right,' she assured us.

Mary had arrived home at about half past ten. She had been spending a couple of days in London with Anne. Phyllis had been with them for the afternoon and had left for her employers' house, first extracting a promise from Mary to phone when she reached home safely. Mary tried but there was no answer.

'Are you sure you tried the right number?' I queried.

'Of course I am,' snapped Mary. 'Why don't you try?'

I tried. No answer. I tried again. Still no joy. That morning Phyllis, who had a job as a nanny, had seen her employers off on a week's skiing holiday leaving her in charge of the house and six months old baby. She couldn't possibly be out at eleven o'clock at night.

Anne was not best pleased. After an exhausting day with her two sisters, following a week of night duty, she had just dropped off to sleep when I phoned. I explained the situation.

'Look,' I said. 'You try to get hold of her. If you have no luck, then ring the local police. Establish the fact that you're a responsible staff nurse in a reputable hospital and not some hysterical idiot and explain that there is no way Phyllis would be wandering round London with a baby at eleven at night.'

Anne phoned half an hour later. 'Phyl's OK,' she told us. 'She'll ring you in a minute. Now, please may I get some sleep?'

Phyllis explained. 'I'd been up since five - they were catching a flight at eight thirty from Gatwick. I did all the usual chores in the morning and met the girls for lunch. We had a lovely afternoon and I came home, bathed and fed Martin, put him in his cot and got myself some supper. I thought I wouldn't go to bed till Mary rang so I sat down in front of the telly and must have fallen asleep. Any way, I didn't hear the phone but the policeman told me that there had been no response when he rang the bell so he hammered on the door. This woke the dog, which started barking in the entrance hall. The policeman kept on knocking and the dog must have jumped up at the door and set off the burglar alarm. That woke Martin and he started howling and that's what woke me. So there I was, snatched from the arms of Morpheus, the baby screaming, the burglar alarm ringing, the dog going berserk and someone trying to batter down the front door. I've sorted it out now but the policeman was laughing so much I don't think he's safe driving his Panda car. Now I'm going to bed so please don't let anyone else phone me.'

She rang off.

The phone rang. It was Anne.

'I've had an awful day,' she wailed. 'I'm just ringing to wish you many happy returns and then I think I'm going to bed.'

'What happened?' I asked.

'Well,' she started, 'I arrived in the ward this morning and found the night staff absolutely shattered. They'd had three cardiac arrests, one after the other. By the time they'd sorted those out, another of their patients had died and they couldn't get hold of any of her relatives. Anyway, I took that on and spent half the morning trying to get hold of her daughter with no luck at all, so I phoned the local police and asked them to try to find her and get her to phone us.

'Then one of my patients wanted a bath. I knew she'd take a bit of time so I waited till all the others had finished with the bathroom and then turned on the taps and went to get her ready. Would you believe it? At that moment it all started and two of the three arrested all over again. By the time we'd dealt with that it was lunchtime and that kept me busy for another hour. I was just thinking I could do with a bite when I noticed water creeping into the ward. Then I remembered.

'I rushed into the bathroom, turned off the taps and pulled out the plug. The water was over my ankles and I'm sure I've ruined a good pair of shoes. I went down the passage, which was just like a river, and found it was flowing under the door to the fire exit so I opened that and there it was, pouring down the stairs. I went down to the next landing and there, under the waterfall, was a trolley with a body on it. Well, it wasn't one of mine and someone had very thoughtfully covered it with a sheet of plastic, so I went back upstairs to assess the damage.

'The water was inches up the door of the linen cupboard and, when I looked inside, the clean sheets on the bottom shelf were soaked. I thought I might as well use them for mopping up and had got most of the job done when in walked the Laundry Supervisor. She started ranting on about how her staff weren't sweating away all day to produce floor cloths and went off in a huff.

'Now I'm in trouble with Sister for not bathing a patient, I'm in trouble with the maintenance staff for flooding half the hospital and I'm in trouble with the laundry staff for misusing clean linen. I don't think I'm going to bed after all. I'm going down to the "Fleming" to drown my sorrows. Then I'm giving in my notice and going to Hong Kong. Happy birthday!'

She rang off.

The phone rang. It was Mary.

'How are you?' I asked.

'I'm fine,' she replied. 'Anne met me at the airport and has found me somewhere to stay while I sort myself out. You've no idea what the rents are like in Hong Kong. She's OK. She lives in the nurses' hostel.'

'So what are you going to do?' I enquired. 'Your Mum is out and she'll do her nut if I can't give her a full report.'

'You won't believe it,' she told me, 'but I've got a job. One of Anne's friends was leaving and I rang her employer and talked myself into her place.'

'What do you do?' I wanted to know.

'It's a fashion export business,' she said.

'That should suit you down to the ground.' Mary had always been able to wear a potato sack and a piece of string and look like something from a Paris fashion magazine.

'Well,' she went on, 'it has some drawbacks. For instance, only one person speaks English and he is one of the two directors. I'm supposed to be in charge of seeing that everything the subcontractors supply is up to standard, sort of quality controller, but the man who speaks English is always away in America and I have to explain what's wrong to a bunch of Cantonese speaking workers who are convinced there's nothing wrong anyway.'

'How on earth do you manage to do that?' I demanded.

'With great difficulty,' she explained. 'It usually ends with me putting on one of the offending garments and pointing out where it doesn't fit. Of course all their wives and daughters are a different shape from me, nine inches shorter for a start. So they are all convinced that it's my fault and stand around jabbering to each other and poking me with their fingers to make sure I'm not doing something on purpose to ruin their efforts.'

'Sounds like fun!' I told her. 'Still, you must be able to pick up some first class clothes very cheaply.'

'You've got to be joking,' she exploded. 'Can you imagine me setting foot out in the street wearing a fluorescent micro-skirt?'

'The mind boggles,' I chuckled.

'I must go,' she told me. 'I'm running out of money for this phone. I'll call again at the weekend when Mum's home. Byeee!'

She rang off.

The phone rang. It was Cormac.

'Well I went to a party last night,' he said in answer to my query, 'but we didn't get there.'

'Sounds like a lot of fun,' I remarked.

'Not so much fun,' he replied. 'More like interesting. Four of us were invited to this party near Bournemouth so we set off in Jim's car. Well, he calls it a car but it's much older than he is and hasn't travelled that far in years. Still, we were all third year students in the engineering department and we reckoned we ought to be able to get it there between us.

'We left the University just as it was getting dark and had only reached the edge of the New Forest when it started to rain. That was where we hit the first snag. The alternator wasn't working properly and the battery was flat. We found that if we used the wiper the lights went out and vice versa. Of course, I, being the only electrical engineer, was expected to do something about it but there isn't a lot one can do to a dodgy alternator in the dark when it's pouring with rain. Luckily I remembered one of your stories about your old Austin Seven. I looked over the hedge and saw potatoes growing so I pulled some up and we managed to find a knife and cut one in half. Then we rubbed it on the windscreen and it worked!

'Anyway, we pushed on but the engine started misfiring and we were going more and more slowly and when we got to a steep hill it just refused to go up it. Nigel suggested doing what the boys in "Cannery Row" did with the old Model T Ford, and try going up in reverse so the rest of us got out and Jim turned it round and tried going up backwards but even with us pushing it only went a few yards and then the engine died completely. We tried everything we could think of but it wouldn't start.

'Nigel remembered that a friend of ours lived about two miles away and his parents owned a farm, so we thought we would try leaving the car there. The worst part was pushing it up the hill but we made it at last and after that it wasn't too bad, if you don't think pushing a car through the New Forest in a downpour is too bad. It was all right till we reached the village, but we didn't know where the farm was and took a lot of time finding it. Just as we pushed the car through the gate, the front offside wheel fell off. Just as well it didn't happen on the motorway out of Southampton. Luckily Ted, that's the friend who lives there, was still up and made us welcome, but I don't think his parents, who had gone to bed and had to be up early for milking, were that impressed. We had some coffee and managed to rake up enough money between us to get a taxi back home.

'Next weekend we are staging a sponsored "Car Push" through the New Forest to the University in aid of charity. Will you sponsor us? OK, I'll put you down for a quid. Mum too? Thanks. Cheers.'

He rang off.

The phone rang. It was John.

'Tell Mum I won't be home for dinner but I'd be awfully grateful if she'd leave me some in the oven.'

'What is it this time,' I wanted to know.

John's not turning up for meals had become habitual. His evenings seemed to be occupied with assorted Church organisations, youth clubs and the like; he was on first name terms with every priest for miles around and 'I'm going to see Fred' might signify anything from visiting the opposing scrum half whom he had put into hospital with a violent tackle on the previous Saturday to a chat with the Bishop. Only a couple of weeks earlier I had received an urgent call to rescue him from the casualty department whither he had been carried as the result of trying an awkward catch at silly mid-on which resulted in a broken collarbone. For the next few days he had been confined to home, stuffed with painkillers and arm supported by a silk scarf, while a path was trodden deep to our door by a succession of pulchritudinous and callipygian maidens, each eager to bring solace to her wounded hero.

On this occasion, though, we had been confident that he would be home by Sunday lunchtime. He had left on Friday evening for a retreat organised by some of his old school friends. He assured us that Mass on Sunday would be followed by breakfast and the participants would disperse to their homes.

'It's like this,' he explained. 'We had some pretty intense debates all through Friday evening and yesterday, so in the evening we thought we'd relax a bit and we organised a disco. Well, dancing is thirsty work so we agreed to have a whip round and I was sent out to get some drinks. When I say "Whip round", we all sorted out our loose change and threw in all our pound coins. When I got to the wine merchant's I found you can buy an awful lot of beer and whisky for a hundred and seven pounds. We had a whale of a party. This morning Brother Arkwright, you wouldn't remember him but he used to teach me carpentry, took one look at us and threatened to call a policeman with his breathalyser if any of us tried to drive. He's taking us all for a hike on the moor for what he calls "a purification of soul and system".'

'I thought,' I told him, 'that this retreat was being held in a seminary.'

'That's right,' he assured me.

'I begin to wish,' I said, 'that you had followed me into the service. Anyone who can organize a booze up of those proportions in a seminary of all places would certainly rise to be the youngest ever Chief of Defence Staff.'

'Glad you see it my way,' he replied.

He rang off.

The phone rang. It was Jane.

'I just thought I'd let you know I'm back safely in Tokyo,' she said.

'That's nice to know,' I told her. 'Is there any reason why you shouldn't be?'

'Well I nearly didn't make it,' she replied. 'You remember the trouble I had when I first arrived here because the firm hadn't made the proper arrangements about my visa? Would you believe it, they still haven't sorted it out? I'd had a marvellous week with Anne and Mary in Hong Kong. We went to the Rugby Sevens and met all sorts of people and had a party every night. You know I'd just been paid a bonus, so I bought masses of new clothes, which I just couldn't afford in Japan, and had two suitcases stuffed with goodies. When I got off the plane I showed the immigration man my passport and it turned out I was only supposed to be a visitor and I'd had my visit and left for Hong Kong, so what was I doing back again?

'I couldn't tell them I worked in Tokyo if I didn't have a worker's visa and I thought I was going to be sent back to Honkers. In the end I persuaded them that I had only broken my visit for a few days to see my sisters. Luckily I had let Yuko, she shares my office, stay at my flat while I was away so I gave them the phone number and address and she told them I had been staying there and gone away for a few days. She didn't mention that she didn't live there normally and, in fact, she was my visitor! So they let me in. That was OK but then I got to the Customs.'

' "Have you anything to pay duty on?" they wanted to know.

' "What sort of thing would that be?" I asked as innocently as I could, trying hard not to eye my cases, which were bulging at the seams.

‘ “Anything, perhaps, that you might have bought in Hong Kong,” they suggested.

‘ “Oh!” I said. “You mean like this,” and I opened my overnight bag and produced the box of chocolates I’d brought back for Yuko.

‘ “That’s all right,” said the man and waved me through.’

‘I have it on good authority,’ I told her, ‘that the interior of Japanese prisons leaves a great deal to be desired in the way of comfort.’

‘Don’t worry,’ she assured me. ‘I’m going to see Personnel and get them to fix my visa chop chop. And all my new clothes will be worn clothes by next week. Now I’m going to bed. It may be time for you to have a preprandial drink but it’s two o’clock in the morning here. Goodnight.’

She rang off.

Jo and I were sitting peacefully on either side of the fire, she knitting a heavy sweater and I disposing of the *Times* crossword and a glass of beer.

'I've had an idea,' announced Jo.

I groaned and sank lower in my chair.

'You ought to write a book,' she told me.

'That, my love, is one thing I am definitely not going to do,' I replied.

Jo smiled.

www.ingramcontent.com/pod-product-compliance
Lightning Source LLC
Chambersburg PA
CBHW030820310726
48980CB00006B/562/J

* 9 7 8 0 9 5 5 6 8 7 3 0 3 *